AQUATIC HUMANOIDS
(APOCALYPSE 2)

Gary W. Babb

AQUATIC HUMANOIDS (APOCALYPSE 2)

DOUBLE DRAGON

Chapter 1
(The Plan)

As I stood facing the Apsaras Assembly in our city's main dome, I blurted out, "No Shit! Finally we get to invade Earth!"

Bart, my father and head of the Assembly, quickly countered, "It's not an invasion, it's an immigration. Your English is better than that, and I notice it is becoming somewhat colorful and crude."

Our race's own language had been banned almost two years ago when we made the decision to migrate to Earth. The Assembly decided to establish English as our common language. They said total immersion into English was the best way to learn the language, and if our future was to be on Earth in the United States, this would be necessary. With our obvious physical differences, they believed it would help us to be more easily accepted, or at least tolerated, by the human race if we were at least fluent in their language.

Our explorers, when we still had them, traveled many times to Earth to observe humans and had established a permanent advanced technology communications satellite orbiting Earth. As a result, we had maintained communications through intercepts and in filtered Internet access. We all had been studying English and watching English language movies ever since, and many of us felt that we could blend right in. Well, except for our blueish color, we were after all a different race from any that existed on Earth, although obviously humanoid with common genetic roots.

"Sorry, father." I said, "We've been preparing for so many years, I was just shocked to finally get the Assembly's approval. What made you decide now?"

Bart said, "The situation has changed. Our remaining scientists have been studying the future on Earth with our technology and discovered a looming civilization collapse. They are overpopulated and are going to destroy themselves in the near future. This means our accumulated wealth in advanced technology, gold, silver, platinum, and precious jewels will be useless unless we go before their apocalypse. Unfortunately, the scientists see Earth's civilization end before we can get there. When their civilization falls we can't buy our way into their society or battle our way in with our advances weaponry, because there will be no civilization to negotiate with or sell to. This forces us to rethink and alter our plans."

Oh crap! This changes everything and could quite possibly destroy any hope for our own future survival. Our race is dying. Over the last two hundred years every generation of our people produced even fewer children, and this last generation, my generation, hasn't produced *any* offspring. The population of our race had been decimated to less than one thousand people, which we concentrated in one last domed city. When father's generation passes we will be only a hundred or so. Our scientists, what's left of them, tell us the only way to save our race, in part anyway, is to inbreed with humans. The influx of new and diverse humanoid DNA might alter and stimulate ours and allow our race to survive. Otherwise, our entire species becomes extinct with my generation. Our explorers traveled the Galaxy in search of other humanoids, and Earth hosted the only race close enough in DNA. Mixing our DNA with the humans of Earth was our only chance for survival.

I said, "So what do we do? How can we survive in a new world in chaos without wealth and friendship? We couldn't even build a facility to live in or feed ourselves."

Bart said, "That's the problem isn't it? Most of the humans on Earth won't survive either for the same reason. Still, if we hope to survive as a race we must go now before they kill themselves off. One suggestion that has been brought up is go there and capture some human males and bring them back here for breeding stock, since our reproductive problem is primarily the extremely low sperm count of our males. This method could work, but we're not sure how they can adapt to living on a water world. Humans have not evolved enough to handle our environment. Another thing to consider: this planet is polluted and dying, so any solution involving remaining on Apsaras would only be a short term solution."

Bart said, "Do you have any suggestions? After I pass you will become the leader of the Assembly, and it will be your problem then."

I said, "I have no immediate ideas. Let me think on it, and we can meet again in a few days." We agreed, and I took off to my own personal dome.

I dove into the water and gave an undulating squeal to alert my escorts and friends. Almost immediately I saw one of my pod's porpoises, Dobe, streaking through the water toward me. My pod was never far from me. Dobe, easily recognizable by the white scars along her left side where she had been burned by red acid algae when she was young, quickly nuzzled against me, and I hugged her. Her mate, Dubs, followed quickly behind her with his own greeting. I squeaked my instructions as I grabbed hold of their top dorsal fins. We kicked off together and streaked through the water toward my resident dome, surrounded by the other pod members.

This family of porpoises was my self-appointed protectors and guardians, which I greatly appreciated due to the predators abundant in these waters. I had grown up with Dobe and Dubs and had helped raise many of the others. I could hold my breath almost as long as a porpoise, and I was a fast swimmer, but not nearly as fast as my friends. Unfortunately, I had little defense against the predators. I mean I carried a laser pistol in a back holster, but by far the best defense was the always watchful eyes and sonar of my protectors. They missed nothing and charged any stealth predator long before I could draw my weapon. The pod would speed toward a predator ramming it with their nose and killing it. As long as they were around, I was never in any real danger.

It was several miles to my underwater dome, but my friends deftly maneuvered us around floating and hovering clumps of dangerous algae and to clear surfaces for breaths of air. A porpoise's breathing hole, blowhole, is on the top of their head, which means they barely have to break water to breath. Unfortunately, they never understood that I needed more time to raise my head completely out to the water to breath. This meant that I have to constantly struggle to reach clear air and draw a breath before they pulled me back under. I didn't always make it. On more than one occasion they had to push me to the surface to get air.

On long distance swims sometimes I would roll over to swim on my back. This gave me extra time to breath air when I was hitching a ride, but I couldn't see where I was swimming. Our race's ability to internally pinch our nose shut, like closing our eyes, could shut the water out and prevent choking. This ability equated to a porpoise's blowhole. As I thought about this I realized that this trait would look strange to humans. Oh well, a human choking in water would look strange to us.

As we approached the bottom opening of my dome I squealed a "Thank you" and shot up through the opening and landed on my feet on the deck. My mates, Meg and Peg, were anxious to hear why I had been called to an emergency meeting this morning. I told them what was discussed, and understandably, they were both upset and excited. They desperately wanted to have children. These identical twins were considered the most fertile, since they were the only pair of identical twins born to our race in over a century. The Assembly put us together hoping we would produce a son of my lineage to rule after me. We had certainly tried, to no avail. The twins continued to milk my seed during their fertile time, with no success. They wanted me to father their children but were willing to have children, even if the child was half human. Yes, they were eager to leave Apsaras behind and go to Earth.

Sex itself had little interest to either gender of our race, especially males. It actually hurt us. I guess that was the result of the genetic weakening. Our race was ancient with little DNA diversity, maybe too little to continue to reproduce. Still, none of us wanted to see our species extinct and continued to allow ourselves to be milked, a process which the females of our species had perfected through many generations.

Our female's training began at puberty. There was a training ritual that must be perfected by them before they were allowed to milk sperm. The training began with the use of a sea sponge, approximately the size and shape of a male's penis. They were required to develop their internal vagina muscles to the degree of being able to milk (suck) whale milk up through a sea sponge. This training took years to develop, but gave the females the ability to extract sperm directly from a male's testicles, a process designed to assist reproduction. Unfortunately, being milked was painful. As a result the males participated reluctantly and only as necessary, but unfortunately, there were far more females than males. So, each male had to endure multiple milking.

Meg and Peg had prepared fish for our dinner, and we ate, mostly in silence, thinking about any possible solutions for all our needs. We curled up in our hammock net, affectionately cuddled and waited for what we knew would be a troubled sleep. As we cuddled we could see our pod through the circular glass dome circling. They were happy as long as they could see us and know we were safe.

Our closeness to the pod was the major reason we remained in our personal dome and not move into the city. There were abundant living quarters in the dome city, due to the dwindling population, but I did not want to abandon my friends. Many others had, but not us.

I was determined to find a solution to our problem. I knew every one of my generation was counting on me. They always did, and I was not going to fail them. As I usually do with difficult problems, I let my sub-conscious mind work on it during the night. Often I would wake in the morning with a much clearer head and sometimes a solution.

Sometimes I wish I had two brains like my porpoise friends. Well, they really don't have two brains, but they do have two halves that can operate independently of each other, one of which remains

11

conscious at all times, while the other half sleeps. I guess that makes sense, since they must constantly swim to keep from drowning. Still, I sometimes wish I could remain awake all twenty-nine hours of our planet's rotation like my friends.

When I awoke the next cycle I still had no idea how to solve the problem. I was blank.

Meg said, "I see you still haven't found a solution. As your father said, "We can't buy our way in'. But, we still need a partner on the Earth side."

I barked, "Don't you think I know that?" She was telling me the obvious, but I was at a loss as to how to buy or trade an Earth partner into merging and helping us. It would have to be someone wealthy on Earth, and if they were already wealthy, why would they help us? The situation looked impossible.

In lieu of any other reasonable solutions I started checking out "Prepper" websites on Earth's Internet. These consisted of people that already believed Earth's civilization was going to collapse, and they were preparing for survival. I figured they wanted the same thing as we did. I found the postings, some anyway, fairly accurate according to reports from our scientists. One in particular got my attentions. He predicted the fall and described it in fairly accurate detail. His post read:

I am convinced that a catastrophe (from nature or more likely man-made) of some sort will happen in the near future. Our society is delicately balanced and it only takes a small shove to upset the balance. The "Domino Effect" will take it all down once it starts. It could be something as simple as the economy fails, the electric grid fails, war, civil strife, etc. I believe that the average person is totally unprepared and ignorant in the basic skills of "survival". I'm thinking the flow of events would happen something like this:

- *Catastrophe happens – panic, fear, uncertainty, loss of hope*
- *Infrastructure collapses – communication, electricity, water stop,... stores stripped clean, looting, the strong/bully segment emerge.*
- *Average person huddles in their home/apartment hoping that everything will somehow "come back" to normal (or at least for as long as their personal resources last).*
- *After about 3 days to a week of no food, the layer of "civilized man" begins to crack and people begin to do anything necessary to acquire what they feel are the essentials.*
- *The initial grouping would be at the church/family/close friends level because of inherent trust.*
- *People begin to carefully group to gain the protection of numbers... Groups will battle*

13

each other for available resources or power.

- *Areas more remote and miles from metropolitan cities should be in better shape, because in many cases these are ranchers/farmers and as such have a better understanding of living off the land... plus, they stand a much better chance that what they have will not be ravaged by roaming gangs from the cities because of the distances.*
- *The folks in these remote areas may very well have the opportunity to come together (as neighbors which have helped each other in the past) and form a protective group of their own which is charged with defending their homeland.*
- *The gangs will grow larger and canvas further out, and no one or group will be safe.*
- *As food becomes more scarce, without the existence of law enforcement or organized armies the gangs will kill to take what they want and become primitive. Civilization ceases to exist.*

I was amazed to see just how accurate he described the fall. It was almost identical to the description our scientists saw in Earth's demise when they looked into the future.

In other posts he even described how he and a select group hoped to survive, what to stock in supplies, what training these survivors would need. He even provided a sketch of the building he wanted to construct for protection and survival. It was a good basic plan, and I knew we needed a human partner like him.

I clicked on his profile information and discovered his name was Mike Brannon, and he lived in Muskogee, Oklahoma. I quickly logged on to Google Earth to find Oklahoma, then Muskogee. Muskogee was located in eastern Oklahoma in what was described as "Green Country". The area was mostly rural and had many lakes, which would serve our purpose well. I still didn't see any way to entice him to help us, but I sent him an e-mail agreeing with his prediction and complimenting him on his plans. I also bluntly ask him if he had started, and if not, why?

My message transmitted to our communication satellite in geostationary orbit above Apsaras then transmitted out to our satellite above Earth. This transmission wasn't instantaneous between the light years separating our planets, but it was damn close. Actually, the slowest part of the entire network was the Earth-side Internet. Our technology was far better and faster. It had been created by scientists and engineers in our ancient past, but unfortunately, none remained of our race that understood how it worked; it just did. Fortunately most of our existing technology was extremely reliable. In point of fact, none could remember any of our technology ever failing. We even still traveled in space in our saucers built by our ancient engineers, and we have no idea how this technology works, either. They were simple to operate, however, and my mates Meg and Peg have been trained to fly them. I didn't know how long it would take for him to receive the message and reply, assuming he would. So I went about my life and waited.

It was nearing evening as I was swimming with my friends when my mates nuzzled up to me. We had just collected a nice fish for our late meal, a big, sleek white fish, my favorite. Meg motioned for us to surface. I knew it must be something important, so we surfaced. Meg knew I had been waiting for a response from Earth and was anxious.

When we surfaced Meg said, "That response you have been waiting for from Earth came in. I thought you would want to know as soon as possible."

I said, "You're right about that. I've already got our dinner and was just playing. We can head back in now." Peg, usually quiet, nodded affirmative and we submerged, racing through the water back to our dome. The porpoises got excited at our burst of speed and raced ahead of us, even circling us, as if to say, *"You might be fast, but we are faster."* Soon we burst out of the water to land standing on our deck inside the dome.

I went immediately to my computer and opened the e-mail. It was from Mike Brannon and read:

"Hello Brin,

Thanks for your nice note. Yeah, I worry about this pending collapse of civilization. I see it coming, but, sadly, there is little I can do about it. I don't have the kind of money it would take to activate my plans. So, unless I win the Lottery, all I can do is dream up plans and worry.

Mike,"

I immediately began grinning, because he had just solved our problem with that statement, at least I think he just solved our problem. I would have to check with our scientists to see if this was possible. The technology that allowed them to look into the future was unreliable in that the scientists couldn't precisely choose the exact time. Their ability to view the future was dependent upon the technology itself. Once it was probably controllable, but, as with all our technology, our scientists had lost their understanding of how it worked. The vast level of engineering and physics knowledge it had taken to design and build our inventions had been decimated as our race died off faster than we could educate new scientists and engineers. Actually, our so called scientists now were no more than moderately educated technicians...operators. Still, I was positive that the existing technology *could* find the answers I was seeking...if asked the right questions or given the right instructions. We had to try.

17

Meg and Peg were looking over my shoulder at the visual display, reading the same message and coming to the same conclusion I reached. We looked at each other, smiling. I immediately called a meeting of the Assembly, but before we left I worded a response e-mail.

"Hello Mike,

If I help you get the funds you need will you partner with my group and build your survival group and activate your plans? I will await your response.

Brin"

This time Meg and Peg went with me to the Assembly. This affected them, so they weren't about to be left out, besides, they were excited with the possibilities of a potential solution.

Dobe and Dubs sensed that we were excited about something as soon as we dove in the water. The pod gathered around us to allow us to hitch a ride on their fins. I squeaked our destination, and we were off at a fast pace.

Communications with them by formal sounds was limited, but they were gifted with a strong sense of reading emotions. I could often sense their emotions as well, and today they were agitated by something. I quickly realized what it was when they took us off far to the left of our normal path. They knew or sensed a major predator in the area and were taking us around the danger. I saw nothing to indicate danger to warrant this extra caution, but I trusted their instincts.

We arrived at the main dome platform without incident and shot up through the opening. As we stood to allow the water to repel from our snug main body wraps and skin, we noticed the Assembly already seated around the center dais ... waiting. Meg and Peg knew the dais was reserved for me alone and took seats in the gallery, while I took the center position.

Bart said, seeming somewhat annoyed, "Well, you called this meeting. Get to it."

I'm sure my face wrinkled with annoyance at my father's bluntness, but said, "All right. I may have found a solution to our problem." I just let that settle in.

Bart's attitude changed immediately, and he continued, "Oh really? This is good. What is the solution?"

I said, "I may have found an Earth partner to build facilities prior to us reaching Earth, and I may have found a method of financing the entire project with Earth's own money. Of course this all assumes our scientists can deliver information on Earth's future." I had the total attention and tentative respect of the Assembly and my father, which made me smile. I proceeded to lay out my plan and detailed needs I required. When I finished I simply waited for their response, which of course I already knew would be favorable.

The Assembly consisted of elders from many of our previous world governments. As our population dwindled, these leaders and their people joined with us, the once largest floating city. They tended to be

19

arrogant and demanding, accustomed to being catered and listened to; but since our entire population of Apsaras was now only around a thousand people, mostly old like them, their importance and worth had greatly diminished. Still, they remained our leaders ... for now.

The Assembly talked among themselves and agreed with my plan. Bart said, "We will devote all the time of our scientists toward trying to find answers to the questions you pose. In the mean time I suggest you and your generation devote your time towards preparing for the journey. Stock the 'Bright One', our largest space saucer, with supplies and equipment for your survival when you arrive on Earth."

I didn't know if I was understanding him right and said, "You are using words like 'You' and 'Your'. Don't you mean 'Us' and 'Our'?"

Bart said, "No. We have discussed it and decided that this journey is for the young. We are old. Your generation is young, and you have a better chance of survival without us. We would just be a burden to you all on Earth. You are now in charge of this adventure and our future as a race. Take anything you need from us. The Assembly's last order is: Go with our blessing and keep our race alive."

I knew he and the Assembly were right in this assessment, but I hadn't wanted to broach the subject. Immigrating a hundred people into a hostile environment would be far better than over a thousand. Our smaller group had a much better chance of survival. Even so, I had a flood of emotion sweep over me. I felt regret at their loss, and I felt the sudden burden of command fall upon me, like a steel wall. Immediate panic swept over me, while I tried to control any outward signs.

I said, "I understand your meaning and intent. I can even appreciate it. I will immediately move into the city and begin organizing our group. We won't disappoint you. We will survive, and maybe once we establish a base we can bring more of you to us." A flash of pride momentarily filled my father's eyes. Bart always appeared so cold and formal, possibly forced. To see this flash of a father's pride warmed me greatly, and I felt my love for him bubble in my chest. Since my mother's death years ago, my father had devoted all his attention toward the Assembly. Now I saw a slight crumble in his self-established withdrawal from his emotions and his firm Assembly front.

Bart said, "Maybe in the future we can look at that possibility, but the most important goal right now is ensuring you young ones survive."

As I left the dais I could see many of my friends in attendance flash me knowing smiles and some thumbs up like they had seen in the American movies. I acknowledge them with a nod, but my heart still hammered in my chest. As I passed my friend, Trix, I said, "Can you pass the word to the others of our millennial group that we will meet here tomorrow to make plans." Trix nodded.

Peg and Meg gave me a big hug of congratulations, but I didn't feel at all comfortable with the honor. Being given command still seemed more of a punishment than a promotion, but I will get it done. I must get it done.

We dove in the water quickly. I didn't want any display of congratulation in front of the Assembly, knowing just how hard it was for them to turn over control to me. I squealed for my pod, and as always Dobe was first to nuzzle me. The three of us had two proposes each, but Dobe and Dubs were mine. We held the dorsal fins of our pairs and took off. My mind was still reeling from the realization of my responsibilities and didn't notice that Dobe was again steering us around the long way. I didn't realize anything was wrong until I heard a high-pitched squeal of pain from behind us. We spun around in time to see a trailing porpoise thrashing in the jaws of a grapper. Grappers were extremely rare in these waters and very dangerous. This was a large one at about forty-five feet long and weighing around three thousand pounds. A grapper swims like a snake through the water using ridges of fins on top and bottom, and the wide mouth is filled with sharp, deadly teeth. I knew my friend would be dead soon, because the teeth also injects a poison.

I drew my laser pistol, but I couldn't fire because the pod members were all over the grapper, ramming it with their snouts at high speed from all directions. The angry porpoises continuously squeaked and chirped as they launched a coordinated and organized attack. The grapper had released my friend to fight back, but it was too late for the porpoise. I could tell she was already dead. The grapper was aggressive and fearless, but every time it moved to attack one of the pod it got slammed from the opposite direction. It jerked back in forth as it was bombarded, and soon I saw blood floating out of its huge mouth from the internal damage being inflicted. Soon it stopped fighting, rolled on its back and slowly sank out of sight, but before it disappeared from sight I could see the limp, dead body jerking from continued assaults.

Some of the pod members were pushing the injured porpoise up to the surface in a futile effort to force it to breath, but she was obviously dead. Now that the tension of the fight was over, I recognized her. Sadly, she was Dobe's youngest, which I had named Nan. The pod, realizing Nan was dead, took turns nuzzling her, as if saying, "Good Bye". Meg, Peg, and I did the same. It didn't seem enough, but such was life in the water. Regrettably, we watched Nan drift slowly out of sight and out of our lives forever. We then resumed our swim toward my dome. I nuzzled my face to Dobe's side as we swam and hoped she knew I was telling her how sorry I was.

We reached my dome and sprang inside, waving bye to the pod. Once inside, Meg and Peg began crying in grief at the loss. The girls had often played with Nan. They tried not to show it to the others, but Nan was the youngest of the pod, not even fully grown, and their favorite.

Meg bellowed, "Why did that sweet child have to die? And where did that damn grapper come from. I've never even seen one before."

I said, "The growing pollution must have driven it into our cleaner water. Remember, it hasn't been that long ago since we had to move our city due to the pollution. The pod must have sensed or tasted it in the water, since they took us the long way. We will have to warn the city to keep watch for others."

Dubs startled us when he popped his head up through our floor opening chirping his greeting. He was quickly followed by Nate dragging a large white fish. I quickly grabbed the fish and patted their heads in thanks. After they left I said to the girls, "Well, it looks like we have dinner." We all laughed and the girls began carving and dressing the fish, while I went to my communication center.

I was hoping there might be a message from Mike, and I was pleased to see that there was and quickly opened it.

"Hello Brin,

You surprised me with a potential offer to fund and partner with me. If you are serious I would be pleased to be your partner, but keep in mind that I don't have funds to invest for this partnership. I do, however, have the energy and desire to build this community. How large is your group? Let me know what you have in mind.

Mike"

I decided to wait to respond until I actually got conformation from the scientists that they could provide the lottery numbers, to be more precise, when I actually had the winning numbers. I would start pushing hard for that information tomorrow. I also decided not to wait until tomorrow to move to the city. We would start moving after we ate. There was no reason to waste a good, fresh white fish.

When our meal was finished I pushed the button for the underwater squealer, signaling the pod. As always they were close and responded quickly, and Dubs and Dobe's heads popped up in the opening chirping. They loved to be needed and summoned. I began hand signing to them our intention to take our small saucer to the city to stay. I also talked to them while I signed. They understood many vocal English words, but the hand pantomiming helped them understand better. They understood, and I knew they too would move to the waters of the city and be available.

Peg then dove in the water and entered our saucer from the bottom hatch. Soon she was positioning the saucer into our dome bottom entrance. Peg opened the top hatch, and we handed down to her the items we wished to take. We traveled light. I wanted my personal communication center with my files, and a few changes of clothing. For us, clothing consists only of light vests and short skirts made of woven waterweed. None of our race was modest, so the skirts were open underneath to facilitate waste elimination. All we really needed was warmth in

25

sensitive places, and the water weed was light and slick underwater.

When we pulled away we noticed the pod had already gone. I'm sure they would be looking for us at the city, and I would make sure they found us. The saucer lifted out of the water and shot over the waves toward the city. Since we would be taking the largest saucer, Bright One, I planned to move into one of the adjacent sub-domes. The entire floating city was supported by these sub-domes, so there were plenty of them. Unfortunately, the domes went for miles with neighbors crowded all around, well, not so many neighbors anymore. Still, I would miss my dome. I liked the open water space.

The domes all looked the same: There was a large clear dome with nothing to see but other domes, a net for sleeping, an energy radiation oven for cooking, a small cooling container for food storage and a fresh water outlet. Energy for appliances in the city was transmitted through the air. There was no bodily waste facility in the small domes. All were encouraged to go topside to a common facility, where the waste could be processed. Most, however, simply went in the water, which, unfortunately, increased the level of pollution. Thankfully, there weren't that many left.

We entered under the city and chose the dome we wanted and unloaded our personal items. Afterwards, we parked our saucer inside the large dome housing the "Bright One". It was easy to see how the saucer got its name "Bright One". Even after centuries it remained shinny bright. It was also as big as I remembered, and I was pleased that we had been given this one. We would be able to store much equipment inside but not just anything. We would have to be very selective, since space was valuable.

After we settled in, I dove in the water and called to my pod. I knew they would be close, and they found me quickly and began affectionally nudging me with their snouts. I am very affectionately attached to my friends, and they were not to be left behind. I planned to take them with me, but I haven't yet figured out how to convince them. Traveling to another planet and going into cryogenic hibernation were concepts they would not understand, especially sleep, since they never slept. No, these concepts would not readily be accepted, but a way must be found. Not all of my generation were attached to a specific pod, few actually. Most had contact with many pods but not to the degree I was with mine. Well, Blane did a lot of underwater farming and he had many friends among the porpoises that helped him. I'm sure he will want to bring some of his friends as well. I would have to discuss with him how we might explain to our friends of our plans.

I frolicked with my friends for a while, then indicated that I had to go to work. They seemed happy and understanding as I shot up into my dome. I said to the girls, "Let's check in with the scientists to see if they have any news for us." They quickly nodded and we went up through an airlock into the city.

There were four scientists hard at work as we approached the Research Center. I say four, but one of them was our friend Flay. She was of my generation. Her mother and father were engineers/scientists, and she had been taught by them and worked with them since childhood. They seemed excited to see us and waved us over, and I got enthusiastic at their excitement.

Flay's face flushed with excitement and said, "We got it!"

I said, "What do you got?"

"We got the winning lottery numbers and date of the drawing. It takes both to win."

As she spoke she handed me a slip of paper. I read it and exclaimed, "No shit! $280,000,000.00? This is fantastic!"

Flay continued, "I think we may also get another winning set of lottery numbers. I'll let you know tomorrow when we meet. I have a couple of names for you too, people that are somehow involved in the future human community. It didn't make a lot of sense to us, but it might help. Our ability to look into the future is unreliable, but dad says it's probably not wise for us to know too much, since our action might change the future."

I said, "Thank you all very much. You have helped us greatly. Actually, you have saved us by making our plan real. Now I need to develop the plan and make it happen on Earth. I can't thank you enough." I was profusely thankful and rushed back to our dome to send an e-mail to Mike. The date they gave me was only a couple of days away, so that added to my rush. I didn't want to have to depend on them finding another set of winning numbers.

"*Mike,*

I want you to go out and buy a lottery ticket with the numbers I am providing. The drawing is for the date I'm also providing, which is soon. Take this request seriously and you will win $280,000,000.00. When you win, I will assume we are partners. My group will consist of about one hundred, 75 females and 25 males, all younger. I would suggest you plan on about the same number, maybe reverse the female versus male ratio, since we may be sequestered for a while when civilizations collapses. Let me know when you win, and we can begin discussing more details.

Brin"

After the e-mail was sent, the girls and I spent the later hours discussing personnel and how best to use them to ready our operation both on Apsaras and Earth. There were several obvious picks. Due to her training, Flay was the only pick for engineering and science. We would rely on her heavily for recommendations for equipment to take. Blane was another easy pick. He did much of the underwater farming here, and was perfect to head up ecologically sound underwater food production for us on Earth. He would know what plants and fish stock we needed to take from Apsaras and how to introduce them there. Tina was the closest we had among the millennials to a medical professional. She would know what equipment we should take and how to use them on Earth. Hopefully we will get along well with Mike's human group, but just in case we would require someone to head up security. My girls suggested Trix. She was a weapons expert, along with Meg and Peg, but I needed them for communications and piloting. Trix would make a good choice.

Due to the lack of genetic diversity, most of us had common features. We look very much alike: slim, athletic, aqua-blue in color, green eyes, black hair with some orange. Meg and Peg, however, had no orange at all, and mine was slight, so slight I kept my orange plucked out. Trix, on the other hand, stood out among our race. While some of us have orange patches of hair at our temples, Trix had an extra-large swath of bright orange hair at her temples that stood out in appearance. I remember how she would braid her hair using only orange in one of the three braiding bundles. It was definitely different. Because of this difference, she had taken a lot of ribbing as a child from the other children. As a result she was quick tempered and quick to fight, which had earned her a reputation. Trix didn't take any crap from anyone, and most of the others of our generation had felt her anger at one time or another. Yes, she would be good at security.

We continued to make notes for the next day's meeting, but soon tired. We decided to take a swim to relax. It wasn't as bright as usual, since the second sun was hidden over the horizon, but it was still plenty sunny from our main sun. We dove into the water and were quickly greeted by the pod. We played for a while, as the pod took us around the city, exploring. Dobe even showed us the large domes housing the two other, slightly smaller saucers than Bright One. When we returned we had swam off any anxiety and were ready for sleep. We rolled together in our net and were quickly asleep.

Chapter 2
(Planning)

We were still asleep when my communication devise chimed. It was Trix telling me that our generation group was assembled and waiting. I jumped up bringing the girls with me. I said, "Shit, we overslept. They're waiting for us in the Bright One dome." I had changed my mind about the meeting area. I felt it was not appropriate to dislodge the Assembly from their formal area. Having given up authority to me would be hard enough for them to accept without adding insult to their injury. I had notified Trix afterward of the change of location. I also knew there would be some anger venting from the millennials, which should be done in private. Most believed we should have been authorized to leave long ago.

We took the quicker route and dove in the water to swim to the adjacent dome. We sprang up to the large deck. Being late for the meeting brought some sniping and jeering from my friends, but it was lighthearted and quick. They knew I was in total and absolute charge and didn't want to push my buttons too hard. They had positioned my chair at the head of the group with the others facing me.

I didn't wait, I plunged right in and said, "We have a lot to do, and we must get organized with our various tasks and establish department leaders. I already have some of these leaders picked. They will run their department both here and on Earth.

Peg and Meg will be in charge of the Bright One." They looked startled when I said it. We hadn't discussed that part. "They are trained pilots and communications and weapons experts and will be in charge of packing and stowage of equipment and supplies. They and myself will be the only ones awake during the trip to Earth. Everyone else will go into cryogenics during the actual trip."

"Blane will be in charge of underwater food production when we reach Earth. Your tasks here are to make sure we stock plants to transplant into the ecology of Earth...food we can grow and eat there. Also gather fish, hatchlings or eggs, whatever is necessary, to cultivate on Earth. Volunteer whomever you need to help. Blane, we have plenty of cryogenic chambers available for us to use. I expect you will want to take some of your porpoise friends," He nodded, "I know I want to take my pod. You might also try to figure out how we will get them to agree to go into cryogenics." At that last statement all laughed at the obvious complexity of that."

"Tina will be responsible for our medical needs on Earth. You must plan the equipment and supplies necessary to do this." I could see the heads nodding in agreement at my choices. They knew as well as I, that Tina was trained in this field, the only one of our generation.

"Trix will be responsible for security on Earth, which will most likely be needed. You will pick some to be full-time security and train them in our weapons. It may be necessary for all of us to

33

eventually be trained to supplement security if needed, but we don't have the time to do it here."

"Flay, I saved you for last because you may have the hardest task both here and on Earth. Our survival on Earth hinges on your engineering ability to help the humans design and build the necessary facilities for both our races' survival. You will help me choose a location for the survival community to be built and engineer and design some of the facilities. The humans will, actually, must have the facility built before we arrive. This makes it imperative that your designs be used. You must also decide what large equipment will be taken, since space on the ship is limited. I'm talking about waste processing, power generation and the like, especially utilizing our advanced technology. I will want satellites to monitor for our security, and we will need a dome to hide and store Bright One in. We will talk after the meeting."

"I know I have not covered everything, so I encourage you to think about our future situation and make suggestions or recommendations. Even as I'm talking, I realize we will need a meal preparation team. On Earth they call them cooks or chefs. I'm sure you will come up with other ideas. Think about it and let's meet again tomorrow." Everyone cheered in excitement, and as we ended the meeting I could hear congratulations being offered to those I had chosen. I waited for Flay's congratulations to settle down and her to show up for our meeting, which she quickly did.

Flay said, "Thank you Brin. I wasn't expecting to be made a department head, but I will do the job as best I can."

I laughed out loud and said, "Don't be modest, Flay. You are by far the most knowledgeable in engineering and the sciences of our generation, and you are already doing the job. Speaking of your tasks, what have you discovered?"

Flay said, "We found two people that are probably in the Earth's early team. Nancy Macintosh and Jeremy Hodge. We don't know who they are or what they do, but they are important."

"OK." I said, "I'll check them out on the Internet."

Flay said, "Oh, another thing. My dad seems excited about the stock market. He says that if you can get some money in a special Earth account where he can buy and sell stock, he can make you a fortune before the economy fails. By getting glimpses of the future he will know what stock to buy and when to sell."

"We also have a better feel for the beginning of the actual collapse of the economy. At best we only have a few months. At least we think this is correct timing, because this date is the last lottery paid out. I've got the winning numbers for you, also."

I said, "Damn, only months doesn't give us much time. We had better hurry."

"Help me research and pick out a location for the settlement. I'll send you my suggestions and information I've accumulated so far. See if you agree. I'm also sending you a basic set of plans for

35

the main complex I got from my contact on Earth. Please work your engineering magic and formalize them for construction. Do it quickly, please."

Meg and Peg were hungry, so we went up to the cafeteria and stuffed ourselves. It's a good thing we did, because I hadn't realized how starved I actually was. Satisfied, we went back to our dome. The girls took a nap, while I went immediately to my communicator to begin my research.

I was curious about the names Flay gave me. As it turned out, Nancy Macintosh was a real estate agent working out of the Cherokee Nation. A picture of Nancy showed a petite and stunningly beautiful, brown Cherokee Indian lady. Not only was she pretty, but she was apparently smart, also. Upon further research I found that she was also an attorney and a tribal member of the Cherokee Nation. I remembered from my research on Mike Brannon that he too was a Cherokee tribal member. Interesting.

I had also been researching areas to build the colony. I had previously settled on the Lake Tinklier area, because of the clean, clear and deep water. I quickly went back to the area and discovered that my chosen target area was also within the territory of the Cherokee Nation. I was beginning to see a pattern that could be helpful. The Cherokee Nation was a sovereign country within but outside the United States with their own laws and enforcement. This could be very helpful in reducing red tape.

My research then turned to Jeremy Hodge. I discovered that he is a private architect working out of the Tulsa area, a large city near our potential site. He had some impressive credits of accomplishments. I would keep him in mind as the project progresses.

I went back to Google Earth to finalize a definite target location. I found a remote area on the shore of Lake Tenkiller and carved out a hundred acre swath of property. The property included a fair sized Island, which would be perfect to house our main building. The adjacent natural deep-water harbor would be perfect for our underwater dome, also. I sent this information over to Flay for her to review then joined Meg and Peg in the net.

I woke up alone and quickly reported to the meeting the following day. It looked like a scurrying school of fish. There really wasn't a general meeting. Everyone seemed to know what was needed and had evidently been working through the sleep cycle. Meg and Peg had even gotten up after I came to bed and had taken charge of the storing of equipment and supplies, and it looked like a steady flow of bodies and lift equipment into and out of the Bright One.

I walked up the bottom hatch and noticed that the larger and heavier equipment such as the power generators, two of them, the waste treatment units, had been brought on board first and secured. There were also three crated satellites stored near the hatch, obviously for quick deployment in orbit around Earth. I also noticed several rail-guns and EMP pulse generators stored inside. What surprised me most was the two smaller saucers inside. Now that I thought about it, this was a great idea. Now that these big items were loaded, every square inch of space around the large items in the lower deck was being filled by smaller items. It was a very efficient use of space, and I was impressed.

When I came out of the ship I was greeted by my chosen department heads. They apparently were ready to brief me on their progress. Peg remained onboard to supervise, but Meg quickly joined us. Actually, Meg did the talking for the group.

Meg said, "We met while you were sleeping and decided to get started with the loading. Most of us already knew what we wanted to take to the new world, so we got started. We also took the liberty, with your approval of course, of selecting a head chef, as they are called on Earth. You know Kit." Meg reached back and pulled Kit forward. "She has been training with the older ones for years. Both her parents and her work in the cafeteria, so we have been eating her cooking for years."

I said, "Of course I agree with your recommendation. Welcome to the group of department heads."

Meg continued, "Also, the way we see it, most everything will be completed on Earth by the time we get there, and we must assimilate into their team. There are many professions and skills lost to us already, but our technology still could be of much benefit to them. We believe our best plan is to fall into their organization and work with them where they need help. They would already have made plans for survival, and we can benefit from their planning and staffing of the necessary skills. Assuming this, we don't have to have everything covered. The humans would have done it already."

I said, "Thanks Meg. You all are making me more confident of our survival. Your assessment sounds very reasonable and probably accurate. What we lack in skills we can make up for with technology. It sounds like the two groups can complement each other. Anyone want to add anything?"

Blane said, "Well, there is one thing I would like to do before we leave. There have been reports of other grappers being seen in the area. The grappers will eat the fish supply in the area or run them off. I would like to sweep the area and kill them. It is the least we can do to protect the old ones before we leave. I feel bad enough leaving them alone without having to leave them with a grapper problem."

I said, "Sure. I can go out with you and bring my pod. Your pod and mine can find them and we can kill them, but let's tell the pods to let us laser them. I don't want to lose any more friends to grappers. Both suns are bright today, so it should be a good day for hunting. Want to get started now?" Blane looked pleased and nodded, so we left the loading to the girls to continue, while we hunted.

Once we were in the water we both squealed for our pods. When the pods gathered there were about twenty-two porpoises, all excited and chattering. As best we could through hand signing, we described a hunt for grappers in a circular pattern. We showed them our laser pistols and hoped they understood to let us kill the grappers, but they were a mortal enemy to our friends, which meant there was no guarantee. The pods took off in search, leaving guards with us. Blane and I both knew they would search and smell them out if there were any near. The pods would follow an ever widening circular path until they found one. Hopefully they would return to get us if they found one. We waited and after about fifteen minutes two of our friend came streaking back chirping with excitement. I grabbed hold of Dobe and Dubs dorsal fins and we quickly followed the excited scouts. I looked back to see a grinning Blane close behind. The pods had obviously found a grapper, and as we got closer we could see the pods circling a large, agitated grapper, darting in and out. They had not launched an attack, just kept it stationary until we got there. Blane and I readied ourselves and waved the pods out of the way. When the pods pulled back the grapper came directly for us. We didn't let it get too close before we fired, mutilating the hideous water beast. The pods immediately took sport ramming the dead body. After driving it to the depths they continued their search.

All total, we killed four grappers, a predator whale and one large water snake within a three mile radius of the city. Water snakes are extremely dangerous but not terribly aggressive like a grapper, but the pods singled it out for destruction and we complied. The predator whale was of particular threat to porpoises, so we were happy to take it out for the pods. I'm glad we cleared the danger out the area for the old ones. They wouldn't acknowledge that we did them a favor or service, but we felt better for having done it.

When we returned, I noticed that the work was still in progress in the dome, so I dove back in and swam to my dome. I was eager to see if there was a message from Mike, but before I got started with the search Flay popped up into my dome.

Flay said, "That site you picked is perfect for us. Lake Tenkiller is mostly fed from artisan springs, which is pure water. This lake is the best one for clear and clean water, and I like the location. It's remote and the water is deep at that location. Mostly, however, what I wanted to tell you is that my analyzer completed the engineering and drafting on the complex drawings you gave me. I sent the file to you already."

I quickly pulled her file up and scanned through the various layers of rendered drawings. I noticed that she had greatly improved the design. I said, "This is great, Flay. Now let's see if we have the money to build it."

When I connected with Earth's Internet there was indeed a message from Mike … a short one but massively relieving to my anxiety.

"Brin,

41

I won the lottery. Now what?
Mike"

I was so ready to hear this news. All the planning so far needed this money to happen. I gave Flay a thumbs up and said, "I believe we have a deal going." Flay made suggestions as I typed the response.

"Mike,

"Now you start building the off-the-grid compound ... quickly. I suggest that you deposit the money in several banks for diversity and protection, set up a $30,000,000 password account with a stock broker, immediately start negotiations with several of the major Muskogee/Tahlequah area contractors capable of building fast and, if necessary, can build night and day. We have developed detailed construction plans for the complex you described, which are attached to this e-mail. We have added to and improved your plans to accommodate some of our needs."

"I have also done some research on you. I discovered that you have a Business Management degree from the University of Oklahoma, making you skilled in running this project. I also know you currently live in Muskogee, Oklahoma. This is an acceptable area of your country to base our complex. Through Google Earth I have also located a prime location in your area. As you will see on the attached map, this one hundred acres is on the banks of Lake Tenkiller just east of you. This acreage also includes an island, two in fact. The big island provides the perfect protection for the

main complex. It has water on three sides and access to the island from land will be by bridge, which should be a draw bridge, also for protection."

"You will need an aggressive real estate agent to purchase this property for you. It could be complicated and difficult, so be ready to pay incentives and bribes. I'm currently researching an agent and will let you know what I find. I also discovered that you are 50% Cherokee Indian and are a member of the Cherokee Nation. This property is within the Cherokee Nation, so it might be beneficial to seek their help, possibly even partner with them."

"This is a good beginning. Good Luck."

I thought to myself how strange it was to be talking about land and property. I had only seen land once in my life. The dolphins had taken me to see land once. They called it the "Bottom on Top". This was before we started studying Earth, and I didn't understand the concept of what they were describing, so they took me to show me the bottom on top. It was far away, but it was in fact the bottom of the water extending above the water. I walked around on the dry land and found it strange, because it was rigid and there was no rhythm of the sea under my feet. Now I was dealing in purchasing the "Bottom on Top", called land on Earth.

My thoughts vanished when Meg and Peg came through the airlock bringing food. I didn't realize I was hungry until I smelled the food. It had been a stringent and busy day killing predators, but pleased we had done so. I showed the girls Mike's message, and they cheered. I let them see my message to Mike. They nodded agreement, so I made all the attachments and sent it to Earth's Internet. As soon as I had eaten, I was ready for sleep. Flay left to go back to the large dome, and the girls and I rolled up in the net. I was asleep almost immediately.

When I awoke I nudged the girls up. We took a quick cleansing swim, jumped up in the large dome and went up to the cafeteria. We ate well then headed back to the Bright One dome for a meeting. As we entered the word spread fast and the department heads came quickly. We gathered and I said, "I want all of you to give me and the others of the group a status report so we can identify what else needs to be done or maybe what we might be missing."

Blane was the first to speak saying, "Well, it doesn't have anything to do with mission, but Brin and I made a sweep of the area to hunt the predators that have been reported. We did kill four grippers, one whale predator and a large water snake. The area is now clear." The others cheered.

"As to the mission, I have recruited several helpers to gather plants for transplanting to Earth's lake. We will load them into a cryogenic chamber next cycle. We are also selecting several species of fish to transplant. These too will be put into cryogenics. This cycle we are harvesting fish and plants for food storage for the trip and after we get to Earth. We know we must adapt to different foods on Earth, but I plan to have food stored so we can adjust slowly, if necessary. Plus, we want to grow our on food supply on Earth. Bye the way, how many will be awake during the trip, and how long do you expect the trip to Earth to take?"

I looked toward Meg and Peg, and Meg took the hint and said, "All but the three of us" waving her hand to indicate herself, Peg and I, "will be in cryogenics for the entire trip. Normally a long distance trip like this takes six months, three months in each solar system using gravity drive only. As many of you know, our ancient scientists passed down these instructions. Evidently, the use of time bending technology, other than communications only, is dangerous to use within a solar system due to collisions with space debris and asteroids. Once we are in clear space we can engage the time bending technology safely and instantly transport across vast distances. In this case we don't have six months. For this trip we will take as many shortcuts as safely possible to make the trip in under three months."

"The bottom two decks of the Bright One are almost completely stocked. We will finish the loading this cycle. That leaves the third deck stocking for tomorrow, but Tina should speak of this. This is all her department."

Tina said, "As soon as the work requirement slows we will begin putting our people into cryogenics. We have already loaded as much medical supplies and technology as we have room for. Only the people and Blane's plants and fish

45

remain to be loaded. Oh, and of course the porpoises if you have figured out how to get them to agree. They're too big to force. As for the people, everyone should start saying their 'Good Byes'."

Trix said, "I have picked a few for my security, mostly those that are already familiar with our weapons, since there was no time for training. Training for the whole team will have to wait until we are already on Earth, but I made sure we have plenty of weapons, including a few of the larger ones. Our weapons are easy to use anyway, just point and pull the trigger. We should be all right."

I said, "I've already heard Flay's report. It sounds like we are almost ready to launch. Let's plan on launching the second cycle from now. Are all in agreement?" I looked around the group and received nods from all.

Tina's suggestion to say my "Good Byes" seemed appropriate. My father was my only family left, my mother having passed several years earlier. I told the girls my intentions, and they decided to go see their parents as well. I approached the Assembly, since that is where my father stayed most of the time. I thought I could detect a slight smile on his face as I approached.

Bart said, "We have been monitoring your progress, and it looks like you are almost ready."

"Yes, father," I said, "We plan to leave in two cycles. Our partner on Earth has been funded to build the survival complex. He won the lottery with our advanced knowledge of the winning numbers. That part of the plan has worked out successfully.

We have another set of winning numbers we will give him just prior to Earth's total economic collapse. Funds will not be an issue. We are, of course, taking our own wealth. Eventually, civilization will begin again, possibly with our help. Our wealth, combined with the funds generated on Earth, will ensure that we prosper on the new world. Once we are established and stable we will communicate with you, and the remainder of you can join us."

Bart said, "Thank you for the consideration, but we have decided to remain here on Apsaras and finish out our lives. Rebuilding what we now have would be a difficult task at our stage of life. We are comfortable here and have everything we need. We are hopeful that you can keep our race from going totally extinct, and we give you all our blessing."

I was touched by his comments. This was the first time he had ever heard his father say, "Thank You" and offer any encouragement. As long as I remembered he had always been rigidly strict and formal. He was saying his "Good Bye" in the only way he knew how. I bowed low toward the Assembly and said, "We will do our best." I held the tears back and turned and walk away.

I went back to my dome to check for messages from Mike. I was beginning to worry about Mike. Maybe he just took the money and ran. I certainly hope not. The waiting was nerve-racking, so I sent a message:

"How are things going?"

I was eager to move the Earth team along. Since Flay had already told me about Nancy Macintosh being involved in the glimpse of the future and liking the information I had discovered about her, I structured a message to her. I sent her a map of the property and asked her to get started on the project and that Mike Brannon would be contacting her.

I decided to continue with Mike and sent a second message:

"I found a real estate agent for you. She actually works for the Cherokee Nation, so she can be doubly helpful. I gave her name, Nancy Macintosh, and contact information. Please contact her as soon as possible. I have sent her the map of the property, and she is already working on it."

I decided to take a swim and try to talk with my pod, especially Dobe. If I could convince her the others would follow willingly. As usual, Dobe and Dubs joined me after only a few moments in the water. In my old dome they could keep better track of me and the girls by viewing us through the glass, but since coming to the city this had been more difficult for them. We made up for lost contact by playing and racing around under the city. We eventually popped up into the large dome to view the Bright One being loaded. Through hand signing and words I told her we were going away to a new home in the saucer. Dobe seemed to understand and looked sad and agitated. I continued and told her I wanted her and the others to go away with me. This seemed to please her greatly, and she began chirping excitedly. I asked her if she wanted to go with me. Dobe started shaking her head up and down and chirping even louder. I continued to explain that she would need to go into the saucer. I let that settle with her then asked, "Will you go with me on the saucer to a new home?"

Dobe actually said in a chirping way, "Yes, Yes, Dobe go ... ship ... we go ... new home ... go with you."

I said, "I'm very pleased that you will go with me. Please explain to the others that they must go in the saucer and sleep. They will be safe. When they awake they will be at the new home." Dobe understood the concept and seemed to accept it. She nuzzled me and took off to explain to the others of her pod.

When I returned to my dome there was a message from Mike.

"Brin, first I have done all you suggested. The money is in four different banks, and I set up the stock broker password account for $30,000,000. I hope you know I don't know a damn thing about buying stock. Next, I will go see Nancy Macintosh tomorrow and see what we can work out on the property."

"Now, for you. You need to provide me more information about where we are going with this and why such a fast rush. You also need to tell me more about you and your group. I have lots of questions which need answering."

I was reluctant to respond to Mike. I could tell he was becoming suspicious. I decided to think on

49

it for a while and maybe talk to Meg and Peg about how to respond. The girls were smart, and I valued their opinions, besides, they weren't bashful about sharing their opinion.

I was tired, but I ventured back to the large dome to check on progress. It looked like they were winding down. I noticed Tina was taking charge now and directing some of our group into the ship, presumably toward the third deck and the cryogenic chamber room. She must have started much earlier, because there were fewer workers in sight. Blane saw him and he waved Blane over. When he approached, I said, "I think I managed to explain to Dobe about loading up in the ship and going with us. She is ready to make the trip and is explaining it to the others. I suggest you talk to your pod leader also and send them to talk to Dobe. It might make it easier to explain. We will have to start loading them tomorrow."

Blane said, "Oh, thanks. I have been dreading trying to explain it to them. Dobe understands the concept? I know she's a smart one."

I smiled and said, "Yeah, I think she does. She actually used words to say, '*Yes, Yes, Dobe go ... ship ... we go ... new home... go with you.*'" I knew Blane would understand the significance of her using actual words. It was difficult for them to chirp out words, and they only did it for emphasis in communication with us. Dobe summed up her understanding of our conversation quite well.

Blane smiled and said, "That's great. I'll talk to my pod and send them to Dobe. We'll be finishing up gathering fish and plants by late meal. I'll talk to them then."

I think Blane had lost track of time, because I was already hungry and ready for my late meal. As if to accent my thoughts, Meg and Peg came nuzzling up to me smiling.

Peg said, "We're glad you're here. We just finished with the loading on decks one and two, and we were about to come get you for dinner. Tina still has a crew working in cryogenics, but once she is done we will be ready to launch."

I slipped my arms around my girls and nuzzled their cheeks and said, "I was just looking for you. I'm hungry, too. I'm also tired, but I need you two to snuggle with."

We went up to the cafeteria and picked up a large meal of boiled fish and green, water salad. Obviously the word got out about us launching in tomorrow's cycle. Many of the old ones dropped by our table to wish us well and give us their blessings. I was also surprised to see Meg and Peg's parents join us at our table. They weren't saying "Good Byes'; they had done that earlier and in private, but I could see all their eyes tear up as we talked about trivial things. I often wish I had a relationship with my father like they did. I did not rush the girls, but eventually it became apparent that the stalling must end. We eventually left and went back to our dome, where both girls broke down crying onto my shoulders. I had previously told the girls what my father said about the old ones staying, but I said, "I know what my father said, but once we

51

get established on Earth we can try again, even if it's only a few that want to come to Earth. I mean there are two other saucers. Hell, maybe we can come up with a reason for some to come, like bringing special supplies or fish stock we need." I had thought about it, but when I brought it up the girls stopped crying and showered me with warm kisses. I liked the attention, and we cuddled up in the net and went sound asleep.

I nudged the girls when I awoke and we took a quick swim to clean ourselves, then popped up into the large dome. The girls went to the control center in the uppermost part of the ship, while I met with Tina and Blane. I asked, "How are things going?"

Tina said, "We have all but ten people, excluding Meg, Peg, and you, in cryogenics already. All of Blane's fish, fertilized eggs, and plants have also been stored in cryogenics. All we have left are the porpoises. I have twenty modified chambers ready for them, more if we need them. We just need you to bring them in and get them to position themselves in the web harness so we can lift them to the third deck."

I looked at Blane and asked, "Did you talk to your pod? Are they ready?"

Blane said, "Yeah, I talked to them and they communicated with Dobe, also. I think they are ready."

I noticed that the deck iris had been opened wider for a water access into the lower decks and that the web harness was already lowered into the water. I nodded to Tina and dove into the water and squealed for my pod, and Blane did the same. Both pods surfaced around us. I said, "Dobe, are you ready to go into the ship?" She chirped loudly, shaking her head up and down, then chirped "Dobe go ... ship ... new home." I said, "Trust me and don't be afraid." She chirped again, "Dobe ... trust." I pointed to the web harness and guided her into it. She swam directly into the harness. She didn't even shake when it slowly lifted her out of the water and up through the lower hatch. I told Dubs and the others I would return soon and quickly ran up the hatch. I was there when Dobe came up. I could tell she was nervous, but she calmed when she saw me. Tina guided her to the open chamber and settled her down in the liquid. Once there, Tina detached the harness and slipped a breathing cup over Dobe's blowhole. Tina patted Dobe's back and closed the chamber lid. Once closed, Tina pushed a button and the process quickly began. Dobe was out and stored for space flight in a matter of seconds. I rushed back down into the water and guided Dubs into the harness. He was no trouble at all. He was eager to follow Dobe. After Dobe and Dubs, the rest followed quickly, swimming themselves into position. By the time all my pod was loaded, Blane had no problem at all. They seemed eager to load, even lining up. I had worried about this process so much. I was afraid I might have to leave my friends behind, but they were evidently not about to be left behind.

Once all the porpoises had been stored in cryogenics, Tina began putting the remainder of our people in chambers. She was the last one to go into cryogenics, but before she went under she instructed Meg, Peg and I in how to bring her out. There wasn't anything to it. All we had to do was push a button, but Tina made sure we knew which button to push. There was nothing left to do but launch.

Chapter 3
(The Launch)

The girls and I went to the control room. The girls had already fired up the gravity engines. Meg sat at the console and opened the dome's iris deck fully. A digital image brightened in the air before her, showing the outline of the ship and the surrounding structures. As she began maneuvering the ship, I noticed through the translucent top dome some of the old one gathered outside. Among them was his father, Bart. His shoulders were stooped and his face ashen and forlorn. As we started sinking beneath the water he actually waved. I waved back and fought back tears. They both knew this was probably the last time they would see each other. Brin had never seen him like this, and it broke my heart. Damn him! Why, after it was too late did he now show emotions. Brin waved again as they sank out of sight, and this time he didn't fight the tears.

Peg, seeing my tears and understanding, slipped her arms around me and nuzzled my neck. I silently wiped the tears away and concentrated on the monitor. Meg was guiding the Bright One under the city toward open water. When we cleared the city she took us up out of the water and increased speed. The image changed from the digital representation to visual. We shot up fast. We took our last look at Apsaras as we shot up into space. Our poor planet was dying. Even from here we could see huge splotches of red algae taking over the water surface of our planet. Our city had been moved several times to clearer water, but from our vantage point we could see there were no other clear areas to move it to again. Once the algae reached the location of our last city, life would be over for our race on Apsaras. We were the last hope for our race.

Meg plotted our course out of our solar system and let the ship take over the controls. With nothing more to do, I needed a distraction, so I went to my communicator and reread Mike's last message. I would eventually have to answer him, now was as good a time as any. The girls, also needing a distraction, were looking over my shoulder and helped me write a response.

Meg said, "You're going to have to tell him eventually. You might as well start now, just do it in stages so you don't scare the crap out of him. We don't want him to run off with all the money, so start with the impending apocalypse. Make it personal to him."

"Mike, Thanks for the quick action on depositing the funds and making contact with the real estate agent. As you will soon see, it's very important."

"Mike, I understand that you have many questions, but you will have to trust me for a while yet. You must admit, though, that we have given you a massive amount of money. It's all in your name, and it's yours; although we are hoping you will use it to further our plan and goals. You can't

say that I am taking advantage of you. Of course we chose you and expect you to partner with our group as agreed."

"Additionally, you need to understand that you were chosen by my group for a reason, because of your original posts warning of future chaos and an apocalypse. Your descriptions of the fall of civilization were and are more right than you know. The apocalypse is coming and quicker than even you know. I tell you this with certain confidence. So you will believe me I must share one of my secrets with you, which must be held in strict confidence. Our group has the limited ability to look into the future, as evidenced by us giving you the correct lottery numbers. I know you will believe this. How else could we have given you the right numbers? Now you must believe that we have seen the future apocalypse. It is real and WILL occur in the near future."

"We needed an advanced partner to prepare us all for survival, because our arrival time there will be too late to prepare. We needed someone like you and the group you will gather to assure our and your survival. We must be self-sufficient and be able to defend ourselves before civilization collapses. I hope now you understand the need for rapid compliance toward our plans. There are other secrets I must share with you, but those secrets must wait."

"As to the stock broker account for $30,000,000, we are already working via the Internet with it. Because of the previously disclosed

secret we have, in fact, more than doubled this amount in the time we've had with the account, and it will continue to grow at an accelerated rate each day."

"I hope that you understand better now and will push an accelerated pace, and an important part of that, excluding the physical property and buildings, is the gathering of a vetted group. You will need to advertise for potential members of this group to consist of a hundred members. You will need twenty-five females and seventy-five men, all need to be educated, healthy, unattached and mostly under thirty-five. They will need an incentive to join the team, because they need to commit to be sequestered for two years in a, what we shall call, survival study and experiment. I suggest offering them one million at contract end. This will provide the incentive, but the apocalypse will occur within this two year period and money will be worthless afterwards. But, they will survive the destruction of civilization, so it is not like they are being tricked."

"I hope everything is well with you. You are important to all of us. Please let me know if you remain a team player."

The girls agreed with my response. Peg wondered if maybe I had given Mike too much information, but Meg thought I should have given him more. This was uncharted territory, and I didn't have a firm direction or course. I only knew Mike from his messages, but I liked him and, for the most part, trusted him. Actually, I had no choice but to trust him. We had one very important interest in common ... survival. Hopefully, this will be enough. Still, I would worry until Mike gave us a response.

Traveling in space we had few options: sleep, watch English movies, exercise or swim. Our forefathers had designed and built in a circular swimming pool. The pool was ten feet wide and ten feet deep and completely encircled the control room, leaving plenty of room in the center. Intermittent retractable walkways reached out to the outside translucent observation dome. As a result we could swim as long as we wanted or until we got dizzy from going in circles. Of course our race depended heavily upon swimming. Swimming hydrated our bodies and provided our hygiene. I mean we had separate facilities for waste elimination, but water provided much of our other needs. Plus, swimming gave us our exercise, and it was something to do with our time. Our food was simple but healthy, so preparing food didn't take up much time either. We would have a lot of time to kill.

Our kitchen, food storage, waste management facilities, and sleeping quarters were one deck down, but we planned to spend most of our time in the control room monitoring communication or swimming. One of us would remain awake at all times. It wasn't really necessary, because nothing ever failed in centuries of use. Still, we felt more comfortable with one of us on watch and monitoring. Who knew when an asteroid might intersect our path or other outside factors might sound an alarm. Peg had programmed my communicator to sound an alarm when I received a message from Earth's Internet, which now startled all of us when it sounded. I recovered, laughed at my reaction and went to view the message. It was from Mike.

"Yes, Brin I am onboard with this project. What you tell me is believable and what you are not telling me is also clear. I'm not stupid. I believe you are not from Earth! Earth technology does not exist that can view time, and there is nowhere on Planet Earth that you couldn't get here within a month. Now, before you panic, I really don't give a shit if you're an alien. I'm in for survival. Still, I would like to know who you are and what to expect."

I initially felt a rush of panic, but I quickly began smiling when I realized Mike did not seem to have a problem with it. My worries were wasted. This was going to work out well.

Peg said, "I told you he was smart. We gave him too much information, but luckily it didn't make any difference."

Meg said, "At least we can stop worrying and wondering about his reaction. He is going to do what is necessary. Now we can tell him all and openly help him accomplish the task. There was little else we could do except open up."

I responded: *"Well, Mike, it seems that I underestimated you. I was afraid to tell you everything in fear that you might run away screaming or not believe me. We need you to get most of the project completed before we get there, otherwise we will all die. This is a fact."*

"Now, as for us. Our race IS from another planet, but we are, in fact, humanoid, at least we came from a common ancestry, human. We are called in English the "Water People". Our evolution developed on a world that is mostly covered in water. We breath air just like you; we speak English; we walk upright, even though we swim like fish; we even look like you, with some noticeable differences, which we don't have to go into right now. Our race lives and works mostly in above water floating cities, but many live in water in underwater dome housing."

"You may wonder why we are coming to Earth when your race is also facing extinction. The reason is simple: Our race is ancient and it is almost extinct, with only a hundred of our generation making the trip to Earth. We are almost totally unable to procreate. Our males can't produce the sperm to impregnate our females, and we hope our races are close enough in DNA to cross breed. Your race is the only other humanoid race we have found in the universe. We need our females to milk the sperm of the male members of your team so we can create a mixed in-breed race. It is the only way our race can survive, even if it is only in part."

"As I have mentioned, we bring 25 males and 75 females in our group. We also bring much technology that will help us all survive, but the facilities must be complete before we get there. We

61

are still far out in space and estimate we will arrive within a few months, your time. I will try to answer any other questions you pose. I will hold nothing else back. I'm pleased that you accept our partnership."

That was pretty much out there. It felt good to finally open up. I felt good enough that I was hungry. It was like a load had been lifted from my shoulders. The girls and I went below deck and prepared a meal, ate, then went for another swim. Afterwards, since one of us would have to stay awake, Peg volunteered to stay awake, and Meg and I went to our net and curled up together and slept. I was vaguely aware when they swapped places eight hours later. The stress of the last few days must have tapped my energy, because I slept through half of Meg's watch. I finally disentangled myself from Peg's arms and legs, ate a snack, used the waste facility and joined Meg in the control room.

Meg and Peg are identical twins, and it is difficult to tell them apart for most, but I never have a problem knowing the difference. With our race's lack of diversity in our DNA most of us look very much alike, especially since we all wear the same seaweed woven skirt. Out of habit many of us just look at the shape of the orange patterns in the temple hair to identify the person. In the case of Meg and Peg, neither has any orange at the temples, rare also for our race. This tends to further confuse many, but not me. I don't even notice the lack of orange. The totally black braided hair on each is identical and uniquely appealing, to me anyway.

No, most of the time I just know which one is which, maybe it is a mental signature, but if I ever do get confused I look at their noses. The indenture, or slight crease, in the skin on the nose from the repetition of pinches shutting out water is slightly higher on the right side of Meg's nose. I'm sure no one else has noticed it, but it is obvious to me.

When Meg saw me approach she said, "We had an asteroid warning in our programmed route, and I had to make a slight course correction. Nothing else occurred. Once we get past the orbit of the planet Aquarius in our solar system we should be clear of anymore potential asteroids. I will talk to Peg when she wakes to see when she might be comfortable making an early time jump to Earth's solar system. We have already agreed that we will bypass some of the established safety restraints."

I'm glad they were already working on the shortcuts, because we couldn't comply with the three months recommended time within our solar system. Still, as I remembered, the orbit of Aquarius was two weeks out. This would be our earliest opportunity to take a shortcut. This gives us plenty of time to analyze our choices.

I was feeling jovial, so I suddenly grabbed Meg from behind and jumped in the pool with her. I said, "Let's go for a swim!" The sudden plunk into the pool shocked Meg, and she came up sputtering and cussing me between her burst of laughter. She reached out at me with slaps, but I had already jumped out of her reach and swam off. She chased me for several laps before she finally caught me. She wouldn't have caught me if I hadn't been laughing so hard. After she ducked me under a couple of times we both broke out laughing again. I realized suddenly that I hadn't laughed much lately with all the stress. I also realized that I liked laughing. Our laughing and cutting up must have woken Peg. She came into the control room wondering what we were up to, but she made the mistake of standing too close to the edge of the pool. Meg and I exchanged glances and smiles and jumped up and pulled her in. This time we both took off, pursued by a laughing Peg. We continued to swim for a while until my communication indicator sounded. We jumped out on the deck and shook the water off. When I checked, it was a message from Mike.

"Brin, I understand all that you have said. I will keep everything a secret until much later. Will you need any extra accommodation for your people? Indeed, we will get along well. There is one thing, however, you must explain to me. What do you mean by milking sperm from our males. Is this another way of saying sex, or do you mean something entirely different? Oh, I am attaching a copy of the ad I will be posting tomorrow to find and recruit members to my group. Nancy is working out well. Let me know if you find any more potential recruits for my group. We may need to win another lottery to cover the 100 million retainer I will need to recruit these members. All is well Brin."

The Apocalypse Group is seeking 100 (75 men & 25 females) professional, educated, unattached and healthy individuals to participate in a two year study group of how to live well off-the-grid. We will literally be writing the how-to book on survival after any future apocalypse. We will be learning the best ways to survive. If you feel you have something to offer toward this project, please forward your resume and contact information along with a cover letter describing how you could contribute. You will be required to remain sequestered and under contract during the study in a remote area near Lake Tenkiller, Oklahoma. If you fulfill your obligation you will be awarded $1,000,000.00 at the term for your contribution.

Respond to:

The Apocalypse Group

P.O. Box XXXX

Tahlequah, OK

Flay, before she went into hibernation, had completed the design of the underwater dome for the Bright One and made improvements to Mike's main complex. And since Jeremy Hodge would apparently be one of Mike's group, I structured a message to him providing the detailed drawings of both the complex and dome. I informed him that Mike would be contacting him to discuss the project. I figured it was time to get Jeremy and Mike together. As to the explanation of milking sperm, I decided to let Meg and Peg describe that.

"Hello, Mike, The ad you sent us was excellent for our purpose. Please let us know the responses. As to winning another lottery, I'm afraid we will have to wait for a while longer, closer to the end; because another win so soon would trigger an investigation. We will wait until it becomes too late to investigate but before they stop awarding the money. I will let you know when and provide the winning numbers."

"Thank you for considering any special needs for my group. We plan to completely interface with your group in the structure you are building, but, now that you know of our nature, we will require an underwater dome structure to park our ship in. We want to be able to hide it from view and protect it. It will be our last line of defense, if required. I have already forwarded the plans of the building and underwater dome to an architect. His name is Jeremy Hodge, and he lives in Tulsa." Brin included the contact information. *"We believe he can get the job done in time, and we believe him to be a potential recruit worth considering. Either way will work for us. You might want to give him a copy of your ad and see what he might want to do."*

"Also, since you are going to Tulsa, I suggest that you begin purchasing gold and silver. Eventually, money will be worthless, gold and silver should be reliable in the future, however. We will also be bringing great wealth in the form of gold, silver, platinum and precious stones, but it will be some time before civilization returns. These supplies will benefit us at that time."

"I will let my mates, Meg and Peg, explain about milking sperm."

"Hello Mike, milking sperm is, we suppose, sex. It involves inserting the male penis into the female vagina, but in the case of our race, the process has been modified through generation of training. Our females have perfected a method of muscle control within our vagina that produces a strong suction that milks the sperm from the male's testicles. This method was developed to capture as much sperm as possible for fertilization, since our males produce a low sperm count and have little sexual desire."

We sent this message out and went below to prepare something to eat and didn't think any more about it, thinking it would be a while before Mike responded. So, when the message indicator sounded we were surprised and went up to view it. As expected it was from Mike.

"Hey Brin, Meg and Peg,"

"You're explanation of milking sperm is shocking and appalling to me and will be to any male of my race, and it is totally unacceptable. There is no way I would slip my dick into a vagina that is going to pull out my sperm by force. It sounds painful, and this process apparently completely bypasses the fun and enjoyment of sex. It sounds like this milking process is done without an orgasm, thus eliminating the attraction of sex. I hate to say this, but your improvements have destroyed the intent of sex and its pleasure. It is no wonder the males of your species have little interest or desire for sex. You can't reduce a natural

67

biological process to a mechanical medical procedure. I think your species better relearn how to fuck. The only way any female will get my sperm is when I give it to them through an orgasm. It's no wonder your race is becoming extinct. Maybe we can find another way such as artificial insemination, but I really suggest you reconsider going back to nature's way."

"Now, moving on to business, I will make contact with Jeremy today and attempt to see him. BTW, I think you already know Jeremy will work out like Nancy is. While you are at it, we will need a doctor and a dentist almost immediately to check out and health clear our recruits. You might give me contact information on these people, and any others you might feel necessary. You might also let me know if there are any names I should avoid."

"Damn", I said, "I think we scared him, certainly we upset him." Both girls nodded, but I could see the disbelief on their faces. They had no idea why. The process employed of milking sperm had been passed down to them by their mother and their mother's mother before and so forth. It was just the way it was and had always been as far back as anyone could remember. To a large extent the same process of being milked had been passed down by the fathers. I had never known or heard of anything different. In fact, being the only descendant of the hereditary leader of our race had almost made me the prime target of females for as far back as my reaching puberty. Most of the child bearing age females wanted to be the mother of the next Assembly leader, which required me to be in demand through my early adult years. Mike had also been right in his assessment: It had never been fun. Being milked did hurt, and any thought of sex brought negative connotations. Mike was correct in that I had never had an orgasm. I didn't even know what it was. Maybe he was right about our plight. I would have to give this some thought.

I decided to respond immediately to Mike's message, but not address the milking issue until we had given it more thought.

***

"Mike, I can't help with other names. We did know about Nancy, because we once saw the two of you together at a glimpse into the future, but we didn't look often. It is quite disturbing, knowing what is going to happen, so we only sought necessary details. We do already have winning lottery numbers and Earth date for the immediately future, which we will use when necessary."

"Now that detailed planning and construction is nearing, I wanted to share with you some of the technology we will be bringing. We will be providing clean power sources capable of providing enough power to serve a medium size city. They are relatively small and are fueled by water."

"Also, since we are coming from a polluted and dying world, we have learned and developed a sewage treatment system capable of treating tons of raw sewage, converting it to clean usable fertilizer for adding nutrients to the fields and pure water. We are bringing edible plants from our world that

will grow underwater. We plan to farm and harvest these plants. We also hope to stock the lake with fish from our world. They grow fast to a large size and will provide a stable source of protein to our colony. I'll provide more information in continued communications."

"We will consider your suggestions on the sex issue and address it further in the future"

We went back below deck and finished making our meal and ate in silence. Finally, to break the silence I asked, "Have you girls been considering any shortcuts to our travel time?"

Meg said, "Well, I have been thinking that we could make a short time jump to get us to the asteroid belt. We can't jump through it, it's too dangerous, but we could get much closer. This would only save us maybe a week in travel time. From that point we can maneuver through the belt into clearer space, then do it again. Is that worth considering?"

I said, "Hey, a week is a week. Do you agree, Peg?" Peg nodded in agreement. We all turned our thoughts to accomplishing the task. We went back to the control room and Peg waved her hand over a light control and a graphic image appeared in front of us clearly showing our location in space and the relative locations of all the other planets in our solar system, all of which were indicated to be in rotation far out of our sector of space. The asteroid belt location was also clearly shown indicating the location of each asteroid and its size. Peg moved her fingers in a complex manner that produced a cross target, which she positioned close to the belt. I noticed a string of numbers, which had to be the precise coordinates of the cross cursor. Peg moved her fingers again and the previous indicator location instantly replaced the cross target indicator. I felt nothing but realized the time jump had already occurred. I said, "Is that it?

Peg chuckled and said, "That's it!" She moved her fingers in the air again in an elaborate pattern and said, "Now we are back on course, but we will have to monitor our course closer now to avoid any asteroids. If a problem appears in the projected course, we will get an alarm notifying us to alter our course. Any small space debris in our course will be automatically eliminated by our laser. We wouldn't be able to deal with obstacles like those in time jump."

Well, we had just saves a week's worth of travel time, and I was full of food. It was time to swim. I jumped in the pool and was quickly followed by the girls. It seemed that the strict and rigid life we had led back on Apsaras was softening, and we were beginning to have fun for a change. I liked to hear the girls actually laugh, because there were no authoritarian elders around to stop us. Life was becoming different and better.

There was little to do traveling in space, so we spent much of our awake time swimming and playing games. Bart, my father, had introduced me to military strategy games years ago. He told me that I needed to be an expert in strategy to govern Apsaras. I have no idea why, since our race had no

71

wars with other fractions within our race, and it had been many generations since we had a war with another alien race. But, I loved the game. The girls liked it also, and we spent many hours playing. I always won, except when they cheated and ganged up on me.

The girls and I didn't talk anymore about what Mike had said, but they, as was I, were obviously in deep thought about it. I certainly was. What he had said was beginning to make a lot of sense, and I was beginning to think about sex in a completely different way. For the first time in my life I was daring to question my rigid training. Mike said sex should be enjoyable and not painful. If this is so, it would be worth considering a change. I know my girls are beautiful, and I shouldn't resent sex with them. I really like them and like being with them … except the sex part. That part is repulsive, and it shouldn't be that way. Mike was right. The process of milking *was* against nature's way, and we should rethink our position and, as Mike had said, relearn how to fuck. That sounded crude but a fairly accurate description. Watching English movies seemed to show sex as enjoyable, but I had never made the connection between our races.

These thoughts were going through my mind as Meg and I rolled up in the sleeping net for the first shift. My mind was making an internal adjustment, and everything seemed different now. Meg's soft, warm skin against mine was somehow stimulating me. My whole thought process had changed. Where anything previously that caused a fleeting thought of sex was instantly rejected and pushed far from my mind. Now I seemed to welcome and embrace these thoughts. I began feeling a stimulation I had never felt before. The touch of her skin now seemed to radiate warmth in me, causing a tingling feeling in my penis. I didn't understand it but welcomed it. I held her close, our faces pressed together from the confining effect of the net. Her intoxicating smell seemed different and no longer repressed by my mind. I looked into her deep, green eyes, and she looked back. We both knew something was very different. My lips touched hers. I tasted her warm, soft lips, and she melted into me with a moan. Our individual reactions stimulated the other. We had kissed before but never like this. We fed each other's wakening desires. Whatever this was, I wanted more. Where repulsion existed before now there was only excitement and craving, craving for something we had never experience before. The urge grew and our kisses became more intense. A passion grew in intensity, and I realized suddenly that my penis felt like a hard pole, throbbing with excitement. The word "Penis" seemed inadequate to describe it, and Mike's word "Dick" jumped forward in my mind. My dick wanted inside her and now! I shoved her webbed skirt up and moved between her thighs, but before I entered her I said in a husky voice I didn't recognize, "Don't milk me!"

In the same husky voice Meg said, "Noooo. I want this too!"

I pushed hard into her hot, wet tunnel. I had been inside her many times before. How could I never have felt the pure joy of being inside her before. My whole being melted inside her, and I began a frenzied pounding into this wonderful, velvet tunnel. My heart pounded inside my chest as my hard dick plunged into her. She began meeting my thrusts with her own, trying to take more of me inside her. Our rhythm and speed increased until we both froze in what must be what Mike called an orgasm. It felt like my dick exploded inside Meg. My sperm shot into her in many quivering gushes, as we both screamed with the release. Meg's internal muscle control and undulations was abundantly evident but weaker and this time extremely welcome. I was amazed. I gave her my sperm. She didn't have to take it, although she did capture it all within her.

Peg came running down the ramp from the control room to investigate the screams asking, "What's wrong? What's going on?"

We were still wrapped together as we tried to catch our breath, and I'm sure it was quite evident what was going on by now. We both ignored her while our chests heaved to pull air into our lungs. Eventually I said, "We were doing what Mike suggested, we were relearning how to fuck. Meg and I were still joined, but we both burst out laughing at my joke. Peg soon joined in the laughter.

Peg continued to watch us then said, "It sounded like you learned extremely well."

We laughed again at her statement and I said, "I believe we did, and I'll be happy to teach you what we learned when your turn comes to sleep." Peg smiled and came over to hug us.

Meg and I finally disengaged from each other. When we did, a copious amount of semen flowed and oozed from her vagina, which shocked Peg.

Before Peg could say anything Meg said, "Brin filled me up. This is much better than milking and far more pleasurable. Just wait, you'll find out."

I think Peg would have stayed longer, but a course adjustment warning sounded. We watched her leave to make the change, but we could still see the smile on her face and a mischievous twinkle in her eyes as she left. Yep, her time was coming, and I could hardly wait to experience another orgasm. I knew my life had definitely changed ... for the better, but right now I needed rest. Meg and I cuddled intimately like we had never done before and fell off into a restful sleep.

I woke when Peg replaced Meg in the net for the shift change. I looked at Peg and said, "Hi sweetness. Please remove your sea skirt before you get comfortable." I had already removed mine. I wanted to feel our skin touching. With Meg my burning desire rose unexpectedly, and I didn't quite know what was happening. This time I knew what to expect, and I was much more controlled. Like it had been with Meg, I knew the girls were beautiful, but I watched with far more interest as Peg removed her covering. She was indeed beautiful, and the gentle curves of her body had new meaning. I felt my passion rise, along with my penis. My mental attitude was now completely different. The curse of and repulsion of sex was totally gone now. It was like a switch had been turned on, or maybe generations of training had been turned off. The soft net enclosed around us and Peg pressed against me. I could see a look in her eyes of wonder, anticipation, maybe even a glimmer of fear of not knowing what to expect. There was, however, no hesitation, as she relaxed her warm body against mine. I wanted to take my time with Peg and lengthen our pleasure. I didn't want to miss a thing. It was like I was seeing her for the first time, and looked deep into her eyes, wide with wonder. Those liquid green eyes had streaks of gold I had never noticed before. I watched her nostrils flare open and slam shut with her growing excitement. My lips gently kissed her soft, cupid-bow lips and felt her body begin to quiver. I nibbled her lips and felt for her tongue. We kissed passionately, tasting each other, but I eventually pulled back to view her body, as I began to explore it with my hands. I touched her lips, tracing the curves. My fingers caressed her soft robin-egg blue skin that trailed into the darker, almost purple lips. My fingers traced the area down her side and hip that marked the gradual darkening of her skin wrapping around her back and buttocks. My fingers followed the quivering lighter skin up her stomach to her breasts. I was fascinated with her hard and protruding, dark purple nipples. It was as if I had never noticed them before, and they were beautiful. Peg moaned as my tongue twirled around her nipples. When I started sucking them Peg squealed and pulled my head against her breasts ...hard. The sweet scent of her breasts was like flower blossoms, intoxicating. It was too much for me. I had held back longer than I should have to be gentle, and I lost myself between her warm thighs. I entered her with force. Peg began screaming, but definitely not in pain. Her arms and legs wrapped tight around me, and her teeth clamped down hard on my shoulder, as I continued to drive in and out of her tunnel of fire. Not being experienced with orgasms, I was relatively sure she had several. When mine hit I no longer knew where I was. I just rode the volcanic eruption to its quivering and jerking conclusion. Afterwards, we lay together recovering, as we listened to Meg clap and cheer our performance.

Meg said, "Peg, I think you are a quick learner." We had to laugh together.

After a while Peg said, "Not that quick of a learner. I think I will need more lessons."

For someone that usually is quiet, that was doubly funny, and Meg and I burst out in hysterical laughter, quickly joined by Peg.

Meg returned to the control room, and I decided to rest some more. As we lay cuddling my mind started remembering the old ones' training, and I got angry. They had been terribly wrong in their training of sex and procreation. How could they have been so wrong? Our entire race had been deprived of meaningful and pleasurable love making for generations. I remembered the many painful sperm milking I had endured since puberty and all the missed chances for blissful pleasure I had lost forever. I vowed to question all my past training and strict rules I had been taught in the future, but I wouldn't start until I had more rest.

When I awoke I eased out of the warm net and started preparing a meal, yep, fish, but this time my own recipe. I baked them in fish oil and spices, then lay them on a bed of simmered water vegetables. When the meals were done I didn't have to call or wake anyone. The smell was enticing and even woke Peg. The girls loved it when I cooked, but I had to be in a really good mood to cook, and I was definitely in a great mood. I had never seen the girls happier. They were smiling constantly and touching me in some way, and I was doing the same to them. Our relationship was drastically changing for the better.

There is no morning or evening in space, and I had totally lost track of any cycle time, furthermore, I didn't care. When we got hungry, we ate. When we got sleepy, we slept. But, exercise like swimming was necessary for our hygiene. We stayed clean and the water remained crystal clear and clean and filtered by the water control unit. Flay had explained the water cycle to me once. She said the gravity propulsion engines ran on a water fuel. That was the one main reason for the pool, it was also our fuel. The oxygen content had to be monitored and the engine automatically converted CO_2 to O_2 when necessary to maintain the proper level, which also provided our life support. So, the pool not only served our exercise and hygiene needs, it also stored oxygen and provided our life support and fuel needs for the saucer. Strangely though, we seldom even considered the pool serving any other purpose but for our swims.

We were refreshed after our swim, and I went to the communicator to check on messages. I must have missed the audible notification, because there was a message from Mike waiting. With all the recent excitement it was not surprising I had missed the notification. Oh well, so what? It was still waiting.

"Hello Brin, We added Jeremy Hodges to our membership today, and Nancy and I believe he will be a valuable addition. He is taking charge of our construction and has already broken ground. We are also purchasing another plot of land that has a natural gas well. It's always nice to have a permanent source of gas."

"I will be interviewing a doctor, dentist and electrical engineer tomorrow. I hope they all work out. We need to get a doctor on board quickly so we can health vet all the new recruits. I will let you know how that works out."

"Let me know the size requirements for your power generator and sewage treatment plant, so we can fit them into the design plans. Oh yes, the dome is already under construction. They are being pushed, so it shouldn't be too long."

"Sue, my new accountant, says your stock broker account has around $150,000,000 in it. You must be doing great with the investments."

79

"Things are beginning to get busy here, but I will keep you informed."

After I read Mike's message I said, "Wow! Flay's dad is really doing well with his investments. She said he would have fun playing the stock market. Of course it helps to know the ups and downs of the market before they happen. It also looks like the Earth group is really taking off. I wish we were there to help."

After a few more days of travel, Meg said, "I believe we might can take a few more chances and shorten our travel time. We are through the asteroid belt. If we want to take a chance we can go ahead and make the time jump to Earth's solar system and save an additional month in our schedule. The risks are minimal now. What do you think?"

I looked back and forth between the girls and saw agreement and excitement. The old ones had always firmly ordered to comply strictly with the old rules, but they had been wrong before, which we had discovered. Of course it was taking a risk to alter the strict rules, but I felt adventurous. I said, "Girls do what you feel comfortable doing."

Peg took her usual place at the controls and again waved her hand over an indicator, bringing our star map into focus. Our exact location began blinking in the display. I noticed the other planets were but far distance dots from our trajectory. Her fingers danced in a red light beam forming the cross target on the screen. The scale of the display reduced considerably and now showed a single star system with the cross target outside of the indicated

80

solar system. Her fingers moved in an intricate pattern and we were suddenly there. The scale increased quickly to show our location and the planets orbiting that sun.

Peg pointed to the third planet from the sun and said, "This is our target, Earth. You do know that with only one sun there will be a dark side of the planet, which they call night? The temperature will also be lower there than we are used to. It is within acceptable levels, but we will have to adjust."

I said, "Yes, we must adapt. Tell me though, will we be able to make other time jumps like we have?"

Peg said, "Oh yes, but we will need to give our analyzer time to take in information and process it for an optimal course. We should be able to make another short jump by tomorrow, but keep in mind that this solar system also has an asteroid belt, two actually. We can't jump through them, it's too dangerous."

I was feeling more confident about our schedule and responded to Mike's message.

"Mike, I'm happy to hear things are going well there. Things are going well for us here, also; which is my focus with this e-mail. We estimate that our arrival will be sooner than we originally projected, and I must speed you up on the underwater dome. We must be able to hide our ship when we get there. Even if the building is not done, we can continue to live aboard as long as our ship is hidden. The early arrival also works out well, because we plan to launch a few satellites. This

81

way we can keep up with the progress of the collapse of civilization after communications fails, plus be able to monitor our facility for security. As a reminder, be sure and stock up gold and silver. We will need it later during the recovery. Keep up the good work and progress"

Chapter 4
(Space)

I had been deprived of the pleasures of sex all my life. Now, with the change that had taken place it seemed that the repressed desires were flooding back and making up for lost time. As time went by in space we had little to do to occupy our minds. I just couldn't stop thinking about sex. Since I discovered sexual pleasure I hadn't even bothered to put my woven skirt back on, nor had Peg. After noticing our nakedness, Meg also removed hers, and I was finding their naked beauty intoxicating.

Mike told us we were going against nature's way. This made me wonder just what our natural way was. We are water people, so our ancestors must, at some point in our history, have had sex in water, like the porpoises. I was thinking about this as the girls and I dove in the pool for another swim. I held back and watched Meg and Peg swim ahead of me. They swam with both legs together, making powerful up and down strokes with their long sexy legs, like a porpoise stroke. I could see the rippling muscles in their naked butt cheeks and thighs flexing. Their strokes produced a rhythm, like a rolling wave moving down their bodies to end in a powerful kick to propel them through the water. But, I found myself mostly watching the hips rise and fall in a very provocative manner that was exciting me. I could see the target of my focus in the shadows between their thighs. As I followed behind them the movement of my own hips began to stimulate me. I quickly looked down to see that I was extremely hard, but I didn't give it much thought, because I knew what I wanted already and my body was just complying with my need. I swam up behind Meg and slipped my body over her back and slipped my hands around her and forward over her breasts to grab her shoulders. It was a simple matter then to adjust my strokes to oppose hers, so that when her butt rose, my hips were coming down. We were both shocked when I entered her so easily. Our swimming strokes provided the movement to force my entry into her hot pussy and continued strokes into her. Suddenly our swimming strokes took on a new meaning, and our swimming speed became frenzied. Just before my climax hit I wrapped my legs around hers and pounded into her. I could hear Meg screaming underwater as we sank to the bottom of the pool. We were both out of air, so we soon broke to the top for air. When we did we saw a shocked Peg staring at us.

Peg said, "Damn. That was crazy hot to watch. I'll go swimming with you any time."

Meg and I were still gasping for breath, but we still burst out laughing.

It only got worse from there, or better, depending on how you looked at it. I became insatiable for sex, wanting sex all the time. Over the next few days the girls and I enjoyed sex everywhere, even standing up. If one of them bent over for anything, I was on them instantly. We got little else done, but somehow we did manage to make two more time jumps. I had all but forgotten about our mission and the Earth group, but finally I started to slowly return to normal, a new normal that still enjoyed sex, but within reason.

I think what did it was Peg. She said, "You guys want to see Earth? With magnification we can now see it clearly. It's amazing. There is lots of clear, blue water, but there are beautiful white clouds and many actual land masses."

Her statement seemed to bring me back into focus again. We observed Earth's beauty from inside of the last asteroid belt. Seeing Earth reminded me of our mission, and I went to the communication console to check for messages. There was only one, which worried me since I had been indisposed for a few days. There should have been more.

"Brin, thanks for the information. I will speed up the work on the dome. I gained three more recruits today, the ones I mentioned, and the property looks like a beehive. If you don't know what a beehive looks like ... well, let's just say there is a lot of activity going on. I will make it a point to go get another load of gold and silver tomorrow. I already have a safe. I like the idea of having observation satellites. What type of weapons will you be bringing?"

"We purchased a cabin complex nearby the property to house our recruits. This way everyone will be close to our work, which should allow us to work more."

We structured a response, two in fact:

85

"Hello Mike, we are now actually in your solar system. Yes, we are ahead of schedule and should arrive in a few weeks, but will spend a few days launching satellites in orbit around your planet and trying to stay hidden from Earth's radar. It's not too difficult to stay hidden, but it is risky. I'm not sure I told you before, but most of my crew are in cryogenics. Only myself, Meg and Peg remain awake."

"Mike, I can imagine the activity level there, even though I have never seen a bee hive. It sounds like you have been busy and productive. We are eager to know the status of construction and organization of the community, especially the dome. Although we may arrive early, we can hide our ship in the dome, and I can keep my crew in cryogenics until our teams become sequestered. It would not be good for any of us if our existence becomes known to the outside world before your civilization totally collapses. Your government may try to get involved, and that wouldn't help our situation."

"You asked about weapons we are bringing. We will be bringing many laser pistols and rifles, some large rail guns, and EMP (Electrical Magnetic Pulse) weapons. These weapons are far more technically advanced than those currently in use on Earth."

"Mike, I hope everything is well with you. I'm concerned with your lack of response, but I am assuming you are just busy with all the activities at your end. Please, however, try to keep me informed with your activities. Also, let me know if I can *provide any information or assist you in any way. I advise you to buy as much supplies and equipment as you can, while money is still good. I'm assuming you still have plenty of funds remaining, but, just in case, please note the lottery date and numbers provided. The end is close enough to risk another lottery win, but the high dollar amount on this lottery makes it worth the risk ($320,000,000)."*

I wasn't too terribly concerned with Mike's lack of messages. He was obviously totally committed to the project, and it was apparently coming along beautifully. I felt confident that the project would be completed by the time we got there. My main concern was wanting to help him, which I didn't see a way to do from space.

I did feel a little guilty about my temporary laps of interest in the project, or maybe more descriptive would be my elevated obsession in sex. Either way, I was back on target ... mostly.

I was also hungry. The girls and I decided to eat and went below to prepare something. As we were working, I asked, "Are you going to miss Apsaras?" They both stopped working and seemed to think about my question.

Meg said, "I don't think so. Well, we will probably miss our parents, but Apsaras itself and the rigid lifestyle really was more boring than anything. We all saw the pending doom coming. All our friends are coming with us, so they won't be missed. I will miss the once beautiful planet, but Apsaras is no longer that beautiful. So, I won't miss Apsaras as it is now."

Peg chimed in, "I think we have far more to look forward to. Think about it. We will be emerged into a completely different lifestyle, one founded on a land based civilization and many new friends. I'm looking forward to being part of this new community. I'm sure we will have many challenges in order to adapt, but this is new and exciting, something we haven't experienced in a long time."

I said, "I'm glad that we are all looking at this in a positive way. I feel very much the same. I'm bringing our porpoise friends also. I would have missed them if they couldn't have made the trip."

"Speaking of the voyage, what else should be doing or getting ready to do before we get there? How many more days before we get there?"

Meg said, "Peg and I were talking about that. We think we can make another short time jump safely. That means we could be in orbit around Earth in three days, and to answer your question, we need to be preparing the satellites for launch. We think we should wake Flay to calculate the proper orbit."

I said, "Nice thinking. I hadn't given it any thought, and I probably should have. It's a good idea. Let's do it after our rest time. That will give her some time to recoup before we get there."

Flay was somewhat surprised to be awake before we reached Earth, but very happy that we made the decision. After Flay recouped, the girls made that last time jump, and we were now in orbit around Earth ... finally.

I was happy that we had awaken her early for several reasons, both good and bad. My highly activated sexual desires came to an abrupt and frustrating halt when both my girls came into their monthly cycle at the same time. I guess that was to be expected, being identical twins and living together. This disappointed me in two very different ways. First, I was disappointed that my increased sexual assaults on my girls had not impregnated either one. I really hadn't expected it, but I had hoped. Secondly, it frustrated me that I had no outlet for my renewed sexual desires. Fortunately, there was Flay, and she had joined the other girls in nudity by discarding her woven skirt. Flay was aware of my recently awakened sexual prowess and the reason for the change. She had even witnessed several of our sexual episodes, but my girls always welcomed my sudden urges. With Meg and Peg's temporary condition, I was now summarily rejected by both. When I saw Flay dive into the pool and start to swim, that undulating body motion flared my immediate desire, and I dove in behind her. I stroked hard and slid my body up over her slick back and entered her on the upstroke of her butt. Flay squealed in surprise but continued to undulate through the water. My grip on her shoulders held her tight and our rhythm quickly synchronized and escalated. We both got into the coupling energetically and climaxed together in turbulent water and sank to the bottom but quickly surfaced for air.

When I opened my eyes I met two stone-faced, staring and obviously angry girls. I didn't understand why and said, "What?"

Meg said, "You just had sex with Flay right in front of us!"

I said, "Well, yes. So what? I've been inside her many times. Hell, you brought her to our dome not too long ago to milk me. You have watched me be milked by many. What's the problem?"

Meg said, "That's different."

I said, "I don't know what's different about it. I was inside her, and I gave her my seed."

"But, but you enjoyed it this time."

I burst out laughing and said, "So it would be all right if I didn't enjoy it? Do you know how silly that sounds?"

After a long silence Peg said, "Yeah, that does sound silly."

I saw Meg and Peg look at each other. Their stone-face look cracked, and they burst out laughing together. While this conversation was going on a scared Flay watched on. Now she broke out laughing with us.

Meg said, "That was kind of silly on our part. I guess we were a little shocked and maybe jealous. We were never jealous before when you were being milked. I guess everything changes when you start making love instead of just having sex. Still, maybe we could have accepted it better if you hadn't enjoyed it so damn much." At that we all burst out laughing again.

Meg looked over at Flay and asked, "Now isn't that a better way of getting semen?"

Flay smiled really big and said, "Oh my, by far better. How did our race ever decide milking was a better way?"

We never had any more problems, and I continued to have sex with Flay, but I made sure to give Meg and Peg lots of hugs and kisses. Our relationship returned to normal, which included Flay, at least for a while. We became mission oriented again.

The three girls were busy in the lower storage area preparing to launch the satellites. Flay had completed the calculations, and now they were adjusting the maneuvering arms on one of the smaller saucers. We had decided to launch the satellites this way, believing it would be simpler and safer. Peg would fly a saucer out of the bottom hatch, and Meg would control the maneuvering arms to hold the satellite while the saucer positioned the satellite according to Flay's calculations. We had brought three satellites, which we decided to place one in stationary orbit above the complex and two in actual orbit around Earth, so we could monitor the world.

It was close to time to launch the first satellite, so Flay came to the control room. When the girls reported their readiness, Flay decompressed the lower deck and turned off the gravity there also. She opened the bottom hatch. We watched in the viewing image as the saucer exited the hatch pulling the satellite. Flay watched the viewing and

91

changing numbers as they positioned the satellite. When everything matched the calculations, Flay ordered the release. Meg and Peg then reentered the hatch and attached to the second satellite. This time they had to take the satellite father out. This one would be the stationary satellite and required a different location. Again they maneuvered the satellite and released it at the designated location. The third one was also released without incident, and the girls returned to the ship.

I was puzzled and said, "Doesn't the third one need to be released on the other side of Earth?"

Flay said, "Technically, yes, but these satellites have their own small gravity drive. They don't need propellants to be maneuvered. I've already programmed them, and they can move themselves. We just did it the old way just to have something to do." She laughed at my shocked reaction. "Something else you probably should know is that these satellites also have high powered lasers in them. They can become awesome weapons if necessary. I can aim and fire them from my controller manually, or we can program them to fire automatically and let the analyzer control them."

I said, "Well, shit, Flay. That's nice to know." She just shrugged.

Flay checked her equipment to ensure the satellites were operating properly. Satisfied, she went below to assist the girls. While I was alone I decided to check my messages. This message was already a couple of days old.

"Hi Brin, I just took a tour of the facility and it is progressing very nicely. A great deal has already been built at an extremely fast pace. Crews, many crews, are working around the clock. You would be impressed. I know you are most concerned with the dome. It will be ready for you when you get here, as long as you don't arrive this week. It will take longer for the Castle, that is what everyone calls it here, but it too is also coming along at a fast pace. I think we will be ready before the fall if we maintain the pace we have set. While I think about it, Jeremy will be contacting you for the specifications on the waste processor and power generator you talked about."

"Our staff is coming together. Most of the key department heads are now here. As you suggested, we are buying everything we can find in the way of equipment and supplies. We still have plenty of money, but we will cash in on the lottery ticket numbers you sent. If we don't need it we will convert it to gold and silver for rebuilding."

"The Cave is well underway to completion, and it will house a massive amount of supplies. The Cave is a new addition to the planned storage of the Castle, which Jeremy suggested and designed. He also added a fourth floor to the Castle to make sure we have plenty of room to house 200 members."

"I told the key players here about you and your group, but then I don't really know a lot about you. I think it went well, though."

There was a second message waiting.

"Brin, today I took a tour of the Castle, as we all call it, and was extremely pleased with our progress. We are progressing at an amazing pace. I think you would be pleased. We have stored over $3,000,000 in gold and silver and will increase this amount once we install our vault in the Castle. We should have our internal power plants operational today. The anchors for the underwater dome were poured yesterday with fast curing cement, and the dome parts should be on a barge on site. This place is really taking shape. Do you have an estimated time for your arrival on site?"

The girls finally returned to the control room, and I showed them the last two messages from Mike. I said, "I need to respond. Do you have any suggestions?"

Flay said, "It sounds like they are doing great without us, but I do have a concern. I observed the dam that exists on Lake Tenkiller. I'm wondering about flood control after the electricity goes down. We don't want to have a beautiful lake go dry on us if the dam breaks. I don't know a lot about dams, but I assume they do. Let's mention it so they can build in some safeguards."

Meg said, "Well, we now have satellites. Why don't we take a look at the property through them?" We all nodded agreement. Flay went immediately to the console and started wiggling her fingers in a blue light. The visual image of the stationary satellite flashed into existence showing a view of Oklahoma. She continued and focused in on the complex and expanded the view. We watched the property and complex come into focus.

Peg said, "Wow! They have been busy. Just look at that. There are workers and equipment moving all over. It looks like a small Earth city. I'm really astonished. This is for us, well all of us, but we made this happen. I'm so proud of you. This is your project."

I felt my head swell at Peg's praise, but really, the praise should be for Mike and his team. They were making it all happen. Still, in all honesty, it was my idea, and I deserved some of the praise. But, the project on the Earth's end was apparently going extremely well, and I wanted to encourage Mike. I composed the following message:

"Mike," we are close, close enough to view the property through our onboard telescope and satellites, Oh, we completed the deployment of the satellites. We can see the progress, and we are extremely impressed. Your team has done an excellent job. Your team is preforming well. We can see that you have expanded the property beyond our original plan. This is great. If you have the opportunity to purchase more, please do so. We have the money, so use it while it is still worth something"

"Buy ... buy lots of food, stores, machinery, parts, medicines, anything you can't produce later. Please hurry. Collect your lottery winnings quickly and take plenty of security with you when you go. The world is getting crazy."

95

"We do have one observation, however. We are concerned about the lake dam. After the collapse, we worry about flood control on the dam. Think about securing the dam. We wouldn't want the dam to breach from flooding."

"The US dollar will collapse soon, which will start the decline. After that, start your perimeter security. The fall will start in the major cities, but eventually spread to smaller cities as the food is used up. I caution you again to store up plenty of food."

"We can land when the Dome is completed. Just let us know."

"Keep up the good work."

We continued to orbit Earth for two more days to give the Earth team more time. Flay spent her time studying the complex and reviewing the detailed drawings and plans. Flay smiled hugely and said, "They have taken my original plans and improved them greatly. They have apparently expanded the property more than double. It's fenced, cleared, cultivated and I can see crops growing. I also see roads, barns and storage bins, evidently complete and stocked. It looks like the Castle is complete, at least the level of workers has been drastically reduced. The Castle is much bigger than I designed, with a fourth level added. But, the most impressive improvement is what they call the 'Cave'. They took advantage of the natural terrain and turned a sediment weakness and turned it into a major advantage. They removed the weakness and converted it to a massive cave for storage. The entire mountain foundation, on which the Castle rests, is now greatly improved, not to mention the storage area. I like this Jeremy Hodge. He is very smart and good at what he does. I think I will get him to impregnate me."

I was taking a drink when Flay said that last part and choked, actually expelling water from my nose. Peg and Meg burst out laughing, and as soon as I could catch my breath, joined them. It was even more humorous when we realized Flay was serious. She obviously was impressed with Jeremy, something difficult to do with her.

After Flay's report and a discussion among ourselves, I structured another message:

"Hello Mike, we definitely see progress on the Castle, as you call it, and our scientist, Flay, is impressed with your construction and design progress, especially the Cave. We are all very pleased with this progress. We are also progressing faster than we anticipated. I'm happy to report that we are here, currently orbiting Earth. Let us know when the Dome is ready, and we can land. We aren't in much danger of being seen, however. We have a radar masking transmission to hide us, but we can be seen visually if they happen to accidentally see us. Hopefully, we will not be seen visually. If so, we can hide behind the moon, if necessary, until you are ready. We will come in at night, and I suggest you have a landing area where we can lower our supplies, the sewage treatment unit and power generators before we go

underwater. Should we wait until there are no workers available to see us?"

Mike's response came back fairly quickly:

"Hey, Brin, I am happy to report that the Dome is complete and filled with air. I am about to give it a final inspection, but it is ready for you. We will have an unloading area ready for you, but we still have outside workers going 24 hrs a day. We probably need a few more days of this before we let them go. You could, however, park in the dome, and we can wait until later to unload the equipment, since we have both these needs under control."

"Thanks for pointing out the potential problem with the dam. We had not considered this type of problem. We now have a dam engineer and we will soon be making some changes on the dam to prevent any potential problem we may have in the future.

"One thing I need to know, however. Obviously, there is a way to hide a spaceship in the Dome from being seen, but I'm wondering about you and your people. What do you look like? You've said you are humanoid, but to a casual observer would it be obvious that you are alien? Can your identity be masked from the outside workers?"

After reading Mike's message, Meg said, "Well, we've put this off long enough. It's time to tell all. I agreed and sent the following message:

"Hello, Mike, we can see your progress. Well done. We are pleased to hear that the Dome is ready for us. We will land in two nights. We will

lower the units and supplies at the cleared location behind the Castle before we submerge. We are looking forward to finally meeting you. In answer to your question about our appearance, yes, I'm afraid we will appear alien to humans, but not from our shape or any major abnormal physical appearance of your race. Remember that we evolved on a water world. We differ physically in appearance from humans in that you might perceive our heights as being taller than most, and slimmer. Also, our fingers and toes have a partial web for swimming, but that is not the outstanding difference. Humans have white, black, brown, even somewhat yellow and red skins, where our race will look somewhat blue or aqua. We believe our appearance is more handsome or prettier than humans, but of course, that is a matter of belief. Our eyes have blueish green pupils, and our body hair is sparse, except for our heads, which is kept long and mostly black or orange in color. I'm afraid we will stand out among humans, but no more than a black human would stand out among white humans. The difference is there are no aqua people on Earth. You will get used to us. I hope this answers your question."

We had little else to do so we began to take turns observing the activities of the complex and expanded our observation of the surrounding areas and finally the world in general. We noticed a war break out in what is called the Middle-East. Being unfamiliar with the geography of Earth, it was hard to identify just who was fighting whom, but it was a vicious battle. We watched intently, but it ended abruptly with what could only be simultaneous nuclear explosions. We saw rockets soar into the upper atmosphere and cross paths, then fall to explode at the opposite locations. The mushroom clouds were still bellowing upward.

Flay became extremely agitated and blurted out, "These ignorant humans are going to destroy this beautiful world with nuclear fallout and waste. If it continues we won't be able to live here! No one will be able to live here. Those areas will be dead for hundreds of years."

I said, "What can we do? Anything?"

Flay's fingers were already flicking in the blue light as she said, "Well, we can set our satellite lasers on automatic and shoot down any more of those missiles going into the upper atmosphere. At least we can try to eliminate more of the nuclear explosions. As Flay set the automatic targeting, a digital image flared to superimpose over a digital representation of the Earth's surface. No sooner had the digital image appeared, an alarm sounded, indicating a target acquired. We jumped to identify the target. Another missile had been launched from another location in the same region. We watched as the targeting analyzer focused on the moving target and fired. The target blip instantly disappeared. We cheered, but quickly stopped when another alarm sounded, then another. Within five minutes four additional alarms sounded from that region. The analyzer tracked each one, positioned the satellite and fired. All were destroyed, and no additional missiles were fired.

Flay said, "I don't know which side is good or bad in this conflict, and I don't care. We can't allow them to destroy our new world. This is our future, if we are to have one."

We activated the satellites none too soon, but we were still lucky that the war didn't escalate into other areas. Hopefully, others noticed what happened to those last five missiles launched, and hopefully it might prevent others. Needless to say, the world was falling apart far too quickly, and we would have to close off our survival complex soon.

We had already began monitoring around the US, and it was becoming bad. It was to be expected, but we hadn't expected it to happen this soon. We decided to pass the word to Mike.

"Mike, we must hurry with the closing off of the complex. Your world seems to be collapsing faster than we anticipated. Already battles are raging in your major cities, especially in your largest ones. law and order has disappeared. Looting and fires are epidemic, even in Tulsa and Ft. Smith. The food has apparently been stripped from most grocery stores in the big cities. Chaos is prevalent and beginning to spill out to the smaller communities. You still have a little time but not many days. We should be there by the time we are needed for defense, and we also bring weapons."

Mike's response was sent within a few hours:

"Brin, thanks for the warnings. We are almost totally complete with our construction. We have

had problems with our own government, but so far we have successfully prevented them from hindering our construction, thanks to your suggestion to partner with the Cherokee Nation. That has made a big difference. From your descriptions of yourselves, you don't sound all that scary. Some of us might be scary to you, but we are eager to meet you and your team. I guess we will meet you in the Dome tomorrow night."

Our response was immediate:

"Mike, we will arrive above the Castle at 2:00 am. There should be no reflective moon light tonight, which will help us hide. We have lights to illuminate the offload of our equipment, but please have a crew to take control of the equipment. We will suspend a ramp, but we don't have personnel to move it. Afterwards, we will move our ship under the Dome. I'm looking forward to meeting you."

I said, "We are almost there, girls. Is there anything we need to do before we get there?"

Meg said, "Well, we have picked the darkest night already to land. It's still hard for me to imagine what it will be like not to have sunlight all the time. It's even harder to imagine that we had to worry about reflected sunlight from the orbiting moon asteroid. I guess there will be stranger things we will have to adjust to on Earth, but it should make life interesting, trying to adapt. Our radar jamming has been on since we came into orbit, so that shouldn't be a worry. The absence of sunlight, radar jamming, and the creation of kinetic energy from our landing in the lower atmosphere will also create clouds to hide us. I can't imagine us being seen until we turn on the landing lights. Let's see, we loaded the ship in the reverse order it needs to be unloaded, so there is nothing to arrange below deck. Peg, Flay, have I missed anything?" Flay shook her head indicating nothing more.

Peg said, "Well, I can think of two more things that need to be done ... Meg and I, since our time has passed. Sorry Flay, but it is our time for sex again."

I burst out laughing and was quickly joined by Flay, Meg and a smiling Peg, who was proud of her joke. But, I knew she wasn't joking, and I was pleased that she wasn't. I said, "Let's take a swim, prepare something to eat and get some sleep." I said sleep with a smile and wink. "Maybe Flay can keep watch while we rest." Flay grinned and smiled agreement.

Flay said, "I really like the human's natural way of sex. I wish we had learned it years ago. I've had Brin's attention for the last few days, so I can watch things for a while. Besides, I plan to meet Jeremy tonight." She grinned, and we laughed.

The swim was refreshing, and the meal was filling. I stretch my arms in mock tiredness and gave a big animated yawn, and said, "Shall we go take a nap before we start the descent? We have about eight hours."

Flay said, "Try to keep the screaming down. I have work to do."

We all laughed, and Meg, Peg and I went below. Off came Meg and Peg's woven wrap, I had never bothered to put mine back on. Once discovered, my sexual desires had not abated at all, and I beat the girls into the net to ensure I would be at the bottom. I wanted to be wrapped in their warmth. This would be the first time I would attempt to have sex in the net since I discovered porpoise sex in the pool. I thought it ironic that I was calling it porpoise sex, because it wasn't anything like the way porpoises had sex at all.

I had watched porpoises have sex many times. When they have sex the male swims upside down under the female, and they did it often when they were frisky, which seemed to be most of the time. I remember being envious of them, since they looked like they enjoyed sex. Well, now I enjoyed it immensely, but I couldn't figure out how to make contact swimming upside down. It just didn't work, but slipping on the girls' backs while they were swimming worked out extremely well. Why try to improve on it? Still, there was no bad way to have sex, and they wanted it in the net tonight. Oh well, that works for me also.

I didn't have to wait long before Meg and Peg snuggled in the net beside me. I don't know how their taunt, muscular bodies could feel so soft, warm and inviting but they did. It was an electric like stimulation to me, and it settled directly into my balls and dick, making me hard. Since we awoke the buried sexual desires we had also found immense pleasure in our touching, especially our kissing. Before the awaking we hardly ever kissed, now we sought it in each other. The girls pressed and rubbed their tantalizing bodies against me and showered kisses over my face, and I was raging in desire for them. I wiggled my body between Peg's thighs and began probing. She pushed her thighs up, searching. When I entered her she moaned … loud. We quickly found a fast rhythm. I felt Meg roll on my back. The warmth from below and above drove me insane with lust. I found it more difficult to stroke into Peg with Megs added weight on my back, but Meg began to match my stroking rhythm, almost like she was joining and helping me. I felt Meg's arms around me and even heard moaning coming from her. The stroking into Peg's hot tunnel increased to a frantic pace. Peg began to grunt out chirps in time with the plunges into her. Finally, we both froze in ecstasy, as my jerking cock pumped gush after gush of hot cream into Peg's convulsing pussy. Peg's scream and my bellow rang throughout the ship. I remained inside as we calmed. It was then that I noticed Meg's quivering body against my back. I didn't know it was possible, but I think Meg also had an orgasm, sharing mine and Pegs as she had the rhythm. I managed to move us all so I could embrace both smiling girls. I remember thinking, "Damn, that was great." just before I fell sound asleep.

I was still sleeping soundly when Flay shook us awake. Flay said, "There is activity on Earth that you need to know about."

We were instantly awake and rolling out of the net. Flay had already returned to the control room, so we quickly followed her. When we got there I said, "What's going on, Flay?"

Flay was calm and said, "There were more missile launches, twenty in fact. They launched from Europe and appeared to be headed for America. Two of our satellite lasers took them all out, but one was launched from America, and it looked like it was headed for us. I think we have been identified. I repositioned the other two satellites for stationary orbits at 120 degrees apart. This way we won't have any dark areas, and we can cover all of Earth. But the worst thing I observed are the existing Earth satellites. Our analyzer tells me that there are at least two of their satellites with lasers in orbit, and one is currently positioned above this continent. I don't think they are near as good as ours, or they would have used them against the missiles. I think they are designed to fire only on land targets. Mike, it could be used against us when we land. There is one other curious thing. One of their satellites is being repositioned, and it's headed toward us in orbit. Here is the curiosity: If civilizations has collapsed, who is controlling them?"

I said, "Civilization *has* collapsed, but you can bet the military, parts of it anyway, is dug in somewhere. They are the ones controlling them. Let's take out the laser satellites capable of seeing and firing on us, and I don't trust any satellite being positioned to come after us. If they fired a missile at us, they intended to destroy us. You can bet the satellite is designed to do the same thing. Let's take it out also."

Flay rushed to the console and brought up the targeting image. I could clearly see the target X and our position in reference to it. I said, "I don't want to fire a rail-gun projectile up here, since we can't predict the high velocity range. What do you suggest: Laser or EMP pulse?"

Flay said, "My vote is laser. We can't verify if the EMP disabled what we fire at."

I said, "OK, let's let the satellite laser take them out. Our ship hasn't fired anything yet. Let's not give them this target. Oh, by the way, where did the missile launch from here?"

Flay said, "Several hundred miles north and west of our complex. I expected more retaliation launches but none came. Do you suppose they knew we would take them out like earlier?"

I don't think she expected an answer. Instead, she began the satellite targeting and fired. Again she fired. "They're gone."

I said, "Can the analyzer identify the spy satellites they could use to track us?"

"Yes. Want me to take them out too?"

I said, "If there aren't too many. Right now just target those that can be used to harm us, but I don't really want to help cause the collapse of civilization by killing all communications."

After about ten minutes Flay said, "There were only three ... they're gone now, but we better land soon before more move in orbit. That reminds me, there was a short message from Mike."

Peg brought the image up.

"We will have forklifts and heavy equipment to move the equipment off and store it. We will also have plenty of manpower to help, also. We, too, are eager to meet you."

"Meg, take us down. I'm eager to meet Mike and our new home."

Chapter 5
(Landing)

With gravity drive we could sail against the wind, so to speak. It made our descent through the atmosphere easy, like going through water. It mattered not to the Bright One, and the artificial gravity within our ship overrode the outside gravity or lack of it. Our descent was steady. Images of Earth steadily expanded, and we soon began to focus upon our target area. As predicted, however, once we reached the lower atmosphere clouds appeared around us, masking us from observation. We were also on the dark side of Earth. Still, our digital targeting gave us a clear view of our exact location in reference to the Castle. We slowly settled down above a lighted area and hovered. Peg remained at the controls, but Flay and Meg went below to begin the unloading.

When we opened the lower hatch, we got our first taste and smell of Earth air. The air was rich with new scents but not unpleasant, just different.

The first things to be unloaded were the small saucers. They had to go first to make room to get the other items off. Through our cameras I watched the bottom iris doors open wider, then the first saucer on tethers filled the void and slowly lowered to the ground. I could see humans on the ground maneuvering the saucer to a landing location. Once on the ground, the cable detached and retracted, and the second saucer was then lowered and parked beside the first. I could see humans covering the saucers with some sort of camouflage netting, so they couldn't be spotted by roaming eyes or satellites. I thought that was a great idea.

Peg moved our ship over and lowered it almost to the ground. A ramp extended to the ground from the hovering ship. I watched teams of humans and equipment move up the ramp into the hold. That would be the first exposure of humans and our race, at least in hundreds of years. I chuckled at the reaction that must now be going on, but speed was necessary. Crates and equipment began flowing down the ramp and gathering in a growing mountain of supplies. I also noticed the humans pulling camouflage tarps or netting over the offloaded supplies. The bigger items came off last, which told us they were almost finished. The ramp retracted and the iris door closed. The whole process was efficient and only took an hour. There was only one thing left to do: park the Bright One in the Dome.

Peg slowly drifted the ship up and out over the water and submerged. We watched the graphical representations under water of the banks and anchors of the Dome and our ship in relationship to them. Peg slowly moved the ship deeper and then under the Dome and slowly raised it into position. We watched our transparent ship dome emerge inside the Dome, then felt the ship attach to the supporting structure. I could see many humans standing inside waiting to greet us. My excitement rose as our top iris hatch cycled open and the exit ramp lowered. I was the first to exit, followed by Meg, Peg and flay. For a moment we all just stood on the deck and stared at each other. I recognized Mike from pictures of him viewed on the Internet.

Mike smiled hugely coming forward and said, "Hello Brin. It's good to finally meet you. I'm Mike."

Mike was about the same height as me, about 6' 3" in Earth measurements but heavier and more muscular. He was good looking for a human, dark complected, long black braided hair, and brown eyes. He definitely looked Indian, judging from pictures and movies I had viewed. He was also obviously friendly. I also smiled and said, "Yes, finally we meet." Mike extended his hand, presumably to shake mine, but I embraced him in a strong hug, as is our custom of greeting. He appeared surprised but quickly returned my embrace. After releasing our hug, I said, "Let me introduce my mates Meg and Peg and Flay is my science engineer."

Mike said, "Let me introduce you to Nancy, whom you introduced to me via your messages." I placed my hand on Nancy's shoulder. "She has been our real estate agent, attorney and my assistant." Pointing at Sue I said, "This is Sue, and she has been our accountant handling our money, quite well I might add." Pointing at Bess I said, "Bess here is a Marine Biologist. She runs our greenhouse and diving operation, among many other things in the community. These three girls are sisters and my mates. Bob here," pointing, "is a

111

recent addition, and he provides personal security for my immediate family." Again pointing, "These are Robert and JJ. They head up the community security force"

Embraces were exchanged all around. Mike then asked, "Do you have any immediate needs?"

I noticed that the three mates of Mike were small, at least a foot shorter than he, but very pretty, even among our race. Two of the others were black and the female was tall, almost as tall as myself. The other male was brown, like Mike and the girls. There was so much diversity of DNA in these few humans. No two looked alike, except for the sisters, which was understandable. That was the problem with our race, we were all too close in DNA, family. We would be noticing many more diverse features I'm sure.

I said, "Yes, we are most excited to taste your lake water. We have been cooped up on our ship for a while. We really need to swim and test the lake water."

Mike said, "We can take you out to the docks."

Mike was surprised when I said, "It's not necessary. We can just dive from here and take a short swim. If you don't mind waiting."

"Not at all."

We had done a lot of swimming on ship, but we had not dealt with any changing water pressure. Most of all we really were anxious to taste and feel the water texture. We quickly dove into the water and skirted around the ship to find open water. We hadn't anticipated being almost blind. Our system was unaccustomed to being without sunlight. We did have some light radiating from the Dome but not enough. I would have to remember to tell Mike to put shades inside the Dome. This light might could be seen from above.

As I remembered, the Dome was about 100 feet below the surface. We swam up to the surface, but without sunlight to gage distances we actually popped out of the water. We now had our bearings. It wouldn't do any good to find the bottom, since we couldn't see it at night, and without the porpoises and their sonar we might collide into something. So we just swam around enjoying the clean water. The water, however, was far colder than we were used to. If we couldn't adapt quickly we would have to find better clothing for insulation. We nodded to each other and sped back to the Dome. We shot out of the water to stand on the deck. In the process we startled the humans. I'm assuming they weren't used to seeing an entrance like we did.

Mike said, "How did you like the lake water?"

Peg said, "Cold!"

Meg said, "Dark! Our home world has two suns and we are not used to total dark."

I said, "The water is excellent, though. It is clean and the texture for us is perfect, better than our world, Apsaras."

Bess, the scientist, said, "I hope you realize that this is the summer season in our part of the world, but in the winter season the water will be even colder. I think we can come up with better and warmer clothing for you, something you can swim in.

Mike said, "Bess, would you please go up to the diving locker and get some of those suits for them now? Brin, I certainly don't want to offend you, and I'm sure you feel the same, but I must tell you that the woven clothing you guys are wearing smells really foul to us. I'm sure you don't realize this fact, but this smell is repulsive to us humans. I would appreciate it if you would change into the suits Bess brings back. In the next few days we can have the seamstress make you custom suits to your liking, but please loose those you are wearing now."

I'm sure shock registered in my expression at first that Mike was telling us our clothes stink, but I quickly realized he was doing us a favor. To us they smelled normal, but we certainly didn't want to repulse our new human friends with our smell. I said, "We are not offended. In point of fact, we appreciate your candor. If the smell is offensive, of course we will replace them. To us these clothes have no odor. Maybe we are just used to the smell or have an under developed sense of smell. Apparently our race has not evolved a very advanced sense of smell. On our world there is nothing much to smell. Almost all life on our planet is under water, and we don't smell under water. Maybe that sense will sharpen living on your world, our new world. Mike, please continue to tell us these things, because we do not want to offend. We hope to completely assimilate into your community and want to be liked." Mike and the other nodded.

114

Mike said, "Our cultures could clash out of ignorance, so please tell us if we offend you as well. We will work it out as long as we communicate."

I liked Mike. He went directly at a problem and not, as is often said in English, "beat around the bush." By this time Bess returned carrying some brightly colorful suits. She handed Meg, Peg and Flay some of these suits consisting of shirts and shorts. They were black with pink sleeves and pink strips down the outsides of the short legs. The one she handed me was bright red with short, black sleeves and a black strip down the outsides of the shorts legs. I liked the bright color combination.

Bess said, "These are spandex and one size fits all, mostly. If you don't like them we have many color schemes to choose from including full length if you need the warmth. We also have plenty of human cloths to pick from also."

While she was talking we had all stripped down to nothing and began slipping into our new suits. They looked great on the girls, and they were admiring them and each other, even me. I said, "Thank you Bess, I believe we like these a lot. They fit snug, should be warm in the water and will be easy to swim in."

"From your reaction I believe we may have shocked you with our nudity, but our race is not shy about nudity. In the heat of our home planet, nudity helps keep us cool and is common place."

Mike said with a smile, "Well I for one didn't mind watching, nor do I believe any of the others. But humans, for the most part, tend to be more modest. We will get used to it. It certainly is not offensive."

"Let us show you around a little and maybe go get some food. Are you hungry?"

I looked at the girls for confirmation and said, "Yes, it has been a long and stressful cycle, and we could eat." The girls nodded an animated affirmation.

Nancy said, "Bob, our chef, anticipated you might be hungry and prepared some food. It will be ready when we go up."

Mike led us through a sealed hatch into a tunnel that headed up. He explained that each door must be closed before we could open the next, and there were three doors. He said the sealed doors maintained air pressure to keep the Dome from flooding. It made sense. When we exited the last door we were inside an immense underground facility. This must be the Cave Mike talked about. The Cave was not on the original plans. It was added by the architect, Jeremy, and quite efficiently designed and functional. Massive amounts of stores were inside with plenty of additional room for more. There was a huge door through which I could see the bridge providing access to the Cave. I wanted to see more, but Mike steered us toward what must be the elevator leading up to the Castle.

I had studied Mike's plans for what they now called the Castle. Flay had even re-engineered the plans, which I also studied, but I was not prepared for what I saw when the elevator doors opened in the Castle. We walked out into a massive open room with a high ceiling. I looked up at the center octagon ceiling of the second floor. It was only open in the center, but we could see offices and deck of the second floor lining the walls. People were standing at the rail of the deck watching us and many humans stood in the large open room staring at us.

Mike announced, "I would like for everyone to meet Brin, Meg, Peg and Flay. These are the first of many joining us in this community. Please make them feel welcome." The crowd began clapping and cheering, which did make us feel welcome. After the crowd settled down, Mike continued, "Introduce yourself as time permits. Right now they are hungry, so we will indulge some of Bob's cooking."

As Mike led us toward what was obviously a cafeteria, a large, white man wearing a strange white hat greeted us. He introduced himself as Bob and guided us toward an open table. As we sat down, others brought plates of food and brown liquid for drinking. We waited to see how Mike and his group responded.

Bob said, "I hope you like this meal. We prepared Tilapia, which is an Earth fish, on a bed of spinach and asparagus, covered with Alfredo sauce. I know the names I mentioned probably have no meaning to you. I just hope you like it."

We had seen humans eat in movies we had watched. They used the silver tools provided to us now. We watched the others now use the tools to put food in their mouths. I now did the same thing, but as soon as my mouth tasted the new flavors I forgot all about the tools. The flavor was like nothing I had ever tasted before. I couldn't believe the pleasure I derived from tasting these new enticing flavors. I looked at the girls, and they too had discarded the forks, remembering the name, and were using their finger to allow them to eat faster. I thought, *"To hell with protocol. This shit is good!"* I even like the sweet drink they called tea. I looked for Bob and waved him over. When he came I stood and embraced him and said, "Bob, this food is excellent, far better than anything we have tasted before. Would it be possible to get more."

Bob beamed with the praise and said, "Of course you may. Eat as much as you like. I'm really pleased that you like it."

We finally had our fill of the marvelous meal and set back to have conversations over coffee, they called it. One sip, however, had me sputtering and choking. It was hot and bitter, and I didn't like it at all.

Mike laughed and said, "I take it you didn't like coffee. I personally love it, but not everyone does." He slid a glass of white liquid toward me. "This is milk we produce here on the complex. Many say not to serve milk with fish, but I like milk with most anything."

I took a tentative sip. It was cold and had a thick feel in my mouth, but the taste was great. I gulped it down. I was enjoying this human food, but I knew it was time to get down to business. I guess Mike felt the same.

Mike said, "I'm really glad you guys are here now. Let me just ask right out; how do you want to organize the joint community?"

I said, "That's what I like about you, you just come right out and say what's on your mind. Let me be just as upfront. Mike, as far as I'm concerned this is your community. You and your team have organized it, built it and it seems you are doing a great job of running it. I do not want to change a thing. We do not know your world. We intend to assimilate into your existing organization and departments, not try to create parallel operations. We all have the same common interest: defense, food production, reproduction, in short, survive. Therefore, we will all be working toward the same goals. I do figure that our team is more experience in underwater food production, fish herding and the like. I have an expert, Blane, in these fields. I suggest we establish this department within the existing organization. Other than that, and the obvious Apsaras technology we bring, we intend to merge with yours. In short, you still run the community, and I will only council and advise."

Mike said, "OK, that's the way we will continue, but don't hesitate to offer up any recommended changes. I won't mind."

The girls all seemed to be engaged in their own conversations, but Robert and JJ had remained silent and listened intently.

Robert finally asked, "Do you think you were observed by any government military when you descended?"

I said, "Yes, I believe we were. In fact we were attacked in space twice, but we destroyed the missile and satellite trying to take us out. We also took out the spy satellites so they wouldn't be able to track us here. There are still plenty of spy satellites in orbit, but none when we descended out of orbit."

Robert said, "Damn, why do you think they were trying to take you out?"

I said, "Probably because we took out over 25 nuclear missile launches?"

"Nuclear? How do you know they were nuclear launches?"

I said, "Because we let the first two pass in the stratosphere and watched the mushroom clouds blossom over the Middle East area. We didn't leave a dying world and come halfway across the universe just to settle in another dying world. We don't know who launched the missiles, nor do we care. We just weren't going to let human idiots destroy our new world. I guess we scared someone … everyone I guess. Anyway, a missile was launched from near here, and we weren't going to let it destroy us. We took it out along with a satellite moving toward us. We figured it was designed to explode when it got to us. You should know that we left three satellites with high powered lasers floating in orbit, and they are set on automatic and will destroy any missiles launched into the stratosphere."

Robert said, "I guess the rumors were true. Rumors in the news are that Israel and Iran destroyed each other, but it was only rumors. I guess it was true after all."

"We should get your weapons mounted on our roof as soon as possible in case they want to continue attacking us. This has to be some advanced military operation sequestered, because everything else seems to have collapsed, including the military. I think we are on our own here."

Meg and Peg called out, "Brin, they have a set of identical twins here at the complex!"

This shocked me and I said, "Identical twins on our home world are extremely rare. In fact Meg and Peg are the only set our old ones can remember. I'm sure my girls would love to meet them."

Nancy said, "They may be sleeping. I'll call them and see."

I watched as she punched in numbers in her radio/phone, and almost immediately I heard a ringing out at one of the other tables. When I looked in that direction I instantly saw them, two identical blonde females. They were shorter than most humans and stocky, with wide rounded hips, even though their waist looked narrow. I had to stare as they walked toward us. I mean they were very white with long, almost white hair, but what got my attention was the size of their breasts. They were massive and they jiggled as they walked. I had never seen anything like it before. I stared directly at the breasts, all four of them. Meg and Peg didn't even notice my fascination with the breasts, they were completely mesmerized at the fact of meeting another set of identical twins.

Nancy introduced them to each other. They had strange sounding names, Ella and Ebba. They embraced each other like long lost friends and started chatting like they had known each other for years. I noticed that, like Meg and Peg often did, Ella and Ebba often finished the other's sentence, and their conversation included all four of them."

"I guess I was still staring at the twin's breasts, as Mike nudged me to get my attention. I quickly refocused and looked at a smiling Mike. I said, "Sorry, I guess I was being rude by staring, but I've never seen anything like them before, and I don't mean identical twins." We both broke out laughing.

Mike said, "If you're lucky maybe you will get to play with them and inspect them closer." We both started laughing again but quickly stopped when the girls stared at us.

Mike changed the subject then and said, "I think everyone is getting sleepy. Maybe we should take Brin's crew up to our apartment and get some sleep."

At 4:00 am, everyone was tired and readily agreed. The twins said their "Good Nights" and Mike guided us back to the elevator. As we were going, Mike told us that our group had identical quarters on the fourth floor but felt it best if we just stayed with them tonight so we could get comfortable with how everything worked. I still marveled at how elegant the Castle looked and wondered how he had managed to get it all done in such little time.

I was still admiring the work when we entered Mike's apartment, which set me off again. His apartment was large. The center room was apparently the main gathering area. There were several comfortable looking chairs and a longer comfortable appearing unit where several people could easily sit side by side. Off this central area four doors led into large rooms he called bedrooms, and at the back was what he called a bathroom at the end. This was obviously a waste facility, which I promptly figured out. There was also a glass enclosed area he called a shower. I didn't immediately figure out what its purpose was. I steered us back to one of the bedrooms to survey it again. Finally I asked, "What is the purpose of these?" I was pushing down on a soft platform as I said it.

Nancy said, " Oh, this is called a bed. We sleep on them. They are comfortable." As she said that she fell on it and spread out. "Do you not sleep in a bed?"

I said, "We usually sleep in netting, but like I said earlier, we intend to adapt to human ways. If you sleep in beds we will learn to sleep in beds. We also cleanse ourself by swimming, so you will have to teach us about a shower also. We've figured out the purpose of the waste facility already. It's similar to what we are used to."

Mike seemed surprised at our answers and said, "It's fine if you want to try using a bed, but if it doesn't work out for you we can rig up some netting for you tomorrow. As for the shower. I might

123

suggest you watch Bess take a shower. She can show you how it works. The girls might want to get in there with her to learn."

I noticed Bess smile when Mike said that. I wondered about that but didn't say anything.

Bess said, "Come on girls. It's a big shower and we can all fit. I'll show you how everything works."

Flay had been up much longer than us, taking the last watch before landing. She was practically asleep on her feet, so Nancy took her to one of the bedrooms and showed her the bed. Nancy returned and said Flay was asleep even before she left.

Bess took Meg and Peg and led them to the shower. I followed and watched as they all removed their clothing and entered the enclosed glass area. Bess explained how to adjust the temperature of the water spray. I had seen my girls naked many times. This was the first time I had seen a naked human. Bess was smaller than my girls, but I could see strong rippling muscles in her thighs and buttocks. I was also curious. Where my girls nipples were dark purple, this brown girl's nipples were dark brown. All the girls breasts were about the same size. Bess' instructions including helping my girls preform all the functions Bess was describing. She removed the braids and used a shampoo on their hair, actually washing their hair, then rubbing their bodies down with a soap. Afterwards Bess took towels and dried their bodies and rubbed some kind of lotion all over them, especially between the thighs and breasts. My girls seemed to enjoy the attention from Bess, and the feeling seemed mutual. I was beginning to envy their attention. Bess didn't seem to mind me watching, but I was becoming aroused, so I went back to the center room where the others were. Mike had put a pot of coffee on and offered me another cup. I thought I would try it again. It kind of grows on you. As I sipped it we chatted.

Mike suddenly choked on his coffee when I said, "Meg and Peg are eager to receive your seed. The other girls they were talking to in the cafeteria told them that you shared your seed with them and many others. Meg and Peg want your seed, also. Flay wants Jeremy's seed." Mike quit coughing and said, "We had this discussion via our messages. No one is going to milk or pull my seed from my balls by suction. There is only one way that will happen and that is if I give it during orgasm. I told you that already."

"Yes, you did. You also told us to relearn how to fuck. We have done that during the trip, and you were correct. It is a much better way, but we are still learning, however. Thank you very much for forcing us to face the truth. Those sexual urges were only dormant in us but they are awake now. So, will you give my girls your seed so we can keep our race alive?"

Mike's mates began laughing, and Sue said, "Well, here we go again. Girls, I guess it's up to us to get the party rolling. As soon as Bess and Brin's girls come out of the shower we need to take Mike and Brin to the shower." Looking at Mike and me

Sue said, "We will clean you two all up and basically show Brin how to shower in the process."

I didn't know what Sue was talking about, but I was beginning to like what I thought was the meaning. I also liked her assertive attitude, and would definitely go with the flow. Bess and my girls came out, and Sue led us all in, two girls and two guys ... interesting. Nancy and Sue stripped naked, and I was right behind them enjoying the view as my new spandex shirt and pants were thrown against the wall. Sue and Nancy turned the two water controls and a spray of water came from each end of the enclosure like before. This time, however, I felt the water and its warmth. I stood under the hot water and watched as Nancy and Sue administered to Mike. They undid his braided hair and put the bubbly white shampoo in his hair and began rubbing a bar of something over his body everywhere. It turned white then the water washed it off. As Nancy began rubbing his dick it began to grow. Mike was obviously getting aroused, and so was I as I watched. Nancy dropped to her knees and took Mike's dick in her mouth. I simply stared in amazement. His dick had gotten hard and very big. I couldn't resist and said, "Do all human males have dicks that big?"

Nancy laughed and said, "No. Most are much smaller. Don't get intimidated. We like smaller ones too."

Nancy then grinned at me and shocked me by taking his entire dick into her mouth. She seemed proud of her ability to do so, and I could hardly imagine how that might feel to Mike. I just stood there and watched in total disbelief. I had never heard of this before and certainly never imagined it.

Nancy said, "OK Mike, go take care of Meg and Peg, and Sue and I will help Brin with his shower. I almost fainted with arousal as Nancy and Sue began rubbing that foam bar over me. Now I smelled the scent, almost sweet smelling, but quickly forgot the smell when their hands began rubbing all over me. I was hard, harder than I ever remember being. They took turns stroking my dick, as their lips began nibbling mine.

They asked me to soap them. My shaky hands took the foam bar and began sliding it over their beautiful bodies. The dark brown nipples stood out hard on their soft breasts. I touched them everywhere and slipped my fingers inside their hot slick tunnels. We were all moaning.

Nancy looked into my eyes and asked, "Would you like me to do to you what I did to Mike?"

I couldn't talk. I just nodded. She giggled and dropped to her knees in front of me and slid her hot mouth over my cock. I felt her tongue rubbing me inside her mouth, as she rolled my balls in her hand. All the while, Sue's kisses became very passionate and her tongue flicked against mine. This was far too much stimulation for me and I orgasmed in Nancy's mouth. My legs shook and gave out, sending me sliding down the slick wall on to my butt. Nancy never let go of my cock and followed me to the floor. She took all of my seed, as I lay there quivering. I just thought I had relearned how to fuck. I was now learning things I had never imagined possible. Nancy and Sue stood and helped me to stand up on shaky legs. They washed my hair and made sure all the white foam had been rinsed off.

The girls smiled at each other and Sue asked, "How do you like the shower?"

I just grinned a stupid grin that set them off laughing. We got out of the shower and dried each other off. Afterward, they took me by the hands and led me back to their bedroom. There were two beds there, and Mike Meg, Peg and Bess were already there in one. Nancy and Sue placed me between them and snuggled up on both side of me and we watched the other bed.

It was time for me to be shocked again. Meg and Peg were screaming in passion. I set up in bed to see why. Bess was between Meg's thighs nibbling and licking on her pussy, and Meg was going crazy. I never knew there could be sex between females, but obviously it was possible. I looked at Peg and saw Mike doing the same thing between Peg's thighs. It was obvious my girls liked what was happening.

It was also quite obvious they were having orgasms. I watched Mike move up between Pegs thighs wrap his arms around her long legs and pull them high. From the squeal I could tell he entered her with that big cock of his. Soon he was pounding into her vagina, much to her pleasure. It was fascinating to watch, but when Sue took hold of my dick and started stroking it I lost interest in what was going on in the other bed. I was already hard. It felt wonderful and the warm breasts from both girls were driving me crazy, but before I could do anything Sue slid her leg and soft thigh over me, grabbed my cock and guided it into her hot pussy. I moaned really loud as she pushed herself down over my cock. The slick warmth engulfed me, and I was once again lost in desire. Sue began humping me and seemed to be riding my cock. Nancy began kissing me with great passion. I began driving up into Sue. Her moans and squeals excited me and I soon shot my seed up into that wonderful encasement. Sue screamed as did I with our climax. She collapsed on my chest and lay panting, as was I. After a while Sue rolled off of me and cuddled. It was then I heard screaming coming from the other bed, and I looked to see Mike between Meg's thighs driving into her. Peg was sound asleep. I again lost interest in the other bed when Nancy started licking on my dick. These girls were taking me places no one of our race had been in generations, and I seemed to be insatiable. Nancy began rolling my dick in her hands and sucking on the head of my dick. I was surprised to feel my cock growing. She again engulfed it in her hot mouth, and I moaned. Nancy began bobbing her head up and down taking my whole cock in her mouth. I closed my eyes to enjoy the sensation, but I felt her move her body. I opened my eyes to see that she had straddled my head and was pushing her pussy down on my face. I stared up at it and tentatively probed it with my tongue. She moaned. Encouraged, I slid my tongue between her lips and tasted her nectar. It was sweet, and I liked it. I began using my tongue to touch inside, tasting all of it. When my tongue touched a hard nub she screamed and flooded my face with more nectar. I began feasting on her sweet pussy. Her thighs and pussy were quivering, but I continued. I thought Nancy might be over stimulated when she crawled down my body, but when her pussy passed over my cock she impaled herself on it. I watched cock disappear into her pussy from behind as she pounded down on my cock. This went on for a few moments, then she sat up and began sliding her butt back and forth with me impaled. She got faster and faster until she froze in orgasm. Her quivering pussy triggered my own orgasm and we screamed in unison. We heard clapping coming from the other bed and looked to see a smiling Meg, Peg, Bess and Mike. Yes, I do believe my team had learned much tonight, but we were all done. We stayed with our new partners and fell off into sound sleep.

Chapter 6
(First Attack)

We did sleep late, but when Robert and another man I didn't know came bursting into the room we immediately woke up.

Robert announced, "Armed forces and heavy equipment breached our secondary outer gate and are moving toward our main gate. I have already dispatched our security guards, but we need to meet them at the gate."

We were all up instantly searching for clothing. Someone tossed me my spandex clothes, which I quickly slipped into. It must have been one of my girls. I had a pretty good idea what was happening from Robert's announcement, and I barked orders to Meg and Peg, "Retrieve our weapons from the Cave, or wherever they're stored, and mount them on the roof and be ready. I'll activate the satellite equipment."

Flay came running in and said, "I'll help you."

The other man said, "Brin, I'm Jeremy, and I've already built the mounts and installed some of your weapons, the Rail Gun and EMP gun as near as I can tell. I didn't know about any other equipment, so I will help you with that and show you the communication room."

I nodded and Flay and I began to follow Jeremy out, while all the other humans prepared to follow Robert, but Tom, the bodyguard, blocked their way, holding up his hands.

Tom said, "Wait! Never put all your eggs in one basket, and never put all the generals together going into a potential battle. Some of you have to stay behind."

Tom was right, and I waited to hear the response.

Nancy said, I have to go to talk legal stuff, if that possibility exists."

Mike said, "I'm going if she goes, end of story! Sue, you and Bess stay here. No! Don't give me an argument. If something happens to us you will have to carry on the community."

Sue and Bess reluctantly remained behind, while the others raced toward their vehicles, and my team followed Jeremy.

Meg and Peg followed another man Jeremy instructed to take the girls to the roof, while Flay and I followed Jeremy to the Cave. It didn't take us long to find the satellite control equipment and took it to what they called the Communication Room. Our equipment is all self-contained and is powered by internal power storage units, so it was operational in minutes, and we were soon zooming in our picture on the front gate. We saw a small army of uniformed men headed toward the main gate. Our viewing angle was mostly straight down, but we had a good view. They looked official, and we saw the glint of badges on many of them as they piled out of the various conveyances.

Jeremy said, "That's strange. I see US Marshals, FEMA Officers and some Army soldiers, only federal. I don't see any state officials."

We could see many of our own security pointing weapons at the army, as Mike's group screeched to a halt behind rock barriers. In the rear of the invading army there were five large hauling units, and their obvious intent was to haul off our stores. There were at least thirty armed men approaching the gate, which still remained closed. We had about twenty armed guards holding position behind the covering wall.

I said, "Jeremy, we can see all right, but is there a way to hear what is being said?"

He looked at me, nodded and spoke into his communicator to Robert. After a minute audio sounded over Jeremy's communicator.

It was obvious that the leader of the forces was trying to intimidate us with a show of force. I wondered if Mike knew this was their tactic. I watched as Nancy stood firm in front of them. For such a small girl her stature was like a giant. I was proud to watch her, such a different girl than I had been with earlier. She was now very assertive.

Nancy said, "Stop! This is as far as you go."

Jeremy said, "That's the same government officers that Nancy ran off before. One of them is an attorney that tried to BS Nancy, unsuccessfully. We have several years of food stored here, and they want it. If they get it, we will all die. Nancy is not about to let them in. We may have a war start right now."

The FEMA Officer, the attorney, said, "We are under Martial Law. You cannot stop us. We have the authority now. Stand aside."

Nancy asked, "You feel that you now have authority over a foreign government?"

The Officer said, "Yes we do. Now stand aside."

Nancy actually laughed at him and said, "Well, this foreign government doesn't agree with you, but I would be happy to review your federal orders and any legal release from the State of Oklahoma, from which issued you a standing order of Cease and Desist. I also note that you do not have any National Guard with you, so apparently the State of Oklahoma has not approved of your action."

I didn't understand the legal issues, but Nancy seemed to understand them quite well.

The Officer seemed to be taken aback somewhat but continued, "Our federal orders are verbal, and we do not need anything from the state courts, as federal orders supersede them."

Nancy said, "That's what I thought. You are *not* a legal organization anymore. The federal government has no idea what you are trying to do, and they certainly definitely would *not* order you to invade another country. That's illegal. You are acting on your own, and, I might add, you are acting very stupidly to position your forces in the open against armed forces behind barricades. As I told you before, the Cherokee Nation owns the property all the way back to the first gate you crashed through. So, you have already invaded our land and are subject to our laws, and we find you guilty."

I had no idea what she was talking about, but she did sound convincing. This must be the legal stuff Jeremy had mentioned. Even though I didn't understand it, I loved the way she was standing her ground.

While we were watching the activities on the ground I heard chatter on one of the humans equipment. Jeremy jumped and strained to listen. The only thing I actually understood was the mention of our location. Jeremy quickly picked up his phone and punched a few numbers. In the viewer I saw Mike jump when his phone rang, which he quickly answered.

Jeremy spoke into his phone saying, "Mike, we just intercepted a radio message from Camp Gruber. They just dispatched a helicopter to our location. I don't know what kind, but they do have air-assault helicopters, and they've been ordered to come in over the lake and approach from behind."

Mike responded, which I heard on Jeremy's speaker, "Well crap. We are sitting ducks here from a rear attack. Tell Brin to take it out if he can't disable it."

I watched Mike lean in to speak privately with Nancy. He was obviously telling her what was communicated. I turned to Jeremy and said, "Can you communicate with the roof so I can instruct Peg?" I'm sure they were also watching the video feed and listening to the audio, but they would not have heard Mike and Nancy's private communication. Jeremy punched more numbers and handed me his phone. When someone answered I said, "Let me speak to Meg or Peg."

When Meg answered I asked, "Are you operational with the weapons?"

Meg said, "Yes we are operational."

"There will be an air vessel coming in over the lake to do us harm. Take it out with the EMP gun. We don't want to kill unless it becomes necessary, but if you have to kill, do it."

Louder, so I could hear, Nancy said, "Those sneaky bastards. Tell Brin to take out the last truck in line, also as a show of force." Then she turned back to the FEMA Officer and said, "So, you want to play games do you? If you have anyone in the last truck you better get them out quick."

I also passed those instructions on to Meg and waited. Nancy appeared calm, possibly some anger showing as she asked that question of that leader. Suddenly, I saw a sinking expression come over him. I'm thinking that this FEMA Officer was understanding that he made a mistake, but he still thought he had the upper hand. Still, he quickly yelled back to empty the trucks of personnel. Luckily, there were only drivers, and they were quickly coming armed, but suddenly the last truck disintegrated in an explosion. One second it was there, and the next it was a growing cloud of dust. The "Rail Gun" is an impressive weapon.

The Officer said, "Damn you bitch! You just wait."

Nancy said, "Wait for what? Wait for the helicopter? I don't think it is going to make it here."

As if to accent her last statement, the approaching helicopter from behind began spinning in the sky. I was pleased that Peg didn't have to kill anyone. I wasn't opposed to killing, but killing could escalate the conflict necessary. Peg's timing was perfect, probably intentional. I then watched in horror as most of them, including Nancy and Mike, turned to watch the helicopter as it sputtered and went down in the lake. It feathered down, so it didn't hit hard, and I didn't need to see it to know it was definitely out of action.

In war I was trained to never take your eyes off your enemy, which is what they did. I saw the angry FEMA agent quickly take advantage of their inexperience and drew his weapon and fired. The black man and Robert apparently were not inexperience. They had kept their eyes on the enemy and reacted. Tom pushed Nancy out of the line of fire by a fraction of a second, but in the process put himself into the trajectory of the bullet. His head exploded in a cloudy plume of red goo. Even as the sound of the shot continued to ring out, Robert's pistol reports sounded, placing three shots and three bloody holes in the middle of the FEMA Officer's chest. The officer's look of shock continued as he fell dead. All this happened in a fraction of a second but continued to play back in my mind in slow motion. Immediately all guns on our side took aim at targets, but no one moved on the other side. I think they were in more shock than us.

The apparent ranking US Marshal, as Jeremy had called him, shot his arms up high in the air in surrender and yelled, "Whoa! Hold your fire! He was not authorized to use lethal force. Just hold on."

While the officer was talking, Mike ran forward to check on Nancy. She had survived unharmed, maybe a scrape on her knee, but she was alive, thanks to black man, Tom. I knew Tom was dead, but Mike checked anyway. They had all been lucky that Robert and Tom had enough battle savvy not to take their eyes off the enemy. That saved Nancy and probably Mike also. He would have been the next target. The Army soldiers had not even gone for their guns. I think they really had no idea what was going on. They were just following orders.

Nancy calmed herself enough to assess the situation and said to the Marshal, "Are you in charge now? Your illegal army has fired first and killed one of us. Tell me why we shouldn't finish what you started."

The Marshal registered a look of panic and said, "Wait! Wait! That man was in charge. He organized this, and you were right. He didn't have any orders or authority to do this. He told us a show of force was all he needed to shut you down. We have organized a survivor camp at Camp Gruber and we have been gathering food there. He said you had plenty, and he was going to get it."

The other FEMA Officer said, "Shut the fuck up you asshole. You aren't in charge now, I am. They killed my partner. Now they are criminals and have no protection under the law. I'm going to call up more helicopters and assault this camp. We'll get their food. We need it you idiot."

I even missed the next action. I didn't see it coming. All weapons were focused on this blustery FEMA Officer, which was the second mistake, because the Marshal drew his automatic and shot the dumb SOB right in the face. He immediately dropped his weapon with his hands raised and said, "The dumb bastard was about to get us all killed. The answer to your question is: Yes, I'm in charge... now, and it's over. We just want to leave, if that's OK. I'm really sorry about your man. I didn't know the FEMA Officer was dumb enough to do that. We'll just take our dead and won't bother you again."

Nancy said, "No. Leave the dead. He was right, the FEMA bodies are evidence of a crime. We will bury them where they will never be found. Without evidence ... no crime. I think they just ran off in a panic, don't you?"

The Marshal actually smiled and said, "Yes Ma'am. We all saw them speed away in their car and leave us. Didn't we?" He looked around at his associates and received nods all around.

As they were about to leave, Robert asked, "Are you staying at Camp Gruber?"

The Marshal said, "You do know everything outside is collapsing? It's a war zone out there, and many of our Marshals have been killed already by the rioters. We aren't getting orders anymore. We're kind of on our own, the three of us left."

Robert spoke to one of his officers, who handed him his radio/phone. Robert then said to the Marshal, "I like the way you think. Take this special radio/phone. It's encrypted to our base station. It might be helpful if we stay in touch, just ask for Robert. Maybe we can help each other in the future."

The Marshal nodded and said, "Thank you. My name is Brady, Marshal Brady if you want to call me. They then loaded up and left, minus one truck and two FEMA Officers and their car.

Mike called Jeremy, "Can you get a crew out to the gate to get Tom. We will want to bury him with honors. The Secret Service would be proud." I guess the Secret Service was another law enforcement unit. "Oh, there are also two dead FEMA agents that need to be buried without honors, their car, too. Bury them where no one can ever find them."

In spite of the situation, Jeremy laughed and said, "I'll get right on that. They will become the foundation of our new front gate security building."

I had to laugh also at Jeremy's comment. The confrontation was over and everyone had been exceptional and interfaced well, even with their inexperience and mistakes. Nancy had been incredible. She was smart, strong willed and dominant in the confrontation, but it had all been a front ... a good front. I watched her as the enemy went out of sight, and she then fell sobbing onto Mike's chest.

I was proud of this human team. Mike had obviously planned well and chose the right people to become members, and I had done well choosing Mike. I felt more confident in our ability to survive.

After the conflict Flay, Meg, Peg and I returned to Bob's Cafe. It seemed that everyone was headed that way and assumed the cafe was the gathering place. Mike and Nancy had just returned and were seated at the same table we used before. We got some coffee and joined them.

Bob came over with a sympathetic look and poured something in Nancy and Mike's coffees out of a flask. He said, "Holler if you need more. It's from my cooking stock." Almost as an afterthought, Bob smiled and pored some of the brown liquid into our coffee."

Mike helped Nancy take a sip of her coffee. She swallowed then coughed, but it did seem to wake her up from her stupor. Thankful for the warning I took only a tiny sip of mine, and I thought my mouth and throat were on fire. The brown liquid from the flask was apparently a strong stimulant, but it tasted like fire. The second sip went down more easily, since I was sure it burned its way down.

Nancy said, "I sure screwed that up, and I got Tom killed!"

"No!" Mike said, "You did not get him killed. The FEMA Officer got Tom killed. He tried to kill you, and Tom saved you. That is what Tom was trained to do, and he would do it again. Tom is a hero and will be honored. Know this, hon, you saved a lot of other people today on both sides. You handled the whole situation masterfully. I really mean it."

Nancy looked hopefully at Mike and asked, "Really?"

Mike said, "Oh hell yes! I was so very proud of you, and everyone else was and will be also when they hear how you handled it. You took charge and won the argument against the bully. That's why the bastard wanted to kill you. I still don't know how you prevented the eminent coming battle, but you did it. I think you even made some friends on the other side."

Nancy embraced Mike and kissed him and said, "Thanks my love. I needed that."

I said, "Nancy, Mike is right. You were fantastic. You shut him down. I don't know anyone that could have done better, or even stood up to his argument, certainly not me. I wouldn't have been able to argue with him, I would have just shot him and let the war begin. You did save a lot of lives." When she looked at me strangely I answered her unasked question, "We watched the entire confrontation through our satellite monitoring and heard what was said through Robert's radio."

Bess said, "We also televised it through our complex video system. I think everyone watched and heard."

Nancy smiled and said, "Thanks for saying that, Brin. I really mean that, and thanks for taking that helicopter out."

Meg said, "You like the timing? We made those shots to emphasize your speech. I think it worked out well."

Mike said, "I think we are going to work out well together."

I noticed that things seem to be calming and said, "We need to start thawing out my crew in case we have other attacks. I'd like to start now, and we could use some help from your medical staff."

Mike said, "Of course, I'll take you up to the Clinic to meet the doctors. Sue, please tell Bob there will be more for dinner tonight." Mike then laughed. "You know what to tell him. Also, tell Mary about housing needs for Brin's crew. Oh, Brin, do you want some netting rigged for your rooms?"

I'm sure I was grinning hugely when I said, "It's not necessary. The beds worked out quite well for us last night. Isn't that right girls?" They also grinned and nodded and our group from last night broke out in laughter.

Mike then took us up to the Clinic and introduced us to Dr. Groom and his staff. When we told him of our needs, Dr. Groom was happy to be asked and joined right in.

Dr. Groom said, "I'm glad you asked me to help, since we also need to get blood samples as we wake them up. It's highly unlikely that you bring any diseases we should be worried about, since you come from a completely different world, but we might as well draw a reference sample. I do, however, worry about some Earth diseases you could be exposed to. We might have to give you and your crew some vaccines."

Meg said, "I don't think that will be necessary. Our race has been on Earth before, back when we had exceptional medical personnel. Our race has been inoculated against Earth's diseases, at least those identified back then.

Dr. Groom said, "That's nice to know, but we still need to draw samples for future records." Dr. Groom called Dr. Norcross to help, and we took off for the Dome.

Awaking from cryogenics is done automatically. The machine does it all, even providing a shock to the heart to ensure that it starts again, but standing by with additional equipment provided insurance. I can't remember any necessity for it, but standby was always provided just in case and to assist in any other way. It was like waking up from a dream. We started with Tina, our medical specialist, then concentrated on my department leaders. Blane was next, followed by Trix and Kit the chef, Bob would like Kit. After these we chose at random, but we stopped after about twenty due to tiredness, plus they were hungry. We took the new ones up out of the Dome and went straight to Bob's Cafe.

During the afternoon Bess had brought many brightly colored spandex suits for the emerging Apsaras team. She also brought some custom made suits put together by who she called a seamstress. They weren't as colorful as the others, but I tended to like them better. They were made of the same

144

material, but the color was a uniform silver/grey. I liked them so much that I switched, although I kept the other, also. Meg and Peg also switched, but Flay stayed with her black and pink outfit.

Nancy had put Flay in Toms bed, and when she woke up later Tom was with her. She spent the night with Tom learning sex, and from her screams last night, she learned it well. Understandably, she was upset with his death. We gave her space to calm some. She would be all right.

When our finely dressed crew approached the cafe a smiling Bob greeted us. I presume Bess notified him. He introduced himself to this partial crew and ushered us to a series of tables positioned for us. The new ones all had wide, surprised eyes at all the new sights. I was happy to see many humans taking the time to come over and introduce themselves and make my crew welcome. Bob and his staff brought trays of fish similar to what he had served us yesterday, and I watched my crew take their first tentative nibbles, then plunge in. As before with Meg, Peg, Flay and myself, utensils were discarded and they were feeding themselves with both hands with obvious enjoyment, pleasure shining in their faces. If a chef takes pride in the appreciation of his/her cooking, Bob would have to be ecstatic at their reaction. I asked, "Hey, Bob, do you have more?"

Bob smiled and said loud enough for all my team to hear, "You bet I do. This is as good a time as any to break your team into the buffet. Anyone that wants more, just take your tray and serve yourself. There are also many other different types of foods available in the buffet. I encourage you to take a sample of each to see if you like it. There is beef, chicken, and more fish to choose from, plus many other items. The menu changes daily. Take all you want, but I do ask that you take only what you can eat. We have plenty of food, but we don't want to waste it."

I said, "Thank you Bob. I will be sure and explain the concept of a buffet to the others as they awake and join us."

Mike and his girls came up behind me and sat at their table directly behind me, and Mike said, "I see you have some of your crew awake, and I see that they like Bob's fish."

I turned my chair toward him more and said, "Oh yes. We love the way he cooks the fish. Oh, and yes. This is my first group awakened. Many of these are my leaders. We will wake some of our water friends after we eat."

"Great! What kind of friends?"

I said, "You would call them porpoises, but ours are more evolved and smarter. We can communicate with them better. They will protect our home world fish until they can populate. Mike, I bet you didn't know your Earth porpoises were originally introduced by our race thousands of years ago."

Mike said, "No, I didn't know that. I didn't know your race had ever been here."

I said, "We have been most everywhere in our ancient past. That is how we knew you lived here."

Looking around the cafe, Mike said, "Just look at our members mingling, the human crew and the blue crew. None of them are shy, and they all seemed to be getting along great. The novelty of a blue color is just that ... only a color.

"Blue Crew? Is that what we are being called?" When Mike suddenly looked at me. I just held my hands up, indicating it was OK. "It's not offensive to us, after all we are blue." I then laughed and saw the concern disappear from his face.

A tall woman with bright red hair and tiny brown spots on her pretty, white nose and face came up to me and introduced herself. I had not seen another that looked like her, such diversity in these humans. Actually, she was quite becoming.

She said, "Mr. Brin, I am Mary O'Shay, the Castle Manager. I'm in charge of quartering your crew. Sue said you would have billeting needs tonight, and I see some of your crew has joined us already. Welcome. Our entire forth deck is for your people. There are plenty of rooms, but I would eventually need to know how you want them assigned. I can show you or your assistant the rooms available and the workings of the Castle if you like."

I stood when she came up to me and embraced her. That's when I noticed and felt her large breasts, which I tried to ignore. I said, "Just call me Brin. No Mr. is necessary. Thanks for your assistance." I then yelled, "Trix!" When she rushed up, I said, "Mary this is Trix. Trix is head of our security and the go to girl for the 'Blue Crew'.

147

Trix, please go with Mary and see to our billeting needs. Mary will let you know the workings of the Castle. Mary manages it. Thank you, Mary."

When they had gone I turned back to Mike and said, "I will watch over my crew for a while and see them to their quarters. I must also indoctrinate them in what our race has been missing sexually for centuries." I smiled internally, and I'm sure my eyes glazed over with the memories. "They will be pleasantly surprised, as I was. Afterwards, I'm sure they will want to learn first-hand from many of you humans. Meg and Peg thoroughly enjoyed learning about real sex from you. I'm sure they want to be taught more."

Mike said, "I'm happy to help." He laughed then said, "While I think of it, we usually have a meeting of our department heads in the mornings. We meet in our conference room to discuss whatever needs discussing. You might want to bring your key players also. It's a good time to interface and get to know each other."

I said, "We'll be there, Mike."

Our races continued to interface, but when Trix returned she led us up to the forth level and guided us toward my apartment. It looked just like Mikes, without the large recliner he had in his. All of us gathered in the center room so I could speak to them all at one time. I began, "What's said here, please pass it on to the others. This is a new world. Everything will be different here on Earth. We do not know the ways of humans, so we will assimilate with the humans and do as they do. We will not try to change them to our ways, we will change to their ways. Of course we will help them where we can, but we will take their lead. We need them for us to survive, they do not need us … remember that always. Our technology will help them survive, and they have already seen that. I don't mean to imply at all that it is us against them. They welcome us, so we must feel welcome and appreciative. I want us to totally merge with them and become one group, not separate. Is that understood?" The group was listening intently and all nodded agreement.

"Meg, Peg, Flay and myself have already discovered some major differences. You won't realize this, we didn't, but our race has lost the sensitivity of our noses living on a water world. That sense virtually does not exist in us. We can easily offend humans by assaulting their superior sense of smell. We learned that with our waterweed woven clothing. To humans they stink and is offensive. That is why we have discarded them and now wear these clothing. Personally, I like them better. Just keep in mind this fact when dealing with humans. If in doubt, ask them. Humans are not shy. They will tell you if something smells bad."

"Another major difference is the fact that most humans do not swim regularly for cleansing. They use showers and foaming bars to clean and scent their bodies. I guess that means that we will too, although we can still swim, but we have to go down to the boat docks. I haven't been there yet, but it

149

should be easy enough to find. Trix, did Mary tell you about the showers and beds?"

Trix said, "Yes. Mary took me around and showed me all the facilities and how they work, very impressive. She also showed me around the Castle, and she took me to the docks. I will show the others later."

I said, "I did not understand what a bed was until I spent time on one. Humans do not use netting to sleep in, they use a soft flat platform. It seems more practical than netting, and you will discover that you can do more on a bed."

"Probably the most shocking thing I have to tell you is that everything we have been taught about sex and reproduction has been wrong. The old one have been wrong, and there will be no more milking of seed here. Seed milking will be forbidden here. Meg, Peg, Flay and I, based upon information from humans, have discovered sex is a wonderful and pleasurable act if it is done as the humans do it in a natural way. The humans will teach you as long as you don't try and milk their seed. Am I right, girls?" I turned to my girls for conformation.

The girls actually blushed and Meg said, "Yes, sex can be very pleasurable when done like the humans, and yes, the humans are good teachers."

Many of the other girls crowded about my girls asking many questions. I figured this was as good a time to leave them as any and motioned for Tina and Blane to join me. Tina and Blane would just have to learn about sex on their own. We left the clatter of women and went back to the Dome.

Surprisingly, Bess was already there in the water wearing a diving suit like ours. She had a tank strapped to her back, a clear mask covering her nose and eyes, and something in her mouth with a hose attached. She saw us, smiled and waved. I jumped in the water to investigate her strange rig. I had to take a double look when I saw exaggerated fins attached to her feet, obviously for swimming. I guess she figured the best way to show us was to swim. She settled under the water and sank. Air was bubbling out of the apparatus in her mouth, so she was obviously breathing under water. She took off with powerful scissor strokes of those muscular legs and, for a small girl, propelled herself through the water at a surprisingly, fast speed. Her speed was still slow for an Apsarian, but still fast. I sped up to catch her and swam all around her admiring her equipment and form. Eventually I had to surface for air, which annoyed me, since she didn't. We circled back to the Dome and surfaced inside.

Bess lifted her mask and pulled the hose out of her mouth and said, "This is how we have to swim and work underwater, unless we want to stay on the surface most of the time to breath. Until you guys came I was in charge of underwater activities. I guess those activities will pass to your team, but I still want to be involved."

I said, "Of course you can remain involved. I'm impressed with your diving equipment and how you use it." I really am amazed. I had never imagined using technology for diving underwater, which could easily be done. Carbon dioxide to

Oxygen converters were common place in our old world. Every dome had one. I wondered why no one from Apsaras had ever thought about using one for diving before. I guess it was the same common curse of, "This is the way it has always been done." This was just another reason to despise the old ones. I really loved these humans for making us think differently. My mind was already analyzing how to adapt our technology to toward this goal.

I heard my friend Dobe chatter at me. Surprised, I quickly turned to see her being lowered down to the water in a harness. Tina and Blane must have gone directly to the cryogenics storage room. I chattered back at my friend, and when she reached the water, I quickly nuzzled her, which she welcomed and nuzzled me back with enthusiasm. When Bess and I released Dobe from her harness she quickly took off out of sight, but she was back in a few moments, chattering. Dobe squealed, *"Like Water. New Home Good."* Afterwards, she nuzzled Bess and quickly took off again. The fact that it was now dark outside didn't seem to bother Dobe at all, then with her built in sonar she would be able to see everything, even without light.

Bess said, "I can't believe she just spoke ... well sort of spoke. I guess she likes her new home."

I said, "You can bet she does, but what you don't realize yet is that she likes you, too. Dobe does not nuzzle many people, and I just watched her show you much affection. You definitely made a friend. Maybe she associates you with her new world."

Bess said, "That is fantastic. I feel honored."

Dubs was the next porpoise lowered, and Dobe was there chattering to him until he was released. He took off close behind Dobe. I'm sure she was showing him to the surface. She was certainly happy. One by one each porpoise was lowered into the water and was greeted by an ever growing audience of happy porpoises. At last the final member of both pods was released, and they took off, eager to explore their new world. Blane and Tina finally joined us in the water.

Blane was anxious about his friends and said, "How do they like the water here? Are they happy to be here?"

I said, "My friend they seem extremely happy. Dobe even said, '*Like Water ... New Home Good*'. They haven't stopped chattering and squealing, so they really must like it."

Blane said, "No shit? Really? Where are they now?"

"Oh, Dobe couldn't wait to show them around their new world. Hey Blane, guess what, Dobe came to Bess and nuzzled her."

"Are you kidding me? Bess, she has never nuzzled anyone but Brin, not even me. Dobe must think you are special. Tina and I haven't tried the water here yet. I think we will take a swim."

I said, "You'll enjoy it, but remember it is night and dark here now. You won't be able to see well. Also keep in mind that the surface is about a hundred feet up, so watch your pressure." They nodded and dove in and swam out of sight.

It had been a long cycle and I was tired, plus having an early cycle ... morning meeting, I decided it was time to find my way back to my room.

Bess asked, "Anything else we need to do tonight?"

I said, "Not tonight. Tomorrow is another day. I think I will go try out the bed again. Thanks for all your help."

"No problem at all. Any time you need me just let me know. I'll show you back to your room. Want me to help you try out the bed?"

I'm sure my grin was huge when I said, "I would like that very much."

Bess quickly led us back through the interconnecting tunnel, through the Cave to the elevator, up and through the corridors of the fourth floor. She was obviously aroused and didn't slow down, while she began stripping off what remained of her diving suit. I was right behind her admiring her lithe and little body as I slipped my suit off, tossing it against the wall. My sexual urges were peaked as I dove onto the bed right behind her. I didn't even give her time to roll over, and rolled over on her back. She moaned as my cock slid between her cheeks. I pushed and slid inside her already slick pussy. I was amazed how tight she was, but she began meeting my thrusts and pushing herself on me. Soon we were pounding into each other. This was so different for a human. This was almost like water sex while swimming. Bess met my rhythm with strong thrusts from under me. This coupling was wild and animal-like, and we exploded together with loud growls. I didn't know if she wanted my seed, but she sure got it … lots. Afterwards, I lay over her still impaled. Her whole body quivered and that seriously tight pussy clamped me hard. It hurt, but this time I loved it. I was in no hurry to pull out, so I lay on her enjoying the feeling. I knew my weight on her caused her little problem, as I could feel her hard muscles rippling under me. She could easily have lifted me off if she wanted, but apparently she was enjoying the feeling as well. Eventually, I rolled beside her and pulled her against me.

Bess said, "You know I was left out last night and unsatisfied. I didn't get any of that blue dick, and I've been thinking about sex all day. I'm glad I waited, because that was different. I like this way of having sex."

I said, "This way is almost like we learned about sex during the voyage. We coupled while swimming. This was almost like that."

Bess set up, interested, and said, "Really? You will have to teach me."

"You would have to learn to swim like I swim for it to work."

Bess said, "I'm an expert diver and swimmer. I can already swim the 'butterfly stroke', which is what you do."

I laughed and said, "What about breathing? You can't hold your breath that long, and the tank will get in the way."

155

It was Bess' turn to laugh, and said, "Are you challenging me? I already have that figured out. You will wear the tank. My air regulator has two mouth hoses, since I teach diving and sometimes need to help others. This way we can both stay underwater for a long time, much longer than you can fuck."

I said, "Now who is challenging whom." We both began laughing.

After a bit of cuddling I said, "I wonder where Meg and Peg are. I figured they would be here."

Bess said, Oh they were with Mike and my sisters when I saw them last. Your girls were talking about getting some more seed from Mike. They are probably all at his apartment. You want to go down there?"

"Sure. Let's go see what's going on."

Bess said, "I was going to do you again, but I'll save that for the water, besides, there are probably several girls down there that wants some blue dick."

I laughed, but that thought made my dick tingle with desire. We slipped back into our suits, but that was a waste of time. When we entered Mike and his girls' apartment we immediately heard moans and screams coming from Mike's bedroom. We walked into an amazing scene of naked bodies. Blane and Tina must have come directly here, because the first thing I saw was Blane, Nancy and Sue on one of the beds. It looked like he was learning sex quickly. Sue was on top riding his cock, and Nancy was sitting on his face moaning. I looked at the other bed to see Meg and Peg,

156

apparently already satisfied laying together. A smiling Bess went directly to them and spread their legs wide to feast on their oozing pussies. It was arousing to watch my girls enjoying the attention. They must have liked having sex with Bess last evening. I sure did with the petite brown girls. I heard other moans and watched Mike driving his big cock into Trix. I had a slight pang of jealousy, since my sexual awakening I had thought of Trix several time, and I wanted to try her. Another scream caught my attention. I saw a naked Tina with her legs spread wide taking a hard cock from … Robert. Damn, they were all getting into real sex, and rightfully so. It's fantastic.

I felt someone slide an arm around me, and I turned to see the beautiful black girl, JJ. She must have come in with Robert and Trix. Another arm slipped around me and I turned in her direction to see a petite white girl. Together they led me out of the bedroom and over to an empty bedroom. The white girl had slipped her hand into my shorts and was holding my already painfully hard cock in her hand. JJ was tall enough to kiss me, but the petite white girl had to pull me down some to press her warm lips on mine. They quickly stripped my suit off and their own and pushed me down on the bed. I really liked the take charge demeanor and flowed with it. They partially lay on me rubbing their soft breasts and hard nipples on my chest while kissing me. Both girls were beautiful in different kinds of ways. The tall, black girl had full, soft lips, and as we became more excited her dark black skin glistened in the soft light from a sheen of moisture. She had short black hair, and her body was slim but muscular. The petite white girl was very light skinned, and her skin was very soft and warm. Her breast were large with hard pink nipples. Both girls excited me greatly. I let my hands slide over their bodies, exploring. The white girl had no hair at all on her soft pussy, which I found tantalizing. The black girl had course hair that felt springy, very different and very exciting.

Our playing and exploring ended very abruptly when the white girl swung her leg over me, grabbed my cock and quickly pushed herself down on me, capturing my cock in a soft, slick sheath of fire. She was on fire with lust and began hungrily bouncing up and down on my cock. Somehow she was also rotating her hips. Suddenly she screamed loud and froze, while holding me inside her. It was such a violent scream that I looked into her face. Her head was thrown back, but I could see that her eyes were also rolled back in obvious ecstasy. Her body may have been frozen but her pussy was spasming, and I could feel hot liquid flooding me. Suddenly, it was like life left her body and she fell on my chest. It almost scared me ... almost. I did not orgasm with her, and I was almost insane with animal lust. I rolled her to the side and reached for JJ. My lust needed release, and my intention was to vent it into JJ. That may have been my intent, but nature had other thoughts. I rushed between her thighs to drive violently into her, but she was so tight I was only able to push in a couple of inches.

She was moaning and wasn't resisting, she was just incredibly tight. I'm glad. I had to work hard to build up any rhythm to penetrate deeper but finally managed to sink myself into her with her help. Her hands pulled me and her heels dug into my butt cheeks, and I went deeper and deeper into that hot vice. We found ourselves driving against each other as our moans and groans built to a chorus, as we exploded together. I felt my cock jerking inside her as I shot spurt after spurt into her gripping pussy. We stayed linked together for a while. Her thighs began quivering with exhaustion, and she fell beside me, panting.

I pulled the girls close to me and thought it was over, but I was wrong. The white girl had woken up and reached for my limp dick. It felt good with her hand massaging my dick, but I knew it was dead after two massive orgasms. She continued, however, while I was kissing JJ, then I felt her move her body and take my dick into her mouth and begin gently and slowly sucking on it. She continued sucking while rolling my testicles in her hand, and I felt a tingle of life twitch. She was determined, and it was feeling damn good. Surprisingly, I felt my cock coming to life again. Soon her mouth and head were bobbing up and down on my now hard cock. When the size of my cock was to her liking she again straddled me and sank her hot pussy down over my cock. This time she was grinding her pussy back and forth and sliding her thighs over me. I felt my cock touching her everywhere inside her. This girl really knew what she was doing. She got faster and faster, and I began helping by driving up into her. Soon I was lifting and bouncing her on my cock and she began screaming again. This time I was not going to let her off my cock until I climaxed. She collapsed again on my chest and I couldn't continue to bounce her, so I rolled with her and remained inside. Her pussy was gripping me hard and convulsing, but I pounded into her... hard. She was in overload and fell silent, but I continued driving into her until I grunted and climaxed deep inside her. I then rolled her back on to my chest with my cock still inside her. We lay still for a long while until she revived. She felt me still inside her and set up partially and looked into my eyes.

She wiggled on my cock, giggled and said, "Hello Brin. I'm Janet Walsh with water and sanitation. It's nice to meet you." All three of us started laughing.

Chapter 7
(Second Attack)

Me and my team were the first to show up in the conference room, beating everyone. We had a chance to look around while we were waiting. The design was elegant with glass walls and doors, even the large conference table was made of glass or some other transparent material. All the chairs around the table were some form of black leather, at least that is what they called it. I noticed the outside wall had sliding glass doors that led out onto a balcony with high heavy rock walls. From this location we could see down on the lake and terrain for miles. The water looked clear enough to see the bottom in some places, even though I knew the water depth to be much deeper than it appeared. On Apsaras we never saw mountains except underwater. Seeing them now covered with green trees and vegetation was a novelty. It would take a long while to become accustomed to scenery other than water surface, but I looked forward to the experience.

We came back in when the others began to file in. I nodded to Nancy, Sue and Mike as they came in. I couldn't help but smile at Bess, what a wonderful night. Robert and JJ entered next and nodded to us. I saw Bob and Jeremy come in. They were accompanied by another man I did not know, but I heard someone call him James. He was the Master Farmer I was told. I did recognized the tall redhead, Mary. I noticed that everyone was getting a coffee and did likewise, and as I sat back down, I noticed the large room was almost filled.

Mike said, "Good morning, Brin. I see you have had a busy night reviving a lot of your crew. I also see you brought some of them with you and assume these are some of your leaders. Would you like to introduce them?"

I stood and said, "Yes, by now most of you know Meg and Peg. They are my satellite monitors and pilots. Trix here," pointing out the beautiful lady with large blotches of orange hair, "Is the head of my security. Many of you met Flay already, she heads up our science and engineering. She and her father got you the winning lottery tickets." Many cheered. "Kit is what you would call a chef. Blane runs our underwater food production, including fish herding. Tina is in charge of our medical. You would call her a doctor, but her duties extend to biological analysis and genetics. If you have specific talent needs we have many others to draw from, otherwise we will interface as best we can."

Mike said, "Thanks Brin. We welcome you all. Now to my team, as time permits introduce yourselves to your counterpart and show them around."

"Now, does anyone have any problems or situations requiring immediate attention?"

Jeremy stood and said, "For you new ones, I'm the architect and master builder of this project, and I'm eager to spend time with Flay. She did a great deal to help design the Castle. Again, for the new

162

members, our project is virtually complete and operational."

"Well, we are building a new guard building. I think everyone knows why. It is going well. The foundation is already dug, packed, backfilled and will be poured today. We stocked up a lot of building material, so let me know if you need anything built. I'll get right on it."

"Oh, I haven't reported yet to the group, but I dispatched two boats to recover the soldiers from the helicopter crash in the lake. None were hurt, and they have no idea what happened to the helicopter, and we didn't tell them. We dropped them off at the docks by the dam and sent a radio dispatch to Camp Gruber telling them where to pick them up. They consider us friends for helping them. Hell, I'm even sending some divers out to strip the helicopter of usable items."

Robert stood next and said, "There is no longer any organized law enforcement. They have been either killed, neutralized, or run off by the large forces of rioters and gangs rampaging. Private citizens are fighting back, but they don't have much of a chance against the gangs. Lots of people are being killed. Even Tulsa and Oklahoma City have collapsed. Without police protection the few remaining firefighters refuse to go out. As a result, cities are burning across the country. To put it bluntly, civilization no longer exists. I've put our security on high alert. Anyone trying to get in now will be hostile. I've ordered them to shoot to kill."

Mike said, "This is sad to hear, but we knew it was inevitable. This is what we prepared for ... survival, and we will survive."

Robert continued, "We have learned even more, thanks to the Blue Team, no offense meant with the name. We have been monitoring the satellite images. It's not of immediate concern to us yet, but I need to report that Oklahoma City, Ft. Smith and Tulsa, our closest large cities, are all in flames from the riots, and people are pouring out of the cities in alarming numbers. Tens of thousands have already died in the food riots, outright race wars and fires. Anything that is believed to have any stores of food is already sacked and destroyed. These ravaging gangs have begun to move into the country and are decimating the farms. Some of the hostile groups are combining and organizing into small armies and attacking any other group competing for food. Unfortunately, the stronger groups are based at or near National Guard facilities or military bases. They can't survive if they share, there are simply too damn many people to feed. These military bands or gangs obviously have the armaments to defend themselves and their stores. Hell, they even have tanks, and they are using them."

Mike asked, "Is the government trying to help in any way?"

Robert said, "Mike, it is like this everywhere. In point of fact, it's worse in most places. It will run its course, like you predicted, and that is likely to take a couple of years. By then 80% or more of the population will likely be dead. The government has gone underground and will most likely stay there until the apocalypse is over."

I said, "What does the rest of the world look like?"

Robert said, "When the dollar collapsed the world economy crashed also. The world economy was extremely fragile to begin with, and it only took a slight push to topple it. So, I guess it is like this everywhere, at least in the developed countries. Many of the 3rd world backward countries hardly noticed. They had little anyway and were living off the land. If it weren't for their massive cities full of starving people pouring out, some might survive."

I said, "OK, we are on our own. Any suggestions or recommendations on what we should or can do?"

I stood to get everyone's attention and said, "Wars are won or lost before the first bullet is fired. We can't win by waiting and defending against an attacking army. We must attack … always. Wars are won by planning. Now we must plan."

"We know eventually the armies will come here. We are probably not a big secret to many, but we must stand firm against those that may come. So we limit their access to us and try to isolate ourselves. Hordes are coming out of the big cities, and we can't save them. We must all understand that. There are simply too many of them. They will die or eventually join the armies we must fight. No, I suggest we try to drive the escaping hordes away from our location and limit our exposure.

Mike considered the statement and said, "We can do that by destroying key bridges crossing the Arkansas River that lead toward us, like Gore, Muskogee, Wagner, Ft. Smith and the bridge on I-40 crossing Lake Eufaula. This won't stop the traffic, but it will sure slow them down and hopefully send them in other directions."

Jeremy said, "That makes a lot of sense, but will the Rail Gun reach that far?"

I said, "I would imagine all these targets you mention are close and should be well within range of the roof mounted Rail Gun. The only limit is line of sight. If we don't have line of sight on all those targets, our fighter saucers also have Rail Guns, and we can make a night attack. I doubt we would be seen, since the Rail Gun has no sound or explosive signature."

Mike said, "Does everyone agree this is the course of action we should take?"

Affirmative nods from all passed around the table, but James said, "Maybe we should expand our reach beyond what we have discussed. I'm thinking that we should also be concerned about influx from the Dallas Ft. Worth metroplexes. These are far larger than the cities here. There aren't too many natural barriers like our rivers to take advantage of, but there are a couple of major highways leading out of that area that cross Lake Texhoma. I'm thinking we should take those out also."

Mike said, "Good idea, James. Brin, how can we help you with this plan?"

I said, "The Rail Gun uses a massive amount of electrical energy. So, we will need to switch over to our Apsaran electrical generators for any extended use of the gun. Don't worry Jeremy, we configured it already to be compatible with your power requirements. Other than that, we could use someone to help us identify the targets, both on the roof and in our saucer. We can start as soon as we make the generator switchover."

Jeremy said, "Your generators are already installed and hooked up and ready to switch over and take our power load. Al, our electrical engineer, did that the first day. I can also volunteer Dam Mark as the target spotter. I think he worked on most of the lake bridges and dams and should be able to easily spot them, or at least know what to look for."

I had to chuckle, along with a few others in the room, at the use of the name Dam Mark, since he was recruited as a result of my suggestion to protect the Tenkiller Dam. We all knew that that joke name would follow him in the community.

I said, "Excellent. Flay, get with this electrician, Al, and finalize the connections and transfer of energy. Meg will operate the roof gun, and Peg will pilot our fighter saucer tonight. Find Dam Mark and make arrangements."

Mike said, "Unless there are other pressing issues that can't wait, let's adjourn till tomorrow and go exercise Brin's plan." None spoke up, so we all left to follow our own schedules.

Jeremy went directly to Frey and took temporary charge of her, but she was more than happy about that, since she had been looking for him. The immediate need, however, was to get her with Al Martinez for the generator transfer, but I'm sure Jeremy would want to show her around his operations more and get her involved. Flay would be one of the few that could appreciate all he had done.

Robert did the same with Trix. His security operation could benefit greatly from her weapons and experience. I kind of figured these two might wind up eventually being more than working partners, and I seemed to remember already seeing Robert between Trix's thighs last night. I was quite sure from what I witnessed that they had gotten much closer already.

I also noticed that Bess went directly to Blane. She would be interested in showing him her operation, getting his ideas and learning more about what he planned underwater.

The human doctors gathered around Tina to absorb medical knowledge from her and show her around the facilities. Plus, they still had many of our Blue Team members to awaken. That kind of left the rest of us alone with nothing to do, so I followed Mike, Nancy and Sue down to Bob's Cafe. I had skipped my morning meal, so I was also hungry. I picked up a metal tray and followed the others down the buffet line. I didn't know what to pick out, and I must have looked lost.

Bob came to the other side of the food line and said to me, "We do have fish, Brin." He pointed to the trays, "But, If you feel adventurous let me offer you a taste sample. We are serving T-Bone steak today, one of the rare human favorites. It will most likely be different than you have ever had, but I'm willing to bet you will like it." He then pulled out a slab of thick, dark meat and took his knife and cut a piece out of it. He then took a fork from my tray and stabbed the parcel. I could see juice dripping from it as he guided it toward my mouth. I looked at it for a short while. I thought, *"Why not?"* I opened my mouth and took it. The texture was tough, and biting into it took far more effort, but the flavor that flooded my tongue and mouth was incredible. I began chewing it in earnest and spoke around my food, "This is good. Thanks. I'll take the rest of it."

Bob grinned and said, "I told you you would like it. Now, trust me." He began dishing other food on my tray. "A baked potato and red beans go well with a T-Bone, but go easy on the beans for the first time until your body adjusts." At the end of the buffet line were glasses for drinks. I figure if I was eating like a human I might as well go all the way. I filled my glass with the white liquid I had seen Mike drinking all the time. I then found a seat at Mike's table and began devouring my steak.

Mike, Nancy and Sue apparently had nothing to do either. That made sense, as they had completed their major tasks of organizing, building a team, and getting the complex built and paid for. They had done a fantastic job.

Mike said, "I see Bob talked you into eating one of his fantastic steaks. How do you like it?"

"It's a little harder to chew, but I love it. I'm not so sure about the potato and beans yet, but I love the milk. Where does it come from?"

Nancy said, "The potato tastes much better with butter and a little sour cream and chives. Potatoes grow in the ground. Beans grow on a vine. Both are considered vegetables, and we grow them on our farms. The white bread you're eating is milled and baked here in the kitchen. It's from wheat seeds also grown on our farms. We also raise the beef here. That is where the steak comes from. Milk comes from our own milk cows … also beef. Milk is the food of young calfs. They nurse it from their mother's utters … tits. When we all get the time we'll show you all around the compound."

I took a second look at the milk. I had wondered about it, but had no idea what it actually was. Oh well, it was good. I said, "Thanks for the explanation of the food. I'm looking forward to seeing the full operation. I have a lot to learn."

I was also looking around at all the various human members … Such vast diversity. I said, "I also have a lot to learn about humans. I'm not used to all the diversity of your members. I guess you have noticed that my group all look quite similar … very little diversity. In humans I see all sizes, shapes, hair and eye colors and skin color and shades. I see all different kinds of white people, many blacks and browns, but I have read about some of your races are red and yellow also. I haven't seen any of those."

Mike said, "Many of us are Indian. I don't know why, but we have been called red skins. For the most part, however, we are just a shade of brown, like the Hispanic and many other races. Now we do have members from China and Japan. They do have a slightly different complexion, some refer to as yellow, but I don't see it. Since you haven't met any Asians yet, while you are waiting, like us, you should go visit the dental office and let them check your teeth and get samples. Ask for Dr. Wong or Dr. Ikiko."

When Mike mentioned this latter, Nancy and Sue started laughing. I knew something was up and said, "OK, what are you getting me into?

Nancy said, "Oh, it's nothing. You will like it."

Now I was curious, curious to know what they were laughing about and curious to see this yellow race. I followed Bob's instructions and emptied my tray and stacked it. I then took the stairs up to the second floor. The sign clearly indicated the entrance to the Dental Clinic, and I went in. There were two beautiful females setting inside. They were definitely different. It was something about the eyes. Maybe they were rounder or slightly tilted. There were dark eyes smiling at me. I'm sure they were thinking the same about me ... different. I didn't see yellow skin, well maybe a slight tint, but the complexion was appealing. I said, "Dr. Wong and Dr. Ikiko I presume. I'm Brin, and Mike suggested that I come here to have my teeth checked."

Dr. Wong stood, shook my hand and said, "I'm Dr. Wong and this is Dr. Ikiko. We're happy to finally meet you, Brin. You caught us at a good time. We can get right on you." Dr. Ikiko giggled.

When they stood I got a better look at both. Dr. Wong was taller than I originally thought, but Dr. Ikiko was small, petite actually. Both were beautiful but in slightly different ways. Both had long, silky and shiny black hair flowing far down their backs, and they were dressed alike in a white uniform looking short dress.

Dr. Wong led me into a back room and had me sit in a chair. My head rested in a support that held my head straight. I had never had my teeth checked before. Apsarians seldom had problems with their teeth. I had been told that our normal diet on Apsaras supported healthy teeth.

Dr. Wong handed me a blue pill and said, "Take this," which I did. I'm going to lean you back in the chair and inspect your teeth, probably give you a good cleaning, too."

I didn't know what to expect, but felt the chair I was in lean far back. She adjusted a strong light to shine directly in my mouth and entered my mouth with some strange looking sharp tools.

As she began inspecting and touching my teeth she said, "While I work on your teeth Dr. Ikiko will take a sperm sample. So, don't move. I don't want to stick you."

172

I couldn't talk to ask, "What the fuck?", so I didn't say or do anything when I felt my spandex shorts being pulled down and off. I think I did moan when I felt a small hand begin to massage my dick. I'm positive I moaned when I felt Dr. Ikiko's mouth suck it in. I forgot about my teeth and wondered if what Dr. Ikiko was doing was a diversion to take my mind off my teeth. Hell, I didn't care, divert away. My cock was standing tall when I felt her stop sucking and rolled something down over my cock. Once it was on my cock she straddled me and slipped her hot pussy down over my cock and started riding me. Oh yeah, you go girl. There is something about being forced to remain still while being fucked. It excited me, and I soon climaxed, filling whatever she put on me. She quickly got off my cock and slipped the thing off.

Dr. Ikiko said, "I've got the sperm sample."

Dr. Wong said, "Oh, good. Help me."

Dr. Wong's instruments never left my mouth, but I felt her body move and her leg slip over me. I felt Dr. Ikiko's small hand grab my cock again and guide it into Dr. Wong's hot pussy, this time without the cock covering. She sat fully down on my lap impaled on my cock. Once impaled, she removed her tools and began grinding on my cock.

Dr. Wong said, "Yours is the first blue cock we've had in here and were looking forward to it. Don't worry about your dick going down. We gave you a Viagra. We plan to use you for a while."

I finally said, "I have no idea what a Viagra is, but it's not about to go down. Use me all you want."

I was now able to lift my head and watch, but the doctors had kept their white dresses on. All I could see was her straddling me, riding. She was good at riding. I felt her pussy quivering just before her pussy clamped down on me in orgasm. Dr. Wong groaned loud and froze, but I was not finished. My hands reached out to grab her hips, and I took over. I began driving up into her, bouncing her up and pulling her down on my cock. If she was trying to keep a low profile or keep the sex a secret, she failed terribly. I took her into another orgasm, a massive one. Her scream echoed throughout the clinic, and her body went into convulsions. It scared me.

Dr. Groom came running in and saw what was happening. He laughed and wrapped his arms around her and forcefully lifted her off my cock. He said to Dr. Ikiko, "OK, finish him off." She didn't hesitate and was on me in seconds, lifting her dress and slamming her hot, slick pussy down on me. Dr. Wong's treatment continued with Dr. Ikiko but more violent, since she was so much smaller. I could almost hold her weight in my hands as I drove, lifted, and slammed her back down on my extremely hard cock. Her screams came in bursts as I pounded. It felt like I drove my cock halfway through her body when I exploded inside her. She fell across my chest when I released her, but she was still awake and smiling. I didn't mean to hurt

174

her. I have no idea why I was aroused to this degree. Dr. Groom allowed us to calm before he lifted her off and sat her in a chair beside Dr. Wong.

Dr. Groom laughed and said, "They gave you Viagra didn't they?"

All I could do was nod my head.

"Don't worry, Brin. It's not your fault. Viagra increases your natural desire. I keep warning them about that, but they like rough sex, and it looks like they got it this time."

Dr. Wong finally said, "Well, we got a sperm sample, and his teeth are in great shape."

Dr. Groom laughed and said, "Yeah, I can see his sperm sample running down Dr. Ikiko's thighs." I joined them in laughing.

Dr. Wong held up a rubber sheath and said, "That was the second one in her. Here's the first."

Dr. Groom said, "They get carried away gathering sperm samples sometimes. We will analyze yours for your sperm count and to establish a reference.

I grabbed a towel and cleaned myself up and slipped my spandex back on. On the way out I asked, "Do I need to come back for anything?"

Dr. Wong laughed and said, "No, not for a while anyway. We'll call you." She then winked.

I went back down to the cafe, and Mike and his girls, minus Bess were still there. They saw me coming and started clapping. I know I was blushing, because it was obvious they knew what had happened. All I could think of to say was, "My teeth are in great shape." This set them off laughing so hard tears were rolling down their cheeks.

Nancy said, "Give it up, Brin. We heard them screaming all the way down here."

I started grinning and said, "Well, hell, they gave me a damn Viagra. It's their fault." With that we all started laughing again. I liked this group, they felt like family.

The timing was perfect. Meg, Peg, Flay, along with a couple of others, came into the cafe. I was then introduced to Al, the electrical engineer, and Dam Mark. Meg even introduced him as Dam Mark, which didn't seem to bother him. He must already be used to it.

Flay said, "Everything is switched over and organized. We are ready."

We all left to go to the roof and Meg and Dam Mark took their positions.

Dam Mark began sighting through the targeting telescope, while Meg sat at the controls of the Rail Gun.

Mark said, "The top of the Castle is a good, high location for line of sight to our targets. There, OK, we're sighted in on the bridge crossing the upper Ft. Gibson lake, but let me give you the signal during a lull in the traffic. I hate to kill people just trying to escape. Now!"

Meg fired the Rail Gun.

Immediately Mark said, "Wow! Most of the bridge just disintegrated. Next, let me find the Arkansas River crossing east of Muskogee." After a few minutes he said, "Ready. Fire! It's gone!

There is a narrow crossing on the lower end of Ft. Gibson lake, but we will have to leave it alone. That crossing is over the top of the dam. We don't want to destroy that one, since it would destroy the dam and flood everything below."

It took him a while longer to find the bridge west of Gore crossing the Arkansas River, but he finally did. He was concerned with a direct line of sight. Finally he was satisfied and said, "Ready. Fire now!"

With the destruction of this last bridge we were, more or less, cut off from any heavy traffic coming from west of the Arkansas River, but not all. The rest would have to be done from the saucer after dark. We were about to leave the roof when Peg came up with a new problem. Flay had just handed her a tablet device showing satellite images.

Flay said, "We were too late on the northern bridges. I'm tracking an army caravan, including tanks, en route toward Camp Gruber or possibly us. The caravan evidently crossed before we took out the Muskogee bridge, but most disturbing is the makeup of this caravan. It includes many of the Tulsa gangs spawned up during the riots. This caravan doesn't appear military, only military led."

Mike asked, "Does anyone have any idea what their intent is?"

Robert said, "Well, Camp Gruber is the designated FEMA food distribution center in time of emergency. The army would know that, and I think this army is invading to get their food. I

177

believe their intent is totally hostile, but we will know soon."

I said, "They could also be trying to combine with Camp Gruber, but either way the army caravan is our enemy. They will come for our food sooner or later. Should they intend to attack Camp Gruber, maybe we should let them fight it out and kill each other. Both are our potential enemies. Remember, this is why we destroyed the bridges ... to keep them out."

Mike listened then asked, "Do we know if Camp Gruber is actually trying to help the local residence?"

Robert said, "There are many cars and trucks there, so I do believe they are trying to help, but we don't know how much food they have stockpiled and how long and how many they can take care of. The FEMA officers were certainly trying to confiscate food from everyone, including us, so they probably do have a major stockpile."

Mike said, "If they are taking in the locals, this is probably good for us, because the refugees have to go passed Camp Gruber to get to us. If the Army takes them in they won't try to come here. If the army is trying to invade Camp Gruber, maybe we should help defend them and keep them alive. They could be our first line of defense from the refugees and other gangs."

When Mike's logic registered, I said, "Well, looking at it that way, I agree. Let's see what happens when they meet."

Peg said, "It looks like Camp Gruber is taking up a defensive position, preparing to repel an attack. It also looks like the approaching army is repositioning for an attack. It appears to be an invasion."

Mike said, "Very well. It's war then, but let's wait until the first shots are fired."

Mark had already gone to the targeting telescope and was viewing the battlefield. He said, "They have five tanks lining up. I'm sighted in on the first tank. Ouch! They fired!"

We huddled around Peg to view Camp Gruber and saw the first explosion. The invaders were targeting the helicopters, and we saw the first one explode. The others were trying to take off.

Mike said, "Go ahead and take out the tanks."

Meg immediately fired, and we watched a tank turn instantly to dust. They continued to target and fire until all five tanks no longer existed. Shortly afterwards several helicopters swooped down on the army, firing upon the gathered invading troops. They cut down many until they were met with rockets from hand-held launchers. Two helicopter exploded in mid-air before they could retreat.

Mike said, "Keep taking out trucks and groups of soldiers, anything else you can see."

We watched the damage inflicted as truck after truck disappeared, and in some instances, crowded areas of the line sprang into dust. The invading rabble immediately turned and ran, followed closely by the returning helicopters. The helicopters were relentless and pursued the running gangs, killing all

179

they could find. They knew there was no choice, that they would have to continue to deal with the survivors. I'm sure some escaped, but not a lot.

Robert said, "I'm getting a call from that US Marshal I gave the radio to."

We gathered around Robert and heard, "This is Marshal Brady. Is this Robert? Was that you guys?"

Robert said, "Yes, this is Robert, and yes, it was us."

Marshal Brady said, "Thanks. We thought we were goners. Colonel Kline offers his thanks, also. The colonel and I would like to come meet with you."

Robert looked at Mike for approval, who nodded in approval, and said, "Come on over. We'll leave word at the gate to let you in. They will give you directions." He then said to us, "I don't guess it matters now if we let the secret out about the Blue Team."

Mike looked at me for comment. I just shrugged and said, "Your right. It's not likely to concern anyone else at this point."

I didn't believe it would take long for them to get here, since they were only a few miles away. We went to the conference room to wait. Since we intended to let it be known about our Blue Team, at least to our new friends, I motioned for Meg, Peg and Flay to follow us down. We had just gathered and was working on our coffee when the front gate called on the radio to let us know they had passed them. Nancy, Mike and I watched at the rail as the two of them came in and went to the security desk. The guards checked them over for weapons and disarmed them before sending them to the elevator. Nancy needed to be there, because the marshal would more easily recognize her. I went back into the conference room and left Mike and Nancy to greet them when the elevator doors opened. They were waiting and introduced themselves. They then led them into the conference room. I could tell they were duly impressed with our facilities, but when they saw me and my girls they stared open-mouthed in disbelief. Even though they obviously were more than curious about us, I chose to wait and not offer any explanation.

Mike said, "You asked for this meeting, so you have our attention."

Marshal Brady said, "Well, first of all, Colonel Kline and I wanted to thank you in person for saving us. They were about to do some serious damage to us, and there was little we could have done about it. Of course, we would have fought back, but they had the heavy power and ground to air portable missiles. It was hard to believe that they intended to attack. At first we thought they wanted to merge with us, but that hope vanished fast. When we saw the tanks start to disintegrate I knew it was you folks. I've seen it before. By the way, I told the colonel everything that happened at the gate and my part in it. I think he suspected, but after society devolved it didn't seem to matter anymore. Those FEMA agents were asshole bureaucrats anyway. They did, however, gather a lot of food stores, which we now have. We can hold out quite a while, even with all the refugees, and there are several hundred of them. I can tell you that we aren't nearly as comfortable as your group though."

Colonel Kline interrupted, "We don't want to compete with you. We hope we can be partners in defense. We were attacked once, it will probably happen again."

Mike said, "We came together as a survival group, and that is what we intend to do … survive. As long as you don't try to attack us or take our food stores we won't bother you. We helped you because that rabble was our enemy too. I'm glad your group didn't go rogue like many of the others. You are actually trying to do some good. We like that."

Colonel Kline said, "That sounds like a truce to me, which I am happy to honor. Unfortunately, the danger is not over. From what we can tell from our radio communications, what's left of it, and incoming refugees of course, most of the big cities have fallen to gangs, and they are now spilling out into the country. That means they will eventually show up here."

Mike stopped him and explained what we had done with the bridges and those we intended to demolish tonight. He knew as well as any of us that it wasn't a total isolation but certainly a big help. He actually began to smile.

Colonel Kline got around to us and asked, "May I ask," pointing at me and my girls, "Who these people are?"

Mike said, "They represent half of our survival team. They are new to Earth, but they are human and our brothers and sisters. I guess you could call them illegal immigrants, but they belong here now. Do you have a problem with that?"

I was pleased with Mike's defense of us. It just reinforced my belief that we had chosen a very good partner.

A startled colonel said, "No, not at all. I was just curious. I'm also assuming they are the source of the weapons you used against the invading army. Marshal Brady told me he had seen that weapon used before. Can I also assume that you also downed our helicopter?"

I spoke for the first time and said, "Yes, we could have done much worse if we had wished to. You sent it to assist the FEMA agent's attempt to steal our food. That made you our enemy, but we used a different weapon that only disabled it. We also retrieved your men and called your base to notify you where to pick them up."

"Thank you for that," he said.

I said, "Thank Mike. I afraid I am not as tolerant and forgiving as he, but he was right in your case. I think we may be able to work together with your group to our mutual benefit."

The colonel said, "Yes, I believe we can work together."

183

I continued, "I'm sure you are curious about us. My name is Brin" pointing, "This is Meg, Peg and Flay, we have no last names. We are from Apsaras, a distant world from Earth. We partnered with Mike early on to establish this survival group, and he and his group have done an excellent job, as you can see. We have only just arrived to assist him in his defense. To answer your original question, Yes, we are the source of the weapons and other technology you have seen. Our race is more advanced, technologically, and we intend to live here on Earth, hopefully in peace."

They didn't need to know more details about us, but the colonel seemed satisfied by what he heard.

After a pause, Mike said, "By the way, are you set up for long term there? I mean, are you set up to grow crops for food for the future and support life there? If not, we can help with equipment and seed for your own crops. We prepared ourselves here for life after the apocalypse."

The colonel said, "We have food to last us quite a while, even with the many refugees, but little else. For long term recovery we would welcome your help, however, we have few women to begin life again beyond the current generation. Most of our military men were National Guard. We were called up at the start of the collapse, and our families were left behind unprotected. We didn't know it would get this bad this quick, and most of our families were killed in the looting and riots. We saved some of our families who lived close but not nearly enough. So, we get our satisfaction by saving other families."

Mike said, "We already knew that you were taking in refugees. Otherwise, we wouldn't have helped you. Nancy, do you think there are any concentrations of women we could salvage for them?"

Nancy said, "Wow! That's a tall task, but we can scan the satellite images to see. Actually, the only groups of only women that might have survived would probably be nuns in a convent way off the beaten path. That would pose difficult to persuade them to break their vows of chastity, however. Meg and I can search around, however."

Colonel Kline said, "Am I to understand that you have satellite feeds?"

Mike said, "Yes we do. You can thank my brother, Brin, and his team for that. They launched them. That's how we knew the army was coming, and we will let you know in the future if something else is coming. Just keep your radio on."

Robert interrupted me saying, "Mike, we have a situation at the front gate. There is a group of herders driving a fairly large number of cattle down the access road."

Mike said, "OK. We better go check it out. Colonel, we can meet often if you like, but we have to go now."

Colonel Kline said, "Thank you. We have learned that we have friends here. I'm sure we will meet again soon, and it was nice meeting you too, Brin and ladies."

Chapter 8
(Nuns Conversion)

When Mike and Nancy took off for the front gate I was left alone again. I had asked Flay to work on a project, so I went to find her. She was in the communication room with Meg and Peg, and apparently they weren't busy. I asked, "Flay, have you had a chance to work on that project I asked you about?"

Flay said, "Well, yes I have, but it isn't as simple as what you described. Simply converting Carbon Dioxide to Oxygen doesn't completely solve the problem and provide the solution you desire. There are many other gases and compounds in "Air". Oxygen is only one of them, the critical one, but still it must be regulated. Did you know you can poison yourself with too much oxygen? Now, I can generate "Air" from water by rearranging molecules without much danger."

I interrupted her and said, "Damn, Flay. I don't need a lesson in physics, I just need to know if you worked something out to breath under water without hauling a big ass tank around."

Flay laughed and said, "Yes I did. I just wanted you to know that I'm the smart one, not you. Your idea made sense, but it could be dangerous." She went to a bag she often carried and brought out two fiber molded cylinders about a foot and a half long and four inches in diameters. "I merged a few of our technologies together to make these. One of these will replace the tank, but it requires the other apparatus from the tank. You breath in and expel the used air out into the water through the regulator. Maybe if I work on it I can reduce the size further, but I would say this is a vast improvement. It extracts "Air" from the water and compresses it in the back of the tank. You can't use up the air. It has a permanent self-generating power source. It remains in operation until you take it out of water. She handed me one. I studied it. There were two fiber "U" shaped clamps folded down. I lifted them and immediately saw the purpose. They would slip over the shoulders to hold it on the back, while the webbing on the bottom would function as a belt to hold it in place. It was light, and the whole thing could be easily carried on the back in comfort. I said, "I'm Impressed! Was it hard to build?"

"No, not really, once I understood the concept and purpose, I figured out what was required. I had all the parts, I just had to put them together. You know these humans have abstract minds. Working with them may force us to greater things."

"They certainly do," I said, "Can you make more of these? I'm going to go test it now. Do you know if Blane is in the water?"

"Yes, I can make more, and, yes, Blane probably is in the water. He asked me how to get to the boat docks, but Bess came by and took him."

I thought, *"Damn, Blane has probably already shown her water sex."* I smiled when I realized he hadn't learned water sex, yet.

I went through the Cave and out a short tunnel and took the steps down to the boat docks. The docks lay in a cove between our island and the adjacent one, which I remembered from messages and plans from subsequent purchases. We have a great property and location. When I approached the dock I heard Dobe chattering her happiness to see me. I had to smile, since I missed them too. I put the tanks down and dove into the water and was immediately greeted by my pod. They seemed happy. Both pods crowded and nuzzled me in greeting, and I petted them all. I didn't see any others of our blue team, so I asked, "Where is Blane and Bess?"

Dobe perked up at the name "Bess" and started squeaking in excitement and said, *"Bess good ... like."* She pushed her dorsal fin at me, indicating for me to take hold. I did, and we were off. Dubs pushed himself into me and I held on to his fin also. We went streaking through the water out of the cove a ways, surfaced for a deep breath and dove to the bottom. I could soon see them digging into the muddy bottom. Blane had Bess's other hose and bubbling air. I let go of the fins and floated down. I think I startled them with my sudden appearance. Bess hugged me and turned to hug Dobe. Now that shocked me. Dobe really did like Bess a lot to welcome her hug, but she certainly did. The pod continued to circle us, either wondering what we were doing or trying to figure out how to help.

Bess got Blane's attention and pointed up. He nodded and they started a slow ascension, while I sprinted toward the surface intent on air. Once there, I waited. Blane and Bess soon popped their heads above the surface and slid the masks up and pulled the regulators out.

Blane was excited and said, "Brin, I really like the ability to breath underwater. It saves me all the swimming up and back down to work."

I knew that was coming and said, "Well, you're going to love what Flay made us. It's on the boat dock. I'll race you there." I took off and left him sputtering. He spent far more time in the water than I and was a faster swimmer, but I had the lead. I swam full out toward the dock, and I was sure I was going to win when Dobe and Dubs shot past me dragging Bess on their fins. I was so shocked that I lost my concentration and swimming rhythm, and Blane pushed past me, leaving me in his wake. When I got to the docks Blane and Bess were sitting on the docks like they had been there for hours. I said, "Yeah, OK. I lost." After a moment I continued, "Bess, I can't figure out how you have won over Dobe and now Dubs, too. What is your secret? Never have I seen them take to anyone else but me."

Bess looked thoughtful then said, "Well, I am a Marine Biologist. I have worked with many porpoises. I like them. I'm very comfortable around them. I guess they must sense that in me. I have missed being in the water like I was in California, and I look forward to being here and playing with them. I'm also sure that I don't look

189

like anything they have seen before. That could also be part of it."

I said, "I'm almost jealous of you. Seriously, I have never seen them take up with another person like they have with you, and I have never seen them transport anyone but me."

Bess asked, "Should I back off some?"

I said, "Oh my, no. It just shocks me. They obviously like you. Please, keep being their friend."

Blane said, "So where is this surprise Flay came up with?"

I quickly went to the two small tanks I left and brought them back. I held one up and said, "See this? This replaces that big, heavy tank Bess has strapped to her back." They both looked surprised. "Flay made these out of spare parts, and the best thing is they run on water. They don't have to be filled and never run out of air. Bess, we still need the regulators, though. Put your hose on one and try it, but I don't think you will need the extra weight or even the Buoyancy Control of the vest. It should be much easier to wear."

I showed them how the "U" straps folded out and the belt. Blane tried to get it from Bess to inspect it, but she wasn't about to let go of it. She had already stripped off her BC, weights, and tank and was already moving the hose attachment to Flay's tank. Bess slipped the handles over her shoulders ... backwards. I started to tell her so, but it did look more comfortable laying between her breasts and down her stomach. She slipped back into the water to test for air. It must have worked, because she sank beneath the water. We could see her swimming around comfortably and soon surfaced.

Bess said, "I like this a lot. Flay gets a big hug for this invention."

I said, "Well, it was my idea. What do I get?"

She just smiled at me and said, "Blane, go up to the diving locker and take a hose off of one of the tanks and put it on the other Flay tank. You might want a mask and fins, too. We're going for a swim. You'll find us."

Blane was anxious and took off. Bess then wiggled around in the water and tossed her diving bottoms up on the deck and swam away. I knew what she was ready to try, so I jumped out of my shorts and dove in behind her. Bess was doing what she called the butterfly kick. I call it the Apsaras kick, same thing. Her tantalizing brown buttocks glistening in the sun. I was aroused instantly and sped up behind her. I reversed her rhythm and slid up over her back and entered her. She made it easy with her labored upstroke. I slipped inside her deep on our first stroke together, and I heard her squeal with excitement. The pod swam beside us watching and chirping their encouragement. It must have excited the porpoises, because I saw Dubs upside down swimming underneath Dobe as they swam. Bess and I continued to swim, getting faster and faster. She never missed a stroke. Our swimming strokes sped up, and we began pounding against each other. I reached for the other regulator and pushed it in my mouth. I sucked air deep into my lungs and continued my relentless driving into Bess. My climax was coming fast, and I could tell Bess was there also. The water was thrashing around us as we both froze in orgasm. After several deep breaths I rolled off Bess, and I was roughly pushed aside by Blane. He must have been behind us watching, learning, and becoming aroused. Blane slid up on her back to replace me and was inside her instantly, much to Bess' surprise, but she didn't resist and soon quickly resumed her stroking, matching Blane's rhythm with enthusiasm. I no longer had a regulator, so I shot to the surface for air. When I returned below they were both still and quivering in the water, still coupled. They finally drifted apart and began to sink. I guess Dobe was concerned, because she began pushing Bess to the surface, while one of Blane's pod pushed him up. That must have been a strong orgasm for both of them. When they surfaced they both had smiles on their faces.

Blane saw me and said, "That my friend is far better than milking seed. You said it was, but I wasn't sure until I watched you and Bess swimming and having sex. It certainly woke something up in me, long forgotten. Bess I hope you don't mind, but you two drove me crazy, and you are so damn sexy looking."

Laughing, Bess said, "It was a surprise, but I didn't mind at all. I really do like Apsaras sex. I will be down here in the water with you a lot, and I don't believe I will wear my bottoms anymore here. So, any time either of you want me, I'm willing."

We swam leisurely back to the docks and found many of the awakened Blue Team testing out the water. I greeted many of them as I slipped my shorts back on. I was still standing on the docks when a very excited Sue and Meg came rushing down on the docks. I knew something was up and turned my attention to them.

Sue said, "Meg and I have been researching the convents in the area and focused the satellite images in on them to check on their status. Brin, these dehumanized gangs have no respect for them and almost all have been decimated. We only found one untouched, and it won't last long. We already identified a fairly large mob gang moving in that direction. The convent is located a good distance north of Oklahoma City in Piedmont in a somewhat rural area, but we only have a few hours at best before it is attacked. Mike is out of pocket right now, and we wanted to find out if it is possible to take your large craft there and defend them long enough to persuade them to join us, some of them anyway. What do you think?"

I said, "You haven't talked to Mike yet?"

Sue said, "We wanted to talk to you first to see if you were willing to take a chance."

"Yes, I suppose I'm willing. Your government has gone underground. I don't think they will come out to investigate. If they do, we can defend ourselves."

Meg said, "See, I told you Brin would go along. He wants to save people. Let's find Mike and get this done."

We found Mike just returning from the conflict at the front gate, and Sue and Meg jumped him with the same argument they had used on me. He looked at me for conformation. I just shrugged and said, "I'm OK with it. I think we are safe and feel comfortable coming out of hiding. We can remain underwater until we get far away from the Castle."

Mike made a quick decision and said, "Very well, let's do it. Sue, call James to look after the cattle herders I invited here, but call Marshal Brady first and ask him to come here as quick as possible and come in full uniform and armed. Tell him to bring another official looking escort with him. Also call Robert and have him come in uniform with JJ and a few other security officers. I want us to look as official as possible. Oh, by the way, Nancy. You will be doing the talking for us." She looked shocked but quickly nodded.

Within an hour we were all gathered and descending down the interlock tunnel toward the Dome. Many were seeing the spacecraft for the first time and were wide-eyes but followed me down the hatch into the craft. Even Mike looked awed as well, but he tried to act like this was just a normal occurrence, even as the hatch closed behind us. We entered into the large circular open space. The only visible apparatus was a central control panel. Meg and Peg took positions at the controls, while I herded the newcomers out of the way.

I thought how strange this experience might appear to the humans. A previously invisible panel lit up in the air like a Christmas tree I had seen in

Earth movies. A large monitor came to life in the air showing a digital outline of the ship, the Dome and surrounding obstacles. A slight vibration and purr of equipment could be felt and heard as it started but nothing more. Their eyes bugged slightly when the clamps clicked release from the Dome, and a slight floating feeling could be felt as we began to move. It was amazing watching the reaction of the people as they followed the movement of the ship on the digital monitor. There was nothing for the passengers to hold on to, and I noticed they were looking around for something. I announced, "We have artificial gravity in the ship that overrides outside gravity. We could fly upside down and you would still be standing as you are. Don't worry. You are all safe, and you won't need safety belts."

My girls steered the ship clear and away from the dock and remained underwater until we were far away the Dome, we then burst out of the lake at a fast rate. The ship operated the same in water or air, but once we surfaced the video image changed to dual, three-way actually. The digital layout remained, while the rest of the viewing image converted to standard video, forward and below. For the most part they took all this in passing, because the ship took off at a fast pace, and we were not tossed around with the acceleration, even though most of us were free standing without any restraints.

The twins steered the craft away quickly, so we couldn't be tracked easily. Surprisingly to the humans but not to me, it only took us about ten minutes to approach the coordinates Mark had provided.

I said, "We may be too late. It looks like the mob is already here."

We could see in the down view a small caravan moving toward the convent with a few empty pickups already at the convent driveway. As we watched we could see puffs of smoke coming from rifles in the caravan. That's all the excuse I needed and said, "Well, it looks like they declared war against us. I guess we should fire back."

I smiled and waved my hand before the monitor, activating a crosshatch indicator on the monitor. I then moved my hand along a smaller image to move the crosshatch on the monitor to focus on a target. When I flicked my thumb within a red beam the pickup simply exploded. The crosshatch continued to move to target after target with flicks of my thumb all along the caravan until all were disintegrated. It was mostly safe and I pointed down, indicating a landing. The twins landed the spacecraft in the front lawn area of the convent. Flay remained on the ship, while Meg, Peg and I led the group down a hatch and out the lower open ramp. The armed security detail fanned out in front of us as we reached the ground to protect us from any mob attack, but we saw none. We went toward the front door without any encounters, but as we entered the building we heard female screaming coming from down the hall. We rushed toward the screaming and burst through a set

196

of double doors. Inside was a gang of about six men in various degrees of undress. Most had a struggling sister in their arms with the obvious intent of rape in mind. Two of the mob were holding the other sisters at gunpoint, with two of the sisters unmoving and bleeding on the floor. Robert, in obvious rage at what he saw, opened fire on the two armed gang members, killing them instantly. The other four released their struggling sisters they were holding and scrambled for their guns, but they never reached them. Meg and Peg and our security cut them down with a vengeance. I can't remember ever seeing Meg and Peg this angry. They had been carrying their laser pistols ever sense we had been on Earth, but this is the first time I had ever seen them fire them, much less in anger. I gained more respect for my ladies.

Robert barked, "Are there more of them?"

An elderly sister, assumably in charge, said, "I'm not sure. These men just came busting in, but I don't think there are others. They were evil men. Thank you for saving my sisters."

Robert sent some of our security to look for any others, while instructing others to drag the dead out. No other of the gang were discovered, but they took up guard positions just in case.

Mike had intentionally wanted to present our group as official as possible. Robert, JJ and all his officers were fully decked out in impressive Cherokee Marshal uniforms, fully armed, and I was somewhat surprised that Trix was in the same type of uniform. That would have to be uncomfortable

197

for her, since the Blue Team had never worn many cloths on our home world, but here she was, one of them. She even seemed to enjoy the decorations. Marshal Brady and another US Marshal were fully uniformed, plus Brady had brought a uniformed army captain from Camp Gruber. The group did present an official looking front, even though the rest of us were in our normal casual dress.

Nancy stepped forward from the group and spoke, "You are actually extremely lucky that we came to protect you ... this time. Most of the other convents haven't been so lucky. They have been looted and destroyed already, and most likely many of the sisters have been raped, like was about to happen here, killed or imprisoned as sex slaves." This brought gasps from the gathered sisters. "Civilization as we knew it no longer exists. Law enforcement no longer exists, nor does the military for the most part. Life outside has turned primal. This is the fate you will be presented with sooner or later, because we can't come again. We came this once to offer some of you a chance to survive. I'll just put it out to you and let you decide."

"We are representatives from two survival groups, three now actually in eastern Oklahoma. We have banded together and have defenses against these roaming mobs and gangs, as you put it, 'evil men'. We also have stored food and the ability to survive for several years and begin civilization over again after this evil runs its course. What we don't have are enough child bearing females for the next generations. Simply put, we offer a home and a future life for the child bearing age sisters here. I'm sorry we can't take all of you, but our food and facilities are limited. Everything we do is focused on the future and surviving and eventually repopulating."

The sisters gasped again and the elder sister said, "You can't be serious? These sisters have given vows of chastity to God. You are asking them to break their vows. The answer is an emphatic *no*!"

Nancy said, "I understand your concern, but I ask you to consider what would have happened to all of you if we had not stopped the mob outside and in here. Most of you would be dead, or even worse, like the other convents, and your order destroyed. At a very minimum, they would steal all your food, which would certainly kill you in the long run. More likely, many of you would be raped, some killed outright, and some would become sex slaves to the mob of evil men. Think about your vows of chastity in this case. Still, if your answer is no, we will leave."

The sister said, "We must believe God will surely save us."

Nancy said, "God didn't save the other convents and sisters, but just maybe God sent us to save some of you and give you a new purpose. Think about that. The sisters joining us will survive and still have a good life, although a more traditional role. We have been taught that in the beginning God made women to help populate this world, and that basic role hasn't changed. In point of fact, tens of millions of humans have already died in this apocalypse, and many more will die before things begin to get better. The original role of women is now even more necessary for our recovery. Maybe God is saving many of you for this purpose. Discuss it and give us your answer quickly, so we can continue our search if necessary."

The elder sister, whom I assumed to be the Mother Superior, looked thoughtful then said,

"Can you first explain the flying saucer you came in and the blue people with you? Yes, we heard the explosions outside and saw it. Now we see blue people. We need to understand."

Nancy didn't appear shocked and said, "They are ancient brothers and sisters from another world. We are alive now because of them. They came to help us survive. They are also here now to help save you if you allow them."

"Do they believe in God?"

Nancy said, "Well, if it is God's will that we survive, and we have a great chance of that, it is easy to believe God sent them to help us. I don't know their personal belief. Brin, would you care to respond?"

Nancy was doing such a great job of talking for us I was surprised to be asked, but I said, "We know little of your concept of God. Our race, however, believes that a higher benevolent being created us in the beginning, and we inherited a concept of good and evil and right and wrong. We certainly know that what these gangs are doing is, as you said, 'evil'. We also know that what we are trying to create is good. I hope that answers your question."

The sister said, "Yes it does Mr. Brin." She then looked at Nancy, "Can we have a few moments to discuss this among ourselves before I give you our answer?"

Nancy said, "Of course, but remember time is short for us to be able to save others of your kind, possibly too late."

The sister led the others into the sanctuary for a discussion. I had no idea what they were thinking, but Nancy had done an excellent job of explaining the situation and options. After about thirty minutes they all came filing back in, well not all. Many had taken off somewhere. I suddenly noticed that none of the younger ones came back in, which made me wonder.

The sister said, "You have provided a reasonable and convincing argument for us, and we believe you. We have decided that it *is* God's will that you came to us, and we believe God sent these 'Blue Angels' to help. We have decided to accept your offer of physical salvation for our younger sisters. They have been released from their vows and will no longer be sisters, and those have gone to change into civilian clothing. They will be here shortly. The rest of us believe we will be of little sexual temptation to other gangs that may come, due to our advanced age. Our survival odds here will be better with the younger girls gone, and their odds of survival will be assured. We will hide what food we have. We may be able to survive, and if we

201

do not, that will also be God's will. I do have one request, however. Many of the sisters have experienced sex before they became nuns, but we have five sisters that are vestal virgins. They don't have a clue what they are getting into. These sisters have lived a very sheltered life. They will need special care and treatment in the beginning, certainly the first time, from someone with the patience to show them that way of life."

Nancy said, "Mike here" pointing, "is my mate. He will introduce the virgin girls to sex. He is understanding and patient."

The sister looked directly at Mike, then hard at me and said, "I also want the 'Blue Angel' teaching them, also." She pointed directly at me. "Be gentle with my girls."

Angel? She just called me an angel. Could she actually believe I am some kind of angel? I had no idea what to say, so I said nothing. I bowed slightly. I think Mike was also in shock, because he just nodded and said, "Yes Ma'am."

I knew there were quite a few sisters in this convent, but I didn't know the actual count. About twenty-five of the ladies came back in wearing normal clothing. Many were dressed quite fashionable, and all appealing. The sister took the five virgins and brought them to Nancy. Silent looks of appeal and understanding passed between them.

The sisters, now simply young ladies, ranged in age from about 19 to 35; and they were, for the most part, appealing, if not beautiful. But, the five

202

virgins were all young, less than twenty-five, and stunning. Nancy looked at Mike and gave him a mischievous smile. Well, it was her fault, since she volunteered him. Meg and Peg were expressionless, which left me wondering.

That left another twenty-five or so still in habits. Nancy said, "I think you have made a wise decision. They will be safe with us. I wish we could take you all, but what we are building is for the future of our civilization. Can we leave you some guns for your protection?"

The sister said, "No guns, but thanks. We all understand your limitations. We will be fine. It's enough to know our younger sisters will be safe. God knows what he is doing, and we know the 'Blue Angels' will watch over them."

This reference to angels obviously included Meg and Peg, and the shock registered on their faces. I noticed that they moved toward the sisters in a protective manner. They obviously accepted the responsibility and took it seriously.

I interrupted, drawing all eyes toward me, "Mike, we must leave. Another small caravan is approaching, and we must be in the air to take them out."

Mike said, "Sister, we will take this approaching mob out before we leave, but do hide your food as soon as you can. If others come tell them your food has already been stolen. Hopefully, they will leave you alone." She nodded, and I continued, "Let's hurry group and load into the craft."

Security led our expanded group quickly out and rushed us into our ship. Shots were already being fired at us as we lifted into the air. Meg and Peg wasted little time getting us high enough for me to unleash the rail-gun. The caravan was indeed small, but they disintegrated quickly, and we rushed back toward the Castle and Dome.

We were about halfway back when Flay bellowed out, "Incoming. We have planes on an intercept course and we have been targeted!"

I said, "Damn!" and rushed to the console. I flashed my hand over a blue light and immediately saw the crosshatch appear. The blue light controlled the EMP guns. Use of the Rail Gun would be too slow for the five targets in formation speeding toward us. I targeted a wide beam in the center of them and flicked my thumb. Everything electrical onboard those planes instantly died, leaving nothing for the pilots to do but eject. The alarm continued, however.

Flay said, "They fired two missiles before we took them out."

I yelled, "Peg, outrun the missiles. Flay, target the satellite laser. We'll stay ahead of them to give you time."

This action would drive the point of artificial gravity to my guests. Peg took us supersonic speed in seconds, and if our artificial gravity hadn't been on, everyone in the control room would have been turned to mush against the back wall. As it was, the only way of knowing our increased speed was the video image streaking by, but my only concern was watching the approaching missiles fall behind. But they instantly ceased to exist.

Flay said, "They are destroyed."

I ordered, "Take out their surveillance satellites they used to find us, and while you are at it, make sure there are no more weapon satellites orbiting up there that can be used against us."

Flay said, "I've already analyzed all the satellites, and all the weaponized ones are gone. Obviously, another surveillance satellite is passing over. It will be gone shortly."

"Thank you." I yelled, "Brady, where are these planes coming from?"

Brady jumped at my sudden bellow and said, "I have no idea. We haven't had any communications from any military source in weeks."

"Well, call your base and have a helicopter go pick those pilots up. Get the coordinates from Flay. We need to find out where they are based from, and who is attacking us. We are going to have a serious discussion with them. The pilots are a hell of a lot closer to your base than we are right now. Hell, outrunning those missiles took us way off course, and we are now currently over Tennessee somewhere in broad daylight traveling at supersonic speed. There is little chance we haven't been heard and seen, so we are going to have to establish a truce with whoever keeps attacking us. Either that, or we will have to destroy them completely."

Flay said, "I found the satellite, and it is gone now."

I said, "Thanks. Slow us down Peg and take us home."

Things had been so intense that I had almost forgotten all the guests in the control room. When I looked around everyone was staring at me in awe, even Mike. I guess maybe I had been taking a lot of action and barking many orders. I chose to ignore their reaction and said, "The danger is over now. We are going home." That seemed to break the frozen stupor capturing them, and all started talking at once. I even heard a few cheers and noticed a few happy smiles.

Mike came up to me and said, "I'm glad you are on our side, my friend."

All the sisters, ex-sisters and especially the five virgin girls had been wide-eyed from the very first, but the eyes seemed to get wider once we entered the ramp underneath the space saucer, even wider when we had combat and traveled back to the Dome. I was afraid all the eyes might pop out when we entered the water and submerged. Their panic seemed to finely diminish and converted to astonishment as we exited the ship into the crystal Dome. A school of fish swam passed, herded by dolphins and a very fast and sleek Blue Team swimmer, which seemed to capture everyone's attention. We then steered the group to the interlocks. The group was so large we had to break them up into two groups. Nancy waited to escort the second group through. Eventually, we all made it to the elevators and started ascending in groups in the two elevators. It took a couple of trips in the elevators, but Nancy and the last group finally joined the growing assemble in the big room, who by now were drawing stares from everyone in the cafe.

Nancy said, "Mike, I called ahead to have Bob cook enough food for this group. I suggest we eat. I also called Dr. Groom to have his team ready to draw blood samples while they eat."

Mike said, "Good thinking. That's why I like you." He smiled when he said that, but it didn't stop Nancy from giving him a punch on the arm. "Marshal Brady, do you have a doctor at your camp?"

Marshal Brady said, "Yes, we have doctors and a clinic there. We also have some buses to transport the ladies. I'll call the colonel and let him know the success of our outing so he can prepare for their arrival."

Meg and Peg had remained by the five virgins' group since they had been called angels and charged for their protection. I had never seen them act maternal before. It was something new for them. Flay was teamed with Dam Mark, Trix remained with Robert and his group, while I was left alone and remained with Mike.

Mike pulled Brady to the side so he could speak unheard from most, but I was close enough to hear. Mike said, "I don't think I have to tell you to go slow with these ladies. Give them time to adjust."

Marshal Brady looked at us and said, "No Sir. We will treat them like the angels they are and let them set the pace. I also want to thank you, Brin and your teams for your help. We owe you all a great deal."

Mike said, "The five will be staying here for a few days. You heard our instructions."

The marshal smiled hugely and said, "Yeah, tough job. Need any help?"

Mike smiled back and said, "I better not. You heard Nancy and the Mother Superior. Angel Brin and I will just have to suffer through it alone."

Bob came rushing over and started guiding the ex-sisters toward the buffet. Lots of hungry eyes studied the food he had lined out for them. None of the ladies were plump or even slightly chubby. I'm sure their standard diet was just enough to keep them alive. This would be a major treat for them like it had been for the Blue Team, especially having been cooked by a master chef like Bob. He only had to invite them once. They piled in with gusto. I also realized I was famished. The cafe was busy, but tables had been cleared off to make room for the ladies. As I looked around the cafe I was heartened to see my Blue Team females dispersed throughout the population, many paired up with humans of Mike's team. All appeared to share affection. I also noticed that Nancy, although next to Mike, had ushered the five virgins next to her or across from her. Meg, Peg and Sue were at the other end of them. I knew Meg and Peg took their responsibility seriously and obviously Nancy as well. Between them they intended to look after these innocent girls. I didn't know how I was going to service them all but left it to Nancy, Meg and Peg to work out the details. Hell, Mike and I hadn't even been introduced to them yet.

As we ate, the doctors and nurses went through the group of ladies taking names and drawing vials of blood. I noticed that Nancy had them start with the five virgins. I guess she wanted to make sure they were healthy. I don't think she was concerned about STDs, since these five were virgins, but she was being careful about something. She spoke to Dr. Groom, and I saw him nod.

Curiosity got the best of me, and I leaned over Mike and whispered to Nancy, "What are you worried about?"

Nancy smiled and leaned in to whispered back, "Sisters are famous for taking care of sick people others won't deal with, like with serious Earth diseases such as TB, HIV, contagious viral infections, even leprosy that rots your skin. The odds are good these girls won't have any of those infections, since they have been isolated in a convent, but I think it wise to make sure."

All I could say was, "Oh, okay." We eradicated contagious diseases on Apsaras centuries ago. Hopefully, the cures of those diseases still remained in our data banks. I made a mental note to ask Tina about that. Any rate, it would never have crossed my mind to worry about contagious diseases. This precaution was another reason to appreciate the human team.

While we continued to eat, a pretty, young girl of 16 or 17 came up behind Nancy and tapped her on the shoulder. When Nancy turned, the girl asked if she could speak to her privately for a moment. Nancy got up and they walked over in an open area. I could see them talking back and forth for a while. When they came back Nancy grabbed a vacant chair and slipped it in beside her and the young girl sat down in our group.

Nancy leaned toward Mike and me and said, "This is the youngest sibling of the family that brought the cattle today and you let join us. She was the one driving the tractor. She heard we were giving a course in Sex Education 101 for virgins and wants to join it. I let her." When she saw the shock on our faces she added, "Don't worry, I have some Viagra."

Damn, six virgins? I would definitely need some Viagra.

Chapter 9
(Assimilation Process)

Mike whispered to Nancy, "I hope you realizes that sex with a virgin is painful for the man too."

Nancy said, "I know, but I have a plan. Trust me. Mike, when you finish eating, why don't you go on up to our apartment and shower and try to get a nap. Us girls need to talk," Louder she said, "You too Meg and Peg come with us girls. I heard Mike tell Brady the girls would be here for a few days, maybe three. So I suggest they stay with Mike tonight rest a day and move to your apartment afterwards. Is that okay with you, Brin? Let's let them get a little experience tonight, since sex is something relatively new to you, and you are also still learning. We can educate Meg and Peg some, also, and we can help when it's your time."

I said, "That sounds reasonable. I trust you. Just tell me what to do." I know my giggle sounded nervous.

When they got up to leave I said, "I'm going too. I need to see my porpoise friends anyway."

It was already dark and today had been very busy, but I went down into the Dome. I'm glad I did. As soon as I dived in, the water around me erupted in splashes and turbulence as my pod greeted me. I had missed them and they me, even many that don't normally nuzzle did so. We shot toward the surface and broke almost in unison. The squeals and chatters of happiness greeted me, but

211

after the excitement settled Dobe chirped, *"Fib ... hurt."* I recognized Fib as one of Blane's pod. I got immediately concerned and said, "Bring Fib to the Dome. It's too dark to see here."

When I surfaced in the Dome several of my friends had already beaten me there. Among them was Fib. I immediately saw the distress and pain on Fib and I saw the reason. There was a metal, curved spike embedded in Fib's upper back right beside her dorsal fin. The hook was the cause, but there was a trailing white line that looked like it had been chewed into. Unfortunately, Fib had done much of the damage to herself by fighting against it and trying to pull away, which left a long rip down her back. She had been lucky that one of the others had been smart enough to chew the line into. Fib could easily have drowned. I tried to pull it out by applying reverse pressure, but it was stuck solid. I said, "I'll get some help."

I got out of the water and retrieved my radio/phone and called Flay. When she answered I said, "Flay, please call Tina and one of the other doctors and have them come to the Dome. One of the porpoises is hurt. She has a rip in her skin and something is stuck inside that needs to be cut out. You might want to call Blane, also. I think I'm going to need you too. It might also be good to bring a human, maybe Jeremy. I don't understand how this happened."

Flay said, "I'm with Jeremy now. We will be right down, and I'll let the others know."

"Thank you."

Blane beat them all down to the Dome and popped up from underneath. He must have ran down to the boat dock dove in. He went directly to Fib and began comforting her and inspecting her side and back. His concern was obvious. Flay and the others entered soon after.

Flay said, "This is Dr. Jones and Dr. Lopez. They are veterinarians, doctors for animals, and will be able to help."

A nervous Blane said, "Thanks for coming so quick. My friend Fib needs your help."

I noticed that Blane had already lashed a supporting net to the side and Fib was swimming into it. The injury couldn't have been very long ago, because it was still bleeding.

Jeremy said, "Oh crap. I know what that is. That's a fishhook and a big one! It must have swam into a trotline and one of the hooks snagged it."

Blane angrily said, "She's not an '*IT*'. Her name is Fib, and what the hell is a trotline?"

Jeremy said, "Sorry. I meant no disrespect or harm. Fishermen use trot-lines to catch large catfish. It's a series of fishhooks dangling in the water. The hooks are baited, and when a catfish comes to eat the bait it is caught on the hook. Fib must have swam through a trot line."

I said, "No offense taken, Jeremy. Blane is just angry in general at her injury, as we all are."

The doctors lay on the deck and began cutting the fishhook out and stitching up Fib's gash. When they were finished they began coating it with some kind of salve, all the while she was receiving sympathy nudges from her friends. Fib received twenty stitches along her back and the doctors gave her an injection of what they called antibiotic. All the while Fib received many nuzzles. It really didn't take much time. When they had finished they gave Blane a tube of something to rub on the wound every day and instructions to call them if there was any change. The real shock to the doctors came when Fib chirped out a *"Thank You."* The doctors had consoled her throughout the whole procedure but being thanked, utterly surprised them. Flay, Blane, and I laughed at their shocked look, but offered our own sincere thanks. These veterinarians had never worked on anything non-human as smart as these friends. I dare say they gained a new respect for our porpoises.

While the doctors worked on Fib I pulled the others aside and said, mostly to Flay, "We need to establish some form of communication with our friends in case something like this happens again. They need to be able to tell us if we are needed. I've also been thinking about trying to invent and build some tools they can use, like scissors or knives they can use to cut these trot line hooks off with. What do you think?" I saw nods all around, especially Blane. We all knew Fib had been lucky and these human trot lines presented a danger to our friends and to the Blue Team, especially in the dark. Even with the porpoise's sonar they wouldn't spot something so small.

Flay said, "I like your ideas, and I will give it some thought and come up with something."

Even though not a member of the Blue Team, Jeremy said, "Flay, I will help you."

With the crisis averted I told my friends "Bye" and we headed back up to Bob's Cafe. I knew Mike and his immediate group would be busy, and I smiled to myself at what must be going on. Flay, Jeremy and I sat to enjoy a cup of coffee. I chucked to myself at how I had developed a taste for coffee. My first taste was a horrible experience. It was bitter, and I almost had to spit it out. Now, I seemed to enjoy coffee immensely.

Jeremy was a likable human, outgoing and funny, but he could turn serious when it came to engineering. They were deep into those discussions now. I was unnecessary to their conversation and excused myself.

I began wondering around the cafe, meeting my Blue Team, inquiring into their quarters and needs. I noticed few were congregated together. They were widely dispersed among the humans, and seemed happy. Many of my team made it a point to introduce me to their new friends. It was surprising to me, but I was extremely pleased to see them all getting along so well.

I noticed the red-headed Mary O'Shey, the Castle Manager, sitting alone at one of the tables. I wandered over with a fresh cup of coffee and said, "May I ask you a question?"

She had been working over some paperwork and jumped when I spoke. She said, "Oh, hi Brin. You startled me … of course, please join me." She flashed me a huge smile. "How may I help you?"

215

I was still fascinated by her looks. The fiery, red hair seemed to radiate light, but it was the whiteness of her skin with those tiny brown spots, especially on her nose, that disarmed me. I'm sure I must have shook my head to break her alarming spell over me and said, "I'm curious how you were able to so thoroughly get my team assimilated with the humans. My team seems completely dispersed among the humans. What did you do?"

Mary laughed heartily and said, "I wish I could take credit for the assimilation, but I can't. It was more of a mutual explosion between the groups." When she saw the blank look on my face she continued, "I think the best way is to show you. Do you have a few minutes?"

"Yes, of course." Mary stood and took me by my hand and led us toward the elevator.

Mary explained, "Only the larger, central quarters have their own bathroom. All the others have a balcony but no showers. They use a common shower facilities for the general members on both the 3rd and 4th floors. For the most part, the facilities are non-gender. After your 75 female team members joined us it got the attention of the 75 males of the human team. It didn't take long for the human males to begin migrating to the 4th floor to help the females learn how to use soap. Your males made the same move to the 3rd floor for the same reason ... naked human females." Mary was laughing as she led me into one of the shower area.

I was shocked when I entered. Maybe it was slightly innocent when it all started, but the shower areas had progressed into a continuing, churning orgy now. Yeah, they were washing each other, but they were also coupled in every imaginable way. No one was shy, and they may have come in alone, but most were leaving as couples. I said, "I certainly understand the assimilation process now."

Mary was watching a couple. The blue female was bent over holding a support bar and the man was behind her holding her hips and driving into her from behind. They both were totally involved, ignoring everyone around them.

Mary laughed, "That's my normal partner. I guess he won't be needing me for anything tonight. Would you like me to go with you back to your apartment and teach you how to wash with soap?"

I quickly looked at her, and she was smiling devilishly. I had been hard since we first started talking and said, also smiling, "I think I would enjoy that greatly." Mary was tall for a human, being only a few inches shorter than me. She was slim but with large breasts. The contrast made them appear even larger. She took me by my hand and led us down the hall to my quarters. It was a short trip. My mind had been undressing her already. These humans all looked differently, and Mary even stood out among humans. I was longing to explore all these differences.

We went directly to the shower and Mary began undressing me, little as there was, and then it was my turn. I slipped her shirt up over her head, but her large breasts were covered up with a cupping and support binding, something unnecessary for Apsaras females. I kept fumbling around trying to figure it out, but Mary decided to help and unfastened a catch between her breasts. Wow. The support popped apart revealing almost totally white breasts, but what shocked me most were her large, pink nipples. I had never seen breasts this big and never pink nipples. I was fascinated with them and just stared at them until Mary pulled my face into them. Her breasts spread across my face, soft and warm. The hard nipples pressed into my face until I found one with my mouth. I began sucking and chewing on it. My hands and fingers slid up to grope them, but I seemed even more excited with the look of them. I held her breasts as my mouth moved back and forth between them. I continued to hold and massage them as I slowly began sliding down her body. I nibbled her taunt white stomach. My hands finally reluctantly relinquished her breasts to slide down to her hips, pushing her shorts down her thighs. It shocked me to see a bush of that same fiery red hair covering her pussy. I wasn't expecting that, and it captured my attention. The red bush consisted of long but manicured hair. It gave the appearance of her pussy being on fire, and when I pushed my face into it the heat I felt added to that impression. I thought, *"Fuck taking a shower."* I lifted her and took her to my bed. I think I actually ran with her. I was insane with lust, and my mouth began playing with that flaming hair covering her source of heat. My fingers and tongue spread that beautiful hair. That's when I got my next surprise. Her pussy lips were bright pink … shocking. I did stare at them, but not for long. I buried my face into the fire of her hair and steamy pussy. Mary had been moaning loudly, but they turned to screams as I devoured her pussy. Sweet honey nectar flooded my face and her long legs captured my head. I let her hold me still, but when her legs slowly released me I quickly slid up her body and drove my cock deep into the flame and fire. My assault was relentless as my lust drove me forward. I exploded deep inside her and lay quivering and jerking within her furnace.

My mind slowly calmed and returned to me. It was then I heard Meg and Peg cheering. I slowly rolled to Mary's side to see Meg and Peg sitting naked on the side of the bed. I don't know how long they had been watching, but evidently long enough to see most of it.

Meg grinned and said, "Mike had all the sex he could handle down there, so Bess was teaching us some of the pleasures of sex with other females. She likes sex with females as much, if not more, than males. We discovered that we like it, also, and Mary has a beautiful body that we want to explore and experiment with."

That kind of surprised and excited me at the same time. But it surprised me more when they pushed me to the side and sandwiched Mary between them. They began exploring that fantastic body of Mary's. Those very features that fascinated me so completely were now being explored by my girls, and Mary welcomed the attention. Meg and Peg's hands were all over those milky white breasts and those big pink nipples disappeared in the girls' mouths. It was exciting to watch, and I just had to get involved. While my girls nursed Mary's nipples I began kissing Mary. Our tongues circled and probed even through her moans. Soon the girls moved down her body to discover the fiery red hair and pink pussy lips. They were as mesmerized as I had been and began probing and licking. They seemed to have learned well and thoroughly enjoyed doing it. Mary gave herself over to them and floated in and out of orgasm after orgasm, as the girls continually switched. Meg and Peg were both between Mary's thighs, each holding a thigh. I moved to the end of the bed and began playing with my girls' bodies. I buried my face between one set of butt cheeks then the other, which excited them greatly. Before I could mount either, Mary screamed out in a final massive orgasm.

Mary bellowed, "Oh my. Enough! I can't handle any more, girls. You're too good at this."

The girls allowed Mary to close her quivering legs shut and cuddled up beside her to help calm her down.

After Mary's breathing calmed, Peg said, "We will work on Brin now, but we need you to teach us how to deep throat. Nancy told us you taught her how, and we want to learn."

Mary laughed and said, "Yes, I can show you."

Damn, these girls of mine were learning much from the humans. Me too. Suddenly, I was flooded with anger at the old one's teaching and at how much pleasure we had missed by those teaching.

But, the rage quickly turned to lust as the girls began sucking me. Sucking me was something very new, but I really like the thought. Meg pulled me to the center of the bed and immediately took my cock into her mouth. It felt really good, but she could only take about half of it. Peg then tried, with about the same results. They took turns, but they were losing ground, because I was getting really hard. Mary got between them and took my cock and pushed it down into her throat. I screamed with delight. Mary started talking to the girls about gag reflexes and swallowing, but I wasn't paying much attention. I just know it felt good as they swapped attention on my cock. Before I realized it they were all taking every inch of me down their throats, but none of them stayed with it long enough for me to orgasm. It was like I was constantly on the edge but never over it. That's when something changed. I suddenly looked up to see Peg pushing her hot pussy down over my cock. This was something new, also. Peg was so aroused. She bounced up and down back and forth, riding my cock. It didn't take her long to climax and flood me with juices, and just when I was about to take over, she jumped off. I was about to complain when Meg replaced her. They must have worked out a system, probably with Nancy's help. They would take me to the edge and get off. I noticed they were also using some of the internal muscle controls they used to milk sperm, but this was different. Just when I was about to explode they would use that muscle control to clamp down on my cock, stopping my orgasm.

They were perfecting a system of keeping me aroused but not allowing me to explode until they were sated. This went on for some time until I got too close and powered through the clamping, but they had managed to have many multiple orgasms. Having my own orgasm prolonged set off a massive orgasm in me. I flooded Meg with my seed, which left me completely drained. All I wanted to do now was sleep, which I did. I don't even remember her getting off.

My internal clock woke me early as always. Sometimes this was a curse, and today was one such time. I was extremely tired, and Meg and Peg were snuggled against me. Mary was no longer with us, and I have no idea when she left. I kissed the twins both awake. I was really beginning to learn what the humans call love. These twins of mine were becoming very important to me beyond the sexual attraction, but I must admit, they were becoming quite sexual, also. So was I, I guess.

For the first time since being on Earth I had the urge to shower. My body felt sticky from all the sex, and the girls readily joined me, but the shower together was for cleansing only, since we were all sated. Afterward, we dressed and made our way down to the cafe for a morning meal. I was beginning to enjoy the morning bacon, eggs and milk. Once refreshed, we went to the conference room, where the standard group was assembled, minus Mike and his immediate group. I kind of chuckled, knowing why. I didn't consider myself the next in charge, but circumstances tended to force me into that position.

Flay looked concerned and stood to report, "Brin, we have maintained a watch via the satellite ever since we returned from our outing in the saucer. As you know, I programmed the satellite to operate automatically, and it operated as such to destroy another incoming flight of planes. The satellite shot down five more attack planes and two missiles fired from the US. We believe the missiles were fired toward our satellite, but they might also have been fired toward our location. It's hard to say." The room went abuzz in concern.

I said, "I suppose our satellite killed those pilots?"

Flay said, "Mostly. We can't be sure if any ejected, but the suddenness of our attack they wouldn't have much of a chance. The satellite weapons are the lasers, and they are pretty unforgiving. They are designed to kill."

I said, "Robert, why are they trying to kill us? They have been the aggressor in every case. The second question we must ask is 'Who' is trying to kill us? Surely they can't be intent on exploding nuclear weapons. That would be insane!"

Robert stood and said, "Well, the 'Who' has to be some faction of the US government or military. They may have moved underground, but they still represents a substantial threat. The 'Why' I really can't figure. I can't even guess, but they are certainly intent on destroying us for some reason."

"What do you suggest we do, Robert?"

223

Robert thought for a moment and said, "Well, they have tried to attack us by air several times, unsuccessful. If they are that serious, they will try a stealth ground attack. A standing army won't have much of a chance against our weapons. I'm not sure they know that yet but would have to assume the worse. Of course, if they can get close enough without being seen they can take out our roof weapons. I think they might try a secret Navy Seal team attack. We can't defend against what we can't see."

"We also don't really know who the enemy is and where they are located. Marshal Brady reported that they picked up the surviving pilots. Maybe we can learn something from them. Want me to get Marshal Brady and Col. Kline to bring those pilots over here to be interrogated?"

I said, "That sounds like a good idea." Robert took a moment to make a call, which apparently went well. When he returned his attention to the conversation, I said, "You seem to have a healthy respect for Navy Seals. Tell us what we can expect from them, and what to watch for."

Robert looked solemn then said, "When I was in the Marines I was a Navy Seal. Seals are highly trained and a formidable fighting group. They usually fight in small extremely organized groups. Stealth is their signature. They are trained in tactics using sea, air, or land. That's how the name Seals was derived. The hardest part of defending against them is detecting them before it is too late, but what worries me most is that our attackers seem to be willing to use nuclear against us. They would only have to get close to take us out and not even that close. My guess is that a seal team would come in underwater. It would be hard to detect them coming in that way."

I noticed that Mike, Nancy, Sue and Bess had come in during Robert's report and were listening intently. I also noticed that Jeremy was catching them up to speed with what was happening.

I said, "We have water friends that can help us detect an attack coming from the water. Flay, maybe we can expand the weapons arsenal you and Jeremy are building for them. Blane and I can explain the threat to our friends, and we must expand our surveillance on the shoreline. They would still have to access the water to get here. We should also establish a water assault team. No offense to you humans, but this team should consist only of the Blue Team. We are far more agile in water. Blane, you take charge and build this team."

"The other concern I have: is detection of nuclear radiation. Do we have any means of detection if one is brought in?"

Flay jumped up and said, "Oh, we just might. Our satellites are equipped to measure many forms of radiation, and they are extremely sensitive. I will, however, have to contact my father back on Apsaras to find out if it's possible to detect nuclear and how to set up the satellite communications programming."

I said, "Great. Please take care of that quickly. Also, let him know our danger and if he knows any other technology we possibly could use if necessary. Mike, do you have anything to add?"

Mike said, "I'm sorry I'm late this morning. I'm catching up now, but from what I've heard, you're doing well with the situation, and much of what needs to be done must be done by the Blue Team. We are certainly lucky you guys are here. Still, I seem to remember you telling us during the last major engagement that we cannot sit back and take a defensive position. As I recall you said that was an easy way to loose. You said, 'Always attack.' I tend to agree. We need to attack."

I laughed and said, "I love it when my own quotes are tossed back at me. I agree with myself and now you, though." I laughed again, "But in this case we don't know who is attacking us just yet. Maybe we will learn more from Col. Kline and the pilots when they get here."

As if to accent my statement, Robert received a call from the reception desk letting him know they were here.

Mike said, "Hold them there for ten minutes then send them up." Looking around the room he continued, "Stay if you feel like you can contribute to the conversation with the colonel and pilots. If not, let's adjourn until tomorrow.

Mike came to me and said, "Brady called me to let me know they have been unsuccessful in getting any information out of the pilots. He said they have been trained in interrogations and torture techniques and might be impossible to break. We will have to try something completely different, something they have not been trained against.

I smiled at a devilish thought and said, "Let me take the lead. I'll give them something different."

Robert, JJ, Trix and a few other additional security joined us, but most of the others filtered out. Nancy then led the colonel and others into the conference room. We greeted Col. Kline and Marshal Brady, but we ignored the pilots. I noticed the pilots were under Army guard.

Colonel Kline said, "We have been trying to interrogate them, but they have told us nothing. I hope you have better luck."

I'm not sure what they had been told about us, but the pilots were petrified and quickly sat down and tried to look invisible. I noticed they didn't seem overly surprised at the blue color of many of us, so they must have been told something. I decided to take advantage of their fear, and I didn't want the pilots to get comfortable. I stood defiantly, pointed at them and bellowed, "Why did you try to kill us?" Two of the five pilots were female, and I thought for a second they would take off running. They might have if security guards hadn't been standing behind them.

They looked at each other and finally one of the men stood. He said, "We were just following orders."

I bellowed again, "Sit your ass back down." He immediately did. "Tell us what those orders were, who you are and where you fly out from." He started spouting his name, rank and serial number, but I held up my hand for silence. "Stop! We are aliens to Earth and not a member of your Geneva Convention. They would call our tendency of eating human flesh cannibalism. Now, if you don't want to be served up as our next meal you better start talking and telling us everything we want to know. Is that clear?"

Pure and total panic fell across all of them. They weren't expecting this turn of events. One even trickled a tear of fear down his quivering cheek, and from the sudden smell permeating the room, I'm pretty sure one or more pissed themselves. They all nodded in great animation, and I'm quite confident that I got through to them with a change of attitude. I also noticed Nancy and a few others fight back a snicker. Mike even had to turn his back on the group to hide his sudden shock, masked as a coughing fit.

In a last show of token resistance one of the pilots said in a quivering voice, "Cannibalism? You can't be serious."

My expression remained stern, and I said, "Oh, I'm very serious. Unfortunately, however, our human friends here don't much like our feeding habits, so we don't get to eat many humans. But, since you tried to kill them along with us, I doubt if they will interfere. I'm kind of partial to rump roast smothered in brain gravy. Meg, what do you think of her butt roast?" I pointed to one of the female pilots. Meg played her role fantastically and walked behind her and squeezed her butt cheeks.

Meg said, "It looks tender. Maybe we could dress one out now."

That was the last straw of resistance. Her firm expression crumbled, as she broke down and started crying huge sobs. Evidently she was the senior officer, because the others seemed relieved she broke.

After she calmed some she said, "Okay, Okay. We will cooperate with you if you promise not to eat us."

I said, "You have our promise. Now tell us what you know."

She humbly asked, "What will happen to us afterwards?"

I said, "What we have never understood is why your superiors consider us enemies and have tried to kill us on numerous occasions. We have not posed any threat to them or anyone other than the gangs. All we want to do is survive this apocalypse with our human friends. If you cooperate and help us identify the cause and a solution you will be our friends. In that case, you will be allowed to join us as members, or we can try to get you back to wherever you want to go."

They seemed satisfied and relieved and she said, "My name is Jane Holloway, Captain USAF. I was the squadron leader of five F22A fighters on this mission. We are/were stationed out of Holloman AFB in New Mexico. In our preflight briefing we were told you were possible aliens and you attacked the US. We were told to consider your ship hostile. That's really all we know."

I said, "I'm sure you know more, you just don't know it. For instance, where were we supposed to have attacked? Who issued the orders? Who is in command of the Air Force? I'm sure rumors abound in your command. Think about those rumors."

Jane said, "Well, we were told that you destroyed the Pentagon, the White House and the Capital building. Rumor has it that the President, Joint Chiefs and most of our Congress are dead. We were told you launched nuclear missiles on those targets and others."

Flay flared out, "That's absurd. We don't even have nuclear capabilities. Nuclear weapons are an abomination."

I shut her up with a stern look and said, "Check out those targets on our satellites."

Capt. Holloway looked surprised and said, "You have satellites? We were told you took out all the satellites and missiles."

Peg, normally quiet, yelled, "The only missiles we took out were nuclear launch missiles fired mostly toward the US or launched directly at us. We want to survive, not live through a nuclear winter, and the only satellites we took out were surveillance or weaponized satellites that could be used against us. I bet you didn't hear that we saved America from multiple nuclear missiles launched from across the ocean. I bet you didn't know your country and others had weaponized satellites in orbit. Well, there aren't any now except ours, which we use only to defend ourselves."

Peg vented her anger and passion during her outburst, but I'm glad she did, because you just can't fake real anger and passion like she had just demonstrated. I also noticed the pilots knew this also and accepted and believed what Peg had said.

Flay came back in and remained standing looking at a video tablet. Eventually she said, "Dam Mike had to help me identify locations, but I can now report that some of what Capt. Holloway said is correct. Washington DC and the Pentagon have been totally destroyed. I don't know how that happened without us knowing it. They were either destroyed before we got here, or were not the result of a detected missile launch. I don't understand it. Our satellites would have automatically targeted them. It would almost have to be the result of a ground or internal detonation... sabotage, but how could that be?"

Robert seemed to grasp the situation faster than the rest of us. He said, "I'm starting to see a pattern and make some sense of all this, as stupid and maniacal as it is. You might want to call me crazy for even thinking of this as a conspiracy, but it is the only thing that starts to make sense."

Col. Kline said, "For Christ sake, Robert. Spit it out."

Robert chuckled and said, "Fine. I was just adding some drama. But, what if? What if this is all a military coup. Think about it. We certainly aren't the only ones to have seen the coming apocalypse. Hell, everyone with half a brain saw it coming. Millions upon millions will die, that's inevitable. The way I see it is it's all about who will be in control afterward. What if a group of high ranking military officers decided to use this apocalypse to establish their rule afterward. They would have the power, assuming there was no governing president or administration, Congress or loyal military politics or rule. This group would have the budget to set it all up and stock up and survive for years. Flay, what did you see when you looked at NORAD in the Cheyenne Mountain? Were they damaged?"

Flay looked at Dam Mark, and he said, "They looked operational."

"There you have it. To pull this conspiracy off you would need a base of operation and you would have to be in control of NORAD. The Cheyenne Mountain complex is probably the safest place in the world to base your operation, and NORAD controls our missile defense and launch control network." Robert jerked his head toward me. "Didn't you tell me you destroyed a major launch of nuclear missiles from Russia aimed at the US? I think you also said there were no counter launches from here?"

I said, "We destroyed around 25 to 30 missiles launched from Europe, everything launched after we witnessed the first nuclear explosion in the Middle East. I can't say they were from Russia, but they were from Europe. Yes, to your other question. The only missile launch from here was aimed at us."

Robert continued, "See what I mean? Doesn't it seem strange that Russia launches an attack and we don't respond? I suggest NORAD already knew where they were targeted for, maybe even provided the target coordinates to Russia. Your defense of the US messed up their plan by destroying them. They would have had to move to Plan 'B' and detonate internally placed, backup bombs to eliminate any political opposition to their plan. I dare say there were many other locations that didn't get taken out because of your actions. Now they are attempting, somewhat successfully, to use the military against us. We are their scapegoat."

Col. Kline said, "That's just crazy sounding enough to be true."

Capt. Holloway yelled, "Those cock-sucking bastards. They used us to do their dirty work ... and we did it, tried to anyway. And, to answer your earlier question about who generated the orders: the orders came from General Brasley from Peterson AFB, which is just outside Cheyenne Mountain and under their command."

Col. Kline bellowed, "Well crap! I know Gen. Brasley. He's an ignorant asshole. He's not in the military hierarchy, he is with NSA (National Security Agency). He shouldn't be giving orders to the Air Force or any other branch of service. This all supports Roberts scenario."

I had gotten so involved in the discussion I had forgotten about the pilots. I was, however, pleased to see the captain totally on our side now. We wouldn't have to worry about them now. I said,

233

"Capt. Holloway, I apologize for frighting you earlier. It was necessary. We really don't eat humans."

Sue burst out laughing and said, "Yes you do, some of us anyway."

I think I actually blushed, and the entire conference room burst out in laughter, including Meg, Peg and the pilots. Silently I thanked Sue for injecting some humor. I just wished I hadn't been the butt of the joke.

After the laughter died down Capt. Holloway said, "I'm sorry we were so duped into trying to carry out their agenda." She looked at the other pilots for their confirmation and continued. "I agree with Col. Kline. That scenario presented by Robert sounds plausible, especially supported by the facts presented here today. We feel used and will do anything we can to help, but I'm sure you are aware the US military establishment is vast and formidable, even depleted as it is. It is a major enemy coming after you, even though misguided. I dare say most of the military hierarchy has no idea there has been a coup and will take their orders."

Col. Kline interrupted, "Well, we must find a way to tell them the truth. Brin, I'm sure I heard you say you left most of the communication satellites operational. Maybe we should destroy their communications by taking the rest of the satellites out, so they can't issue orders. There will still be landlines and conventional radio, but little civilian maintenance or power exists. Those lines of communication will eventually fail, if they haven't already. Maybe we can take out some of the radio transmitters and towers around Cheyenne Mountain as well. That will severely cripple their communications. That would be my first suggestion. If your satellites are the only ones in operation we control almost all communications. I'm talking worldwide, too. Shut them all down. It sounds like the Russians would almost have had to been involved in our military coup, and they are probably doing the same thing. We need to isolate the groups from each other."

"I'm assuming your satellite technology can transmit standard radio frequencies?" I looked to Flay for conformation and received a nod. "If so, we can start transmitting our own information to the remaining and isolated military establishments still functioning. I suggest we base this part of the operation out of Camp Gruber, at least it could be recognized as a US military base and command center. Maybe we could convince these pilots to tell their story along with us to the world. If there is any US government left they will come to us."

"I don't mean to presume to put myself in charge, but I do know the military end of this better than anyone here and have some rank. I will move to establish myself as the new temporary head of the government military and take control. I think many of the military bases will accept me in lieu of a coup once they know the truth, plus we would be controlling communications. They would have little choice, especially if we find some existing government to legitimize it."

"Once we turn much of the military from the coup establishment they will lose their ability to war against us. At that point, we can move against them and have the forces to do so."

"Our major problem is surviving long enough to get this all done."

Mike jumped in and said, "Col. Kline ... We will make all that you suggested happen, and we will do it quickly. But ... Humm, I think we will need to give you a field promotion to Major General, because you will be dealing with a lot of other generals to accomplish what you described. We wouldn't want them trying to take command due to their higher rank. Brin, what do you think?"

"I like it." I said, "Let's do it, General Kline. Flay, can we do all the things the general suggested?"

"Our satellites will handle it." Flay said, "Plus a whole lot more. Our technology is far more advanced than Earth's. I have already programmed all three satellites to commence destroying the satellites. It will be done in a couple of hours."

"Also, I received a message back already from my father with instructions for the radiation detection. The proper sensors just need to be activated. He also offered suggestions on other technology that can be used, but I will have to study them before I understand even what they are, much less how to use them."

Capt. Holloway injected, "I feel that I must warn you that we are not far from Whiteman AFB in Missouri, and that is the launching base for the B-

2 Stealth Bombers. They could sneak in undetected."

I said, "Thanks, Jane for the warning, but stealth technology does not pose a problem for us. We use a different form of detection technology. Still, thanks for bringing it up and reminding me of something else we must do."

"Flay and Meg please program the satellites to provide immediate indication of other air flights and have your monitoring teams shoot down any planes approaching our location. Try to use the EMP weapons, so we don't kill the pilots, but use satellite lasers or rail guns if necessary."

Jane said, "Thank you for that attempt to save pilot's lives."

I nodded and said, Jane, we don't want to kill anyone, but we also don't want to be killed either.

Chapter 10
(Fighting Back)

After the meeting broke up Mike came to me and said, "You know, while we have a break, while the others set all this stuff up, I should take you for a tour of the outside facilities. I know Bess showed you the Green House. It is fantastic, but you haven't even seen the property and farms."

I said, "Actually, I have been wondering about that also. I would enjoy a tour. Meg and Peg, I'm sure, would love to see it as well." They were nodding vigorously. Sue and Bess excused themselves for other duties, but Nancy came with us, and we all managed to get into Mike's pickup parked in front of the Castle. We drove down from the top and intersected the road just before it entered the Cave. A similar road come down from the other side of the mountain to intersect. The outside walls of the roads were steep, having been reinforced with concrete, also greatly reducing any easy access to the top other than the roads. The Cave had a massive steel door, obviously to secure the Cave in times of emergency, but they mostly remained open with guards protecting the entrance. The secondary security was the bridge connecting to the mainland portion of our property. The bridge was movable in that it could be raised to close off access to our island if necessary. As we drove over the bridge and up a black finished road lined with trees, Mike began to comment on what we could see, or in this case, what we couldn't see.

Mike said, "You can't see it, but we have a tunnel from the Cave and under the water and road. It serves as our utilities connections and runs to the outer buildings. It also provides protected security for moving personnel as may be required into and out of the Cave/Castle."

He stopped at an intersection of a road going left and right off the main road. To the left down the road was a series of three similar barns, and to the right was a series of multiple building in various shapes. There was abundant activity in and around the buildings to the right. That area also had lots of strange, some very large, equipment and many vehicles like Mike's. Many different types of animals, mostly with four legs, wondered around in the fields and pens.

Pointing to the left, Mike said, "We call those our chicken houses. We'll stop by on our way back. That's where we get the chickens to eat and also our eggs." Pointing to the right, "This is our farming/ranching headquarters, dairy operations and various other animal corrals. At the end is our outside security area center. They patrol the parameter of our property. Down in the center is our hog farm. That's where we get our bacon. They're nasty animals, but they taste good."

We drove on up the hill past many large silver tanks. At the top was a series of buildings on the left. There wasn't much activity there, but on the right was a large barn, but what shocked me most were several humans were sitting on top of four legged animals. The humans were controlling the beasts they were riding on, like together they were one, and they were herding other brown beasts to somewhere they didn't want to go. I said, "What are those animals?"

Mike chuckled and said, "The cowboy ranchers are riding horses and they are driving cattle out to the field. Cattle ... well, that's where the T-Bone steaks comes from, among many other food dishes. There, further out in the pasture, those smaller white animals are sheep. I'm not sure if you have tasted any of those yet, but it's meat like a cow, just different tasting."

I said, "Oh. Cowboys. We have seen them in English movies, but we thought that was only in your history." Nancy just laughed.

"The other buildings were our temporary headquarters while we were under construction. I think Jeremy has taken them over as shops. Actually, who knows what Jeremy is doing. He is always building something."

From the hilltop I could see many cultivated fields of crops, orchards and pastures full of grazing animals. I had seen plots and maps of the property, but seeing them in real life gave me a greater appreciation of what these humans had accomplished. I've said it hundreds of times, but I had chosen well when I picked Mike as a partner in our survival community, and he had chosen well also. We continued to drive around the property. Of course I had seen the front gate facilities and wall from video, but I had not seen the fencing around the property. This was new and helped me understand our defenses better. The fence itself probably wouldn't stop an intruder, but on numerous occasions we were passed by vehicles patrolling them. Most of the vehicles had an animal riding with the humans. I asked about that.

Mike said, "Those are trained guard dogs. Their sense of smell is about twenty times better than humans, probably a hundred times better than yours." He laughed. "They can smell an intruder, track them down and bite the hell out of them if necessary. Did you hear them barking when they passed? They were barking at your smell, since they are unaccustomed to your scent. They were telling the guard that you were possible intruders."

Since I had shown interest in the horse barn, Mike took us over and introduced us to a pretty lady he called "Cowboy", which I found strange, since she was female. Mike said she was in charge of the horses. Cowboy showed us around the facilities and horses. They seemed a little skittish around us, but as Mike had said earlier, it was probably our smell. The horses calmed after Cowboy give them assurance by talking to them and petting their necks. As I stood there one of the horses came up to me and nuzzled me. It reminded me of my porpoise friends, which endeared me to them instantly. I began petting her neck and nuzzled her in return. I decided I liked horses.

Cowboy must have noticed the pass of affection and said, "Brin, you and your team are welcome to

241

come ride the horses any time you wish. I think they like you."

I asked, "Is it hard to learn horse riding?"

"Not at all. The horse does all the work. You just have to learn a few direction instructions; go, stop, left or right. I can show you these instructions in minutes."

I said, "I think I would like that. When we get some time we will come see you."

When we left the horse barn, stables, they call it, Mike took us back to the chicken houses. Meg and Peg were getting excited, and I had no idea why. We entered the first barn and I too got excited. The heat was sweltering inside and we were met by thousands of tiny yellow animals. They were so cute, and they had absolutely no fear of us. They ran on two legs and cheeped and chirped and climbed on our feet. In many ways they sounded like a porpoise.

I was startled by voices from behind us and quickly turned to see Ella and Ebba, the identical twins. My jaw dropped when I saw them again. I remembered from meeting them before that they were blonde haired and shapely, but standing I could see they were shorter than average for humans. I suppose they could be considered stocky, but in an appealing way. They were very pretty. In this heat they were hardly dressed at all. Their cargo shorts were short and accented their becoming shape, but their breasts were huge and the center of focus, far bigger than I had ever seen before. The breasts were barely contained in strong supports that appeared they could bust apart at any second. My jaw remained open until Nancy laughed and pushed my jaw closed. I wasn't embarrassed, as Nancy had to also close Meg and Peg's jaws. The three of us continued to stare, however, at those massive breasts until the girls spoke, breaking the temporary spell.

Ella and Ebba spoke in chopped partial sentences, with each contributing to the same thought and sentence. I had often noticed that Meg and Peg sometimes did the same. It must be the closeness of identical twins to be in tune and think identical thoughts and obviously linked mentally.

Ella/Ebba said, "We apologize for the heat. The baby chickens prefer warmer temperatures. We have to adapt to their comfort level."

Mike grinned at us and said, "We don't mind do we?"

All three of us blues gave an exaggerated affirmation of shaking heads, as we continued to stare. Ella and Ebba must be used to it and didn't seem to be bothered. They went directly to Meg and Peg and gave them huge hugs. Like it had been the first time they met, the two pair merged and mostly ignored the rest of us.

"See this," Mike said, "Well, back to business. These are baby chickens. When they are grown they reproduce by laying eggs. Some of them we put back in incubators to grow more baby chickens, but we gather many of the eggs for eating, like we have eaten in the mornings. We also serve many of

243

the grown chickens as dishes in our cafeteria. Try the fried chicken next time. I think you will love it.

After a while Mike got a call. After he talked for a few moments he said, "Col. Kline reports that Flay established communications with Camp Gruber and that they prepared a radio message that has been transmitting repeatedly from your satellite for several hours. He reports that many military facilities have replied already with thanks and pledges of support. He says things are moving fast. I think we better head back and check in."

We finally pried the twins apart and returned to the Castle. It was becoming harder, since each time they seemed to get closer, more linked. It must be some sort of a natural connection between identical twins. Each set of twins had spent a lifetime in each other's heads, knowing the other's thoughts and often finishing each other's sentences. Now it seemed that this level of communications was spreading to the other set of twins. It was hard to follow their communications, because so much of it between them was just understood without speaking the words. Still, I had never seen Meg and Peg so happy, and I enjoyed that. Before we left Meg and Peg had offered an open invitation to Ella and Ebba to visit them at the Castle. Both sets of twins seemed interested in continuing their visiting, and I certainly would be interested in watching them.

After we returned to the Castle we went directly to Bob's Cafe for an early supper. After seeing the chickens I was looking for an opportunity to sample a chicken dish. When Bob greeted us I quickly said, "Do you have any chicken in the buffet?"

Bob smiled and said, "I knew you were going to the chicken houses today, so I planned ahead. I have what we call Southern Fried Chicken. I think you will enjoy it. We also have some Apsaras fish dishes, too. Kit has been teaching us some of your recipes."

"Great." I said, "I look forward to enjoying both." Bob followed us to the long buffet and began pointing out different dishes and side dishes. I wound up with two big brown slabs of crispy chicken, mashed potatoes covered in a white flower gravy, long green beans and corn still attached to a bar. Bob helped us by spreading butter over the corn and sprinkling salt on it. Oh well, I would try anything once. As we reached the far end my eyes must have bulged, because Kit had prepared one of my favorite dishes on Apsaras. In English we called it "Twisters". They are made by twisting two, long slices of dissimilar fish together then wrapping them in a special water plant. When baked together it creates a new and totally unique flavor ... a very spicy and *hot* flavor. I knew Kit had used some of our stores from home. We were destined to run out of our stores, so I grabbed several of them while I had the opportunity. The humans seemed to like them also, and they were going fast.

I liked the crunchy chicken. The texture of the meat was similar to a fish on Apsaras, which we had brought to transplant. The flavor was, however,

245

different, and appealing to my taste. I liked these Earth foods, maybe too well. I pictured myself growing a paunch belly like some of the humans had, another reason to swim more. I had had corn before, but eating it off the stick somehow tasted better. I devoured it. We had our fill, but I still had two twisters left. I wrapped them in my paper towel and took them with me. I wasn't about to go through the waste line and dump food, certainly not under Bob's observation. I would eat them later.

Mike and Nancy excused themselves for other duties, but Meg, Peg and I decided we would have another coffee and visit about today's tour. Meg and Peg suddenly saw something that excited them. When I turned to see what they were looking at I saw Ella and Ebba approaching. They were still dressed as they were at the chicken house, much to my pleasure, and apparently also to the girls. Ella and Ebba sat across from us and jointly said in broken sentences, "We talked about you after we met today. We felt that we have a natural connection. It's probably because of the connection we have as identical twins, but you also seem to have a strong curiosity about us, and we have a curiosity about you as well. We thought we would accept your invitation and come and see if you wanted to explore our connection and curiosity?"

I didn't speak, because I didn't feel I was part of this conversation. This conversation was between the twins, and they maintained constant eye contact. Still, I had no intention of being left out of what I thought was developing. I waited.

My girls said, also in joint broken sentences, "Yes, we feel the connection also. Do you want to go up to our room and explore our differences?" Ella and Ebba smiled and stood up, waiting. Meg took Ella's hand, while Peg took Ebba's and the four walked toward the elevator and our room hand and hand. I followed, but they didn't notice.

Things heated up quickly once we entered the room. It was like the twins were irresistibly drawn to each other and never broke their deep eye contact. Both sets of twins began to passionately kiss, then my girls led their partner toward the bedroom and sat Ella and Ebba on the edge of the bed. Ella and Ebba looked at each other and in tandem pulled their halter tops and binding off, releasing those massive breasts. My girls gasped, along with me. Those huge breasts spread out across their chests, yet strangely firm, considering their size. Without even thinking, Meg and Peg removed their spandex shirts, exposing those beautiful identical, blue breasts with purple hard nipples. Each twin stared at the other's breasts in awe. My girls didn't talk. They simply reached out to fondle those massive, white breasts, while Ella and Ebba explored theirs. But, after only a few moments, my girls gently pushed their partner down on the bed and began playing, licking and sucking on the focus of their attentions. I found it amazing that both sets of twins seemed to also think identical and perform in tandem. I continue to watch and so wanted to explore those breasts, but unfortunately, my advances felt unwelcome. Instead I simply watched.

I was getting so aroused watching and noticed Ella's hips and legs dangled over the edge of the bed. I was drawn to them like a magnet. Ella was obviously aroused and moaning, so I took a chance. Meg was lying to the side and over ... all over, Ella's breasts. I began sliding my hands over Ella's muscular thighs without a reaction, so I undid the catch on her shorts and unzipped them. There was no reaction, so I began to slip her shorts and panties, they were called, off. Once off I spread her thighs to expose a white bush. I loved it. I got down on my knees between her thighs and let my tongue play in that white bush. Her smell of arousal pulled at me. Soon I spread that bush and her lips and tasted the nectar. Ella moaned, but I didn't know if it was Meg or me causing it. I was starting to really get into devouring Ella's pussy when I felt Meg's leg slide between Ella's and push me to the side. Meg continued to slide her body down between her legs and eventually took over Ella's pussy.

I was desperately excited watching, but I glanced over at Peg and Ebba and saw them. Abba was in the same position Ella had been in, but Peg was still engrossed with Ebba's breasts. So, I took another chance and successfully removed Ebba's shorts and panties. As I stared at that identical white bush and pussy I thought, *"If I tasted one, I've tasted both, since they are identical."* I smiled and pushed down my shorts. I was already definitely hard and quickly pushed my dick deep into that hot, wet pussy. Again I thought, *"If I fuck one, I've fucked both."* I laughed at my own joke, but quickly started driving into Ebba. I was just starting to build a rhythm when I felt Peg sliding down like Meg had done earlier. Peg pushed me aside and took total control of Ebba's pussy with her fingers, mouth and tongue. This was becoming a disaster for me.

As I was feeling sorry for myself for being forced out I realized that both my girls were occupied below the waist and Ella and Ebba's breast were unoccupied. Finally. I quickly jumped between them and began to explore those beautiful breasts. Both blonde twins had their beautiful blue eyes rolled up, almost disappearing. I was between them caressing those globes and enjoying all four succulent, pink nipples. I'm sure I assisted in generating those massive orgasms I heard and felt in both chicken girls. Ella fell silent as she calmed. I saw her blue eyes refocus and felt her slip out of my grip on her breasts. She jumped out of bed to lift Meg up and back over the bed to swap positions. Ella was hungry for Meg and began to explore her body. Ella seemed fascinated by Meg's breasts and blue skin, and Meg began moaning.

When Ebba swapped positions with Peg I was again left out, but at least I had my girls, and I began kissing my smiling and moaning girls. This went on for some time until I noticed Ella had slipped down between Meg's thighs and was feasting. I saw my opportunity, smiled and jumped off the bed and watched Ella's butt gyrate as she devoured Meg. I quickly got behind her to lay over her back to feel her warmth. My hands wrapped around her to again fondle her breasts as I pushed my cock inside her. Ella moaned in response as I began to find my rhythm. Meg began to grunt out when my thrusts forced Ella's tongue harder into her pussy. Too soon, Ella screamed out in orgasm and pulled off my cock. I guess she was overly sensitive.

I was about to scream with unfulfilled desire and lust until I heard Peg's squeal and turned to see that Ebba and Peg had also reversed position and Ebba's butt was exposed. I quickly moved over and plunged deep into Ebba again and resumed my fast pace in her. It didn't take long to reach my peak, and I pushed deep and unleashed inside her. This time, however, I held her hips so she couldn't pull away like Ella had, while she erupted in a screaming orgasm, causing Peg to also orgasm.

We were all very satisfied and cuddled together on the bed with me sandwiched between the chicken girls. Still, I was not, nor was I ever, fully included in the foursome. We fell asleep together, but it was the twin partners that were entangled. I really didn't mind, since I was sexually sated and nuzzled by those huge breasts all night.

We awoke and all showered together. There was little need to talk much. The smiling twins seemed to understand each other without words. We then dressed and wandered down to the cafe for breakfast.

Over coffee Meg and Peg said, "Brin, we would like to move Ella and Ebba into one of our unused bedrooms. Would you be all right with that?"

I thought about that and said, "I know the four of you have something special between you that few could understand. I want you to be happy, so as long as you don't exclude me I am fine with that."

All the girls began laughing and together said, "We noticed that you were not excluded last night. You found a way to get involved, and we welcomed it."

I also laughed and said, "I wasn't sure you knew I was involved."

"We knew."

I said, "Have you talked about it? Does Ella and Ebba want the same thing?"

Ella and Ebba said, "There was no need to talk. We all know this is what we want. We must be together, at least close. Brin, there's something you should know. Last night was the first time we experience sex individually with another partner. We have always teamed up on our partner. Last night was different due to the mental connection. We are one mind now and want to please you, too. You will discover special times just for you, and we will team up on you." They all smiled really big and each one kissed me. This was going to work out.

Ella and Ebba left to take care of their operation, and we assembled in the conference room with our coffee for the standard morning

251

meeting. Jeremy and Flay were already there and eager to report, and Blane came in right after us. They had contraptions arrayed on the table, some of which I could guess there uses. Most were configured to fit over a porpoise's nose. I saw what looked like strong scissors, long knives and one that had no meaning to me. I picked it up and looked at Flay.

Jeremy spoke instead, "One of your laser pistols clips inside, which can be fired by the porpoise's mouth closing on the plates, same action as the scissors. As you know, the laser pistol has limited range underwater but can be quite effective at close range. Blane has already presented the gadgets to the porpoises, and they prefer the knifes and this." Jeremy picked up a large, wide, circular hoop with Vs cut out. "These will slip over their heads and fit snugly against the dorsal and side fins. Oh and we have locators attached so we can track them."

On the top was an arched serrated blade. At the end of the blade was a support brace and curved cradle pad that would lay against the porpoise's back. At high speed these could do a great deal of damage, even to boats.

Flay said, "We also rigged up the communications from the Dome to our network, and Blane showed Dobe how to use it. They understand and will be able to talk to us on our phones if necessary."

Blane said, "They now understand that potential enemies may try to sneak in and harm us, and they have patrols out looking. They also like their new tools. In fact, Dobe told me they are already out now cutting hook lines. There will be some surprised fishermen soon."

"Trix and I have a blue team of ten defenders organized for an underwater attack if required. I wanted to keep it all blue team because of our superior swimming skills, but Bess insisted she be part of it. She can kick butts, so we allowed her to join. She is also teaching us some underwater assault techniques. I might add that she is quite proficient in hand-to-hand fighting. She certainly kicked my ass, even underwater, and I thought I was good. What's even more surprising is that Dobe seems to like Bess and accepts training tips from her in the new weapons."

Mike said, "Nothing surprises me about Bess, and she *is* quite proficient. She is a master in many disciplines of martial arts, and she teaches a class in hand-to-hand combat here. I would hate to try and tell her 'NO'."

Blane said, "I didn't want humans on the team because I didn't think they could keep up with us in the water, but she does well in water. Bess has an underwater scooter, too, and she keeps up quite well."

I agreed with Mike, nothing Bess does surprises me. She functions well underwater, the only human female I know of that can have Apsaran sex while swimming. Of course Blane would remember that as well. I didn't, however, know she was an expert in martial arts. I am somewhat of an expert also.

My father believed an Apsaran leader must be highly proficient in combat, and I was trained from an early age. Maybe I should test her, but if she kicked Blane's ass, maybe I shouldn't, since he was my most competent sparring partner.

Robert and Trix came into the room, and we all turned to them. They would have the latest news from Col. Kline, now General Kline.

Robert said, "Wow! It has been busy, and lots of things are happening. While Camp Gruber was putting together their audio transmission, we set up our 24 hr. monitoring team from both teams. Also Capt. Jane Holloway and a couple of her pilots are coming over to help monitor. As we discussed, we are monitoring our areas and the lake for any kind of intrusion, the lake is being paroled by the dolphins, and the satellite surveillance of all three satellites are programmed for automatic alarm for planes and missiles. Flay also pulled the other two satellites in closer to us for better protection. It is a good thing we did all these things, because once the transmissions started we stirred up a hornet's nest. Within an hour of starting transmissions, three B-2 Stealth bombers took to the air heading for our location, well Camp Gruber. We shot them down immediately. Two missiles were launched from Colorado, which we also shot down. They have even attempted massive low level helicopters attacks, but they were quickly identified and the satellite lasers made quick work of them all. General Kline broke into his own transmission and announced these attacks and the results. He declared these actions as proof of the announced military coup and issued warnings to cease the attacks or suffer the consequences. He has received acknowledgment and support from many military activities still remaining active already. He even received a transmission from someone claiming to be a surviving Senator in hiding. This Senator wants the protection of Camp Gruber. He didn't give his location in fear of being attacked by the rogue military.

I interrupted, "Tell him not to try and fly in. He would be shot down, and we can't trust them to get close. It could be a trick."

Robert said, "Yeah, we considered that also and told them exactly that. General Kline told him to travel on the ground into Oklahoma, then check in again with us. At that point we will tell him how to identify himself. We were thinking a number on the roof we give him. It could only be seen from our satellites, since they no longer have surveillance satellites. Once we have found him we can send a helicopter to pick him up."

"We've also picked up on another suspicious activity. The Army base at Ft. Sill has dispatched a large convoy moving toward Oklahoma City. We don't know if they are headed toward us, but we suspect they are. We also don't know if they are pro or con. They have tanks and heavy artillery. Since we haven't received any radio transmission supporting General Kline from them, they might be en route to launch a ground attack. As we all know, the bridges are out over the Colorado River, but if they get serious they can build a bridge."

I said, "Once we know if they are coming toward us, start issuing warnings, verbal and if necessary, fire a warning laser shot in front of them. If that doesn't get their attention, start taking out some of their firepower."

I said, "Flay, have you programmed our satellites to detect nuclear radiation so we can identify them?"

Flay said, "Oh, yes. I did that immediately after I learned how. Sorry, I thought you knew that. And, before you ask, we are monitoring for them. This is our priority for shooting planes down. We target any plane with nuclear weapons in the air or on the ground. If you're wondering, the B-2 bombers and missiles had nuclear weapons."

I said, "These military rogues must be insane. They seem intent on destroying this world just to get us."

Flay said, "My father also sent instructions on how to neutralize an atomic weapon. I haven't figured it out yet, however. Somehow it's possible to radiate the uranium in the weapon from our satellites to prevent the atoms from splitting, thus exploding. I just haven't figured out how to tune our satellites yet."

I said, "That is great news indeed. I'm sure I don't need to tell you to rush on that." She nodded.

No one seemed to have anything to add, so I suggested that we adjourn.

Nancy said, "Brin, Sue has been entertaining the six virgins all day." Nancy laughed and continued, "Well, they are ex-virgins now. They are waiting in your quarters for you. Remember what you promised the Mother Superior?"

Mike laughed and said, "Yeah, it's your turn tonight, Blue Angel."

Oh crap. In all the excitement I had forgotten about them. Damn. Six women? I said, "Blane, I will need your help with them."

Meg and Peg looked surprised and Meg said, "You can't. You promised."

I said, "That woman at the convent wanted a Blue Angel to teach them, and you and Peg are also Blue Angels to her. So is Blane, and I need his help." Thankfully, they seemed to accept my logic and argument. Of course I hadn't expected an argument from Blane. He just smiled.

Nancy laughed at the reaction and said, "OK, Blane. You and Brin come with me. Meg and Peg why not just go stay with Mike tonight, since we will be using your bed. Trix, you might as well come, too, since Blane will be busy. I did promise to oversee the girls education, so Sue, Bess and I will be with the girls. Besides, I like choreographing the action."

Meg and Peg seemed to think about it for a few seconds then smiled. They obviously liked their memories of the experiences with Mike. Trix initially looked shocked, but she too begin to smile.

Nancy led us back to my apartment, but before we went in she handed Blane and I one of those

257

blue pills. Having had one before, I readily took it, while Blane took his because Nancy told him to. He would thank her later.

I stopped mid-step into my apartment at the sight that met us. There were eight completely naked ladies standing there smiling, and there were no signs of modesty. It was like they were proud of their bodies and wanted us to see them. Blane and I were amazed at their beauty and vast diversity. All we could do was stare, but Nancy pushed us into the room and began to undress us. That didn't take long. The girls took over and dragged us toward the bedroom and double king-sized beds. They knew what they wanted. It made me wonder what happened during the night with Mike to free these previously inhibited ladies. I would have to ask Mike later but much later.

Nancy introduced them: Lena, Kathy, Karrie, Tammy, Sarah and Sissy, all beautiful. Nancy said, "They want to show off their groomed bushes Bess designed and cut."

Blane and I were noticing the entire beauty but focused then on the bushes.

Lena was short with an olive complexion, very appealing. Her short, pitch black hair and deep black eyes stood out, and her firm breasts and brown, hard nipples pointed directly at me. But Bess had cut her bush in a diamond shape, which we now stared at. This diamond definitely represented a fantastic jewel.

Kathy's skin was white as alabaster, and she had large breasts for such a small lady. Her bright pink nipples stood out like fingers. The long, bright red hair seemed to flow around her breasts, accenting them even more. Bess had manicured her bush, but left the flaming red hair fairly long. It even looked like a burning fire, that matched the fire burning in me.

Karrie was a hot blonde, beautiful, and openly aroused. She stared at us with a hungry and lustful gleam in her blue eyes. Bess had left a small landing strip and arrow of blonde hair pointing down toward her pussy, but I had no trouble finding her steamy hot and obviously wet pussy.

Tammy was a petite brunette with small but firm breasts and a shapely body. Her bush simply trimmed with no design that I could recognize, but then I wasn't looking at the hair. I was staring at the swollen lips on her pussy. She was also obviously aroused, adding to my building lust.

Sarah was a tall, ebony beauty, with short springy, black curls on her head. She was the only ebony girl in the group. Her pussy was shaved, but Bess had left a heart shaped bush above her pussy. I had to smile, remembering JJ's soft and springy hair ... very erotic.

Sissy was a muscular and beautiful with natural, platinum blonde hair, which was even more evident from her manicured platinum blond bush. Bess had groomed her pussy well, leaving a triangle of the platinum blond hair. I was shocked by her youth, even though she was abundantly mature in appearance, stunningly mature and abundantly endowed.

259

There was so much diversity on display, and it aroused me greatly. I turned to see that Blane's jaw had dropped, displaying a wide-open mouth. I couldn't help but smile at his reaction. Nancy had just removed his shorts and stood, laughed and pushed his mouth shut. Blane didn't even notice and kept staring at the girls in rapt attention, as was my renewed focus.

Now Blane and I were displayed in front of the girls, all with lust burning in their eyes. I remember the Mother Superior telling us to be gentle with her girls. It made me wonder what she told these girls … I hope the same thing. I originally thought this session would be us teaching these neglected girls about sex, but seeing these lustful girls I was beginning to think they might be teaching us about sex. I guess Nancy thought we needed more instructions. But, I was open for instructions, and so was Blane, judging by his raging erection.

A smiling Nancy said, "OK girls. Their blue angel cocks are yours. Show them what you have learned."

The smiling girls moved toward us. Sarah, Sissy and Karrie surrounded me, while Lena, Kathy and Tammy encircled Blane. The girls began sliding their hands over our bodies, and Karrie whispered into my ear, "Hello Angel Brin, my blue angel. We are going to show you what we learned last night with Mike."

Sissy, however, went straight for the meat, literally. She grabbed my pointing cock and began pulling me after it toward the bed. She had my leash, and I followed behind it. My body was burning with desire. Those dormant sexual desires were now fully awake. Sissy lay back on the bed, eagerly pulling my cock between her spread legs, but Nancy stopped her.

Nancy said, "Girls, I did give the angels a Viagra, but there will still be limits to their endurance. I suggest you lay back and let them explore you. See what they have learned first, before you devour them. The girls giggled but followed her suggestion. They were so beautiful and exposed. I got down on my knees to explore Sissy. She was so hungry and ready. The sweet smell of arousal drew me straight to her pussy. My eyes burned with lust, as they watched my fingers explore the depths of her slick tunnel. Sissy began moaning as I spread her lips. The aroma and radiated heat pulled me closer, and I suddenly slipped my tongue into that magnetic source. I had to taste her pussy and did. The taste was incredible, better than anything I had tasted before, and I began to devour her. At first it was my desire that motivated me, but once I heard the moans coming from her enjoyment and felt her body quiver with excitement, I wanted to satisfy both of our lusts. I discovered that I loved pleasing her and increased my tongue action, touching and tasting her soft quivering flesh inside. Suddenly, she screamed, grabbed my hair braid and pulled my mouth hard against her pussy and flooded my tongue with sweet nectar. She was definitely pleased, and so was I. When her tight, hot sheath began a convulsive quivering, I had to feel it on my cock. I stood up and plunged it deep in that quivering flesh. Her tight muscles gripped it hard and began massaging my hard cock. It was wonderful. Her hips drove her pussy against my cock over and over until she screamed again. I felt the hot liquid flood over my cock, then she fell back. I think she passed out from stimulation, but I was still on fire. Someone grabbed my hips and physically pulled me out of Sissy's burning pussy. It must have been Nancy.

I hadn't realized it until now, but hands were rubbing my body, and they pulled me between another set of warm thighs, where my cock was guided into another deep, flaming tunnel. I opened my eyes and saw that it was Karrie. Her eyes were blazing with arousal, and she hungrily drove her hips and pussy against my pounding cock. She was already screaming in climax. I felt like an animal, driving and pounding into her. Her large breasts shook from the slamming. My hands grabbed them and the intensity of her screams increased. I squeezed her jiggling breasts and pounded hard and fast into her hot, velvet sheath and felt my quivering cock explode inside her gripping pussy. My cock jerked with each gush of my seed. Soon, I fell over her and began sucking her hard nipples. Finally, her screams died down, as my breath came in huge gulps. When I calmed I slowly pulled out and was moved again.

I was calmer now and saw that I had been moved between Sarah's ebony thighs. I again sank to my knees and started exploring and playing with her sweet pussy and the springy hair in the manicured bush. My tongue twisted in that intoxicating heart shaped bush, but the more I played and explored the more aroused I became. Her nectar tasted different than Sissy's but very tantalizing, and her moans got louder. I wanted to please her ... and myself. I found the places that increased her moaning and gave those places more attention. I was soon rewarded with several gushes of sweet nectar and loud screams of orgasm. Again, I stood and sank deep into her moist depths. Sarah groaned and wrapped her long legs around me and pulled me deep into her quivering sheath. Soon I was driving hard and fast in rhythm with her groans. When she climaxed her legs locked me in her grasp, which prevented me from orgasming, but I loved the feeling of being impaled inside her. After a few moments she sighed and released her hold.

When I stood, Bess pushed me to the side and dove between those undulating thighs to devour our juices. I guess she intended to follow me for her own pleasure. I idly realized that this was actually an orgy, something I had read about but never understood. Well, I understand now.

As I stood watching Bess devour Sarah, I noticed spread legs on the other bed. I smiled with the devious thought of being inside all of the girls. I quickly went between the spread thighs and saw the red flaming bush of Kathy. She had her eyes shut, as I pushed inside her. Kathy moaned from the unexpected penetration, but quickly joined in my excitement and rhythm. She had obviously recovered from her orgasm with Blane but still remained aroused. Kathy opened her eyes, saw who it was inside her and smiled. Soon she began screaming. I remained deep inside and let her settle down, then I pulled out and moved to the next available girl, which were Lena. She saw me coming, smiled and spread her thighs. Lena was small and beautiful, and I wanted her. I was still aroused and assumed she would get my seed, but I wanted Tammy, also. Lena opened her arms, beckoning me. How could I resist that? I sank deep into her as she moaned a welcome. We started fast and hard, both of us were at heightened levels of arousal. We ground against each other. The sound of wet, smacking flesh got louder until we both moaned our orgasms. Lena kissed me passionately and I kissed her back. This girl was beautiful, and I will remember her always. With my release I knew I was done and rolled over on my back beside her.

I didn't see Blane and began looking for him. I found him between the girls on the other bed. We must have shared the same devious idea. I laughed out, which alerted Tammy. She smiled, knowing the plan and snuggled up against me. I loved the feeling and loved it more when I felt her hand massaging my cock. I didn't think it would do any good, but surprisingly, after a while I began to feel the tingle. Tammy grinned at me and leaned over and took my cock into her mouth. Wow! It began to grow again, much to her satisfaction. Soon, the other two were helping her to excite me by kissing and nibbling me all over my body. Needless to say,

I was simmering again. Tammy mounted me first, then they surprised me by taking turns straddling my cock and impaling themselves on it. It was incredible. They rode me hard, constantly switching and screaming. I just closed my eyes and enjoyed it ... over and over. I could really get used to being milked like this.

This time when I climaxed I really was done. Not only was I done, I fell asleep almost immediately. I have no idea what happened after that.

When I awoke I was tangled in naked bodies cuddled together. It was a beautiful sight to wake up to, but I no longer had sexual interest. Gee, I wonder why? I carefully extricated myself from the intertwined bodies and took a shower.

Nancy handed me a towel as I exited and said, "I think the girls are ready to transfer to the army. Don't you?"

I smiled hugely and said, "Yes, I would definitely agree with that."

She grinned back and said, "Good. I've already called Marshal Brady, and he is en route here with a bus. Mike is already waiting for him at Bob's Cafe, if you want to meet him there. I'll get the girls ready and bring them down."

When I entered Bob's Cafe I noticed I was receiving many knowing stares from both teams and both genders, many accompanied by large smiles and some winks. I thought, *"Oh, crap. Everyone knows what we did last night."* I don't know if they could see my blush, but I certainly felt the flush on my face.

Blane was already setting with Marshal Brady and Mike, and they were smiling and waving me over. I tried to ignore the unwelcome stares, as I detoured through the buffet for something to eat and coffee. I also tried to ignore the knowing grins from Mike, Brady and Blane, but the grins were contagious. Finally, I broke out with my own grin, which set them off laughing.

I looked at Blane and said, "I don't know why you are smiling so big. You were there too."

Blane laughed and said, "Yeah, I know. That's why I'm smiling." They all laughed.

I said, "Well, I'm smiling because I survived." This time I laughed with them.

Mike said, "Brady, you be sure to take care of the girls, all of them. This is a big change for them. But, I think you will find these girls more than ready to begin an active life with your group."

I actually choked on that statement and said, "Oh hell yes. They are ready and very active, thanks to Mike and the blue angels." We smiled hugely but held back our public laughter on this subject.

By the time I was finished eating, Nancy led the girls into the cafeteria and into the buffet line. We turned serious then and began discussing business, although we would be meeting in the conference room soon and saved the information we might normally discuss until then.

Brady waited until the girls finished eating, then said, "Well, girls. Let's load up and go to your new home. Everyone is eager to meet and welcome you."

The girls seemed solemn and reluctant, but each came to Mike, Blane and I and gave us a big hug and kiss, then followed Marshal Brady out to the bus.

Chapter 11
(Attack)

After a busy day and night and good breakfast, we left for the conference room and our late scheduled meeting. Even though we were meeting later in the morning than usual, we beat many of the others and had already taken our normal seats. Mike typically sat at the head of the table as moderator, while I took the secondary chair at the other end. The teams and departments had grown to the point that the large, conference table was completely filled and additional chairs had been brought in. The returning Marshal Brady, General Kline and the Air Force pilot, Capt. Holloway, were the last to come in, dragging three more chairs. I nodded hello.

Mike said, "Who is first?"

Flay jumped up, obviously eager, and said, "I have finally figured out the technology my father sent me, and it is amazing. First, however, let me report on our current status with the nuclear detection and destabilization. I think I have already reported this, but if not, here it is. Our satellites are programmed now to detect the locations of nuclear weapons, and there are many of them. The satellites are now also programmed to destabilize them and are currently in the process of doing so. The process doesn't make the nuclear weapon actually unstable. The formulated energy transmission from the satellites bombards the plutonium core, effectively discharging it. I don't fully understand the technology. I wish I did, but details and the science behind much of our technologies has been lost with our race's population decline. So, how exactly it is done, I have no idea, but I understand the results and how to do it. The atoms will not split to begin the fusion and the results are: no more energy or nuclear weapons. I have already begun to identify those weapons and programmed the satellites to take them down. We started here in America, but will eventually reach out worldwide. There will soon be no more threat from nuclear detonation. We also identified many dumping sites, which we will neutralize after the weapons have been taken care of. The depleted uranium remains dangerous for contamination for many years, but not anymore."

After a moment of silence, Flay sat down. I said, "When you started you mentioned some other amazing technology your father sent you, but you didn't mention it in your report. Would you like to elaborate?"

"Oh, yes. I forgot. It has to do with additional adjustments and alterations of our ship's space skip technology. It is amazing technology, but I haven't figured out what we can use it for. I need a little more time." She then retook her seat.

General Kline raised his hand for attention, and Mike nodded. General Kline stood and said, "We had additional contact with Senator Clayton. He is the senior Senator from Oklahoma and a member of the Senate Armed Services Committee. So far he is the only elected government official we have heard from. He had an emergency and had to rush home when D.C. went up in smoke and ash. He went into hiding until he heard our transmission and contacted us. Thankfully, he isn't far from us, and we dispatched a helicopter. He and his wife are en route to Camp Gruber as we speak. We will get him up to speed and bring him to the next meeting."

"More and more bases are reporting in and coming on board with us, but sadly, there are many not joining us, obviously entrenched with the coup. This is why I am pleased to hear that nuclear weapons are being removed as a threat."

Mike said, "What do we hear about that army convoy coming from Fort Sill?"

Robert said, "They are, or should I say, were coming toward us. The convoy was stopped by the missing bridge on I-40 running over Lake Eufaula, but they simply backtracked and passed north of the lake and continued to follow I-40 until they ran into the missing bridge over the Colorado River at Gore. They are stopped there, while they search for another crossing. They can probably find one eventually either north or south, but once we fired a warning laser slowly burning across their path, they don't seem very serious. If they try to cross at another bridge, I will ask Flay to take it out. They do have long-range artillery that could possibility reach us, but we are watching them closely, and if they attempt to set up and fire them, we will take them out. Unless they do, we don't have much to worry about from them at this point."

"As long as we control the air and ground around us, and a nuclear attack is off the table, I revert back to water as their attack method, since we have excellent ground and perimeter security. It would be difficult to get past our defenses on the ground. If they attack us now, it will most likely come from the water. Navy SEALS pose our most dangerous threat. They are trained to come in underwater in stealth, probably at night. Even if we assume they are aware of the neutralization of their nuclear devices, which I sincerely doubt, they are high explosive experts and could still attack with conventional weapons and explosives. They could do some serious damage to the Castle, Dome, saucer and anyone they encounter very quickly. If they could penetrate the Cave and explode it, they could collapse the entire structure. Our best defense is to spot them coming in and prevent it, but make no mistake, they are serious fighting adversaries above and below water. This remains my worry."

I said, "We will just have to prevent that from happening. I will talk to my friends and double our watchfulness."

Mike said, "Our main concern is defense from attack right now, so I think we will skip over the operational areas, unless any of you feel a need or has a problem." No one spoke up. OK then, lets meet again tomorrow."

I said, "Robert, could you stay? You were a SEAL at one time I understand? Since the Blue Team will most likely be the ones to engage the SEALS underwater, I would like to know more

271

about them, how they fight, what weapons they use, and their fighting tactics." He nodded.

Mike and Nancy stayed, along with Trix and the rest of my team, while the others filed out. When the room cleared I said, "We are constantly monitoring the shores of the lake with infrared. I believe we will see them coming, but it might help to know how they would attempt and launch an attack."

"Well, if they controlled the air they would probably drop into the lake by parachute and go immediately underwater, but I don't see them having that option. I don't see them trying to drive to the lake in trucks, knowing we are closely watching the traffic. Besides, the bridges are out. I suspect a SEAL team of maybe twelve men and equipment will come in by boat, probably several, and spread out to appear to be fishermen. I would imagine them to come down from the upper Illinois River into the lake, get close and come at us from underwater. You can bet they have been able to get some intelligence from satellites, before you took them out, or from recorded data on the lake. They may have also found contractors that worked here to get intelligence on the complex. So, they will have an organized plan."

I said, "Will they expect to be engaged underwater?"

"My guess is no. They believe themselves to be the experts in underwater warfare, but they have no way of knowing about the Blue Team's underwater expertise and certainly not the porpoises. But, if they anticipate engaging in water, which I don't believe they will, they will have spearguns and bang-sticks." When he saw blank stares he said, "A bang-stick looks like a spear with a bullet at the end. It is stabbed or shot at close range into their opponent, firing the bullet on impact. At close range it is lethal. They will most likely, however, be counting on stealth to get them here undiscovered. They can't know about the porpoises or even you guys. They will obviously have weapons but probably no spearguns, although they will have knives. They will anticipate fighting above water, and they are very good at it. They will kill anyone they see … quickly. You don't want them to get that far. Trust me."

I said, "Do you think we can capture them?"

"Humm, it's possible if they are totally overwhelmed, but don't count on it. Be very careful. They don't give up easily, and they are trained to kill without hesitation."

Blane said, "Bess has been down in the Dome working with the pods every day, taking them through various exercises. I will tell her about the spearguns and bang-sticks. They like her and follow her instructions, and Bess has learned the sign language quite well. You should hear her squealing instructions and talking to them. When I go down, my pod just nuzzles me then returns to Bess if she is there. I'm actually jealous of their attention to her. But, the pods are getting quite efficient at organized attacks, and they understand who the enemy is. Bess has made sure of that with pictures and instructions."

"Flay has built for us more of those compact breathing units, also, enough for all ten of the Blue Team. She even made a few with blowhole attachments for some of the pods, and they can stay under for quite a while. They like what it allows them to do, but they don't like wearing them."

I said, "I've got to see this, plus, I'm on the team. And, it sounds like I am not up to speed. Shall we go down and practice?" All nodded.

The first thing I noticed when we entered the Dome were Flay's modified tanks hung on the rail. There was one for each of the team, complete with masks, fins, weapons and identifying name tags. Bess had been busy organizing. I noticed the same organization for the new porpoises' weapons just under the water housed in some kind of press and release mechanism. I picked my tank, slipped it on and dove in the water. I grabbed the mask and fins, too. I figured I would try them out. Trix, Meg, Peg and Blane were right behind me, followed by the remaining members of the team.

The pods saw us coming and immediately broke into pairs and dispersed to each member of the team. Many of the team were unaccustomed to riding porpoises, as were the porpoises, and were shocked but quickly receptive. This must be some of the organization by Bess, that Blane had referred to. It was an efficient way to maximize our speed and power. Now each team had sonar, speed and weapons. We now obviously had ten three unit teams.

Dobe and Dubs were my porpoise team, as they should be. They nuzzled me, then offered their fins to hold, which I quickly did. They already were wearing their modified air tanks, and obviously had been shown how to use them. They rushed me out into the lake and toward Bess, some distance away. She did not have porpoises with her. Instead, she was navigating an underwater, high powered scooter. When we approached, Bess smiled and took off kicking and accelerated her scooter. Dobe and Dubs squealed in excitement and immediately followed her. Bess was fast, but we kept pace with her. I looked around and all the other teams were streaking behind us. I was amazed at the rapport Bess had been able to establish with the porpoises. They trusted her and apparently liked her a great deal. Obviously Bess liked them also, and they must be able to sense that in her, and the pods apparently now trusted her to lead them into battle. Now I understood what Blane meant when he said he was jealous. Bess ruled this lake and everything in it.

I shook off the selfish feeling and concentrated on the team. The porpoises and team member worked exceptionally well together during the speed and diving exercises Bess took us through. Still, I have no idea how she explained the moves to the pods and convinced them to pair up with a team member, but they seemed to welcome the joint cooperation.

After a few hours of exercises the sun was setting, so Bess led us back to the Dome and parked her scooter. Shock froze me when she spread her arms and squealed. The porpoises immediately flocked around her beckoning, churning around her to reach for her embrace or touch. I had lived with the pods all my life and had never seen this kind of open affection from them, other than Dobe and Dubs.

I nuzzled Dobe and Dubs and shot up into the Dome, followed closely by the other stunned team members. A smiling Bess climbed up the ladder. Bess said, "Aren't they wonderful? I think I would love your home world."

I said, "What is your secret, girl? They never show that level of affection to any of us."

"Really? I don't know. I just love them, and I guess they feel it. I didn't know this was anything different for them."

"They are so very smart, far more intelligent than Earth's porpoises, and I've worked with many as a Marine Biologist in California."

Oh, now I understood. She was educated in their biology and obviously loved doing it and interfacing with them. I said, "How did you instruct and teach them?"

"Oh, that's easy. I just talk to them like people and explain what I want and how to achieve it. They quickly envision the purpose. They understand much more than you might think. They are at least as smart as humans, and in some ways even smarter. I didn't mean to get so involved, but they asked me to teach them, and I love doing it."

I said, "We are not upset, but we are surprised. Please, keep it up." Bess smiled hugely.

I asked, "Where did they go?"

I sent them out on patrol. They have two patrol perimeters, one close in and another far out. If they see anything disturbing, one rushes back here to trigger the alarm Flay installed, which sets off alarms programmed into our communicators. As you can see, all we have to do is rush down here and jump into our gear, meet our team and rush back to the target area. If the technical monitors see anything they can set off the alarm also, which activates the sonar alarm to the pods. It should work quite efficient and fast."

After all the exercise I was hungry and said, "Let's go see Bob and get some food. We can talk more there."

As we entered the cafe we saw Mike waving us over. I nodded and pointed to the buffet. Once we had our food we joined Mike, Nancy and Sue at their table. Bess hugged Mike and kissed him.

I said, "We have been practicing with Bess and the porpoises. She has taken over down there, and is very good at it."

Nancy said, "I think that was the hardest part about coming here for Bess, having to give up her porpoises to come here. I'm glad you brought some with you."

I asked, "It's too quiet. Does Robert still think the SEALS will attack?"

277

Mike said, "Yeah, he does. There haven't been any more missiles or planes sent our way, and we are constantly monitoring for army ground movements. There haven't been any more, and the Fort Sill group is camped out at the missing bridge. Flay tells me that there are no more potential nuclear bombs anywhere near us … one less worry. Coming in underwater seems to be the only area we haven't seen any activity. The satellites are closely monitoring the lake, but you have to know, there is a lot of shoreline to watch."

As if to accent our concern, Mike's communicator sounded, and he quickly answered and listened. He hung up and said, "Peg sees something suspicious on the infrared sensors. Let's go take a look."

We rushed to the communication center and looked where Peg pointed. There were two boats seeming to quickly be converging a mile off our Castle. There were seven men in each boat. They must have come in from upriver as Robert had warned and apparently took different routes. Upon closer examination the boats appeared to be the rubber inflatable type called Zodiacs, definitely SEALS or Special Forces. Peg hit the alarm, and our underwater team took off after Bess, who was sprinting toward the Dome. Bess must have ran down the stairs, because she was already in the air-locks to the Dome. Not wanting to wait for the air-locks to cycle, I led the way down to the docks and dove in and swam to the Dome. As we shot up to the deck for our gear, Bess was talking to the pods.

She was pointing in the general direction of the incoming boats telling them, like any another person, fourteen men, two rubber boats attacking. "Take your team member and find them!"

As our Blue Team members jumped back in the water, each member was quickly sided by two porpoises and sped away following Bess and her scooter. The water was alive with their sonar, which located the boats in short order. It was hard for me to see, but the friends had no problem seeing Bess' signals. Soon, one of the larger ones dislodge from his team and shot toward the first boat. I think it was one of Blane's pod named Dex. Dex wore the serrated blade on his back. He sped toward the boat and rammed into the bottom, which ripped it apart. He then rammed the second boat. Both boats and much of the equipment began sinking, as the men inside scrambled to enter the water. Bess turned on lights on her scooter, lighting up the underwater area. Men in black wetsuits scrambled to get into their gear underwater, while our teams circled them … waiting to see if they were going to put up a fight or surrender.

Suddenly, two blasts of expelled air shot out from spearguns and spears shot directly toward Bess's lights and her. Bess dodged to the side, and they missed her, but the porpoises squealed their outrage, dislodged from their team and instantly shot toward the frogmen from every angle. Some of the porpoises were wearing the long knives on their snout and streaked into the frogmen, slicing their air hoses. That ended the battle for about six of them.

They went straight to the surface and stayed there treading water. Two of the unlucky frogmen spouted blood and began to slowly sink. One had been viciously sliced open from crotch to neck by an angry porpoise wearing a knife. I couldn't tell for sure, but I suspect the target was one of them that fired a speargun. The other had his throat slit, probably accidentally, from a knife slice at the air hose too close to the man's neck. Bess squealed and the porpoises resumed their circling, again waiting.

The remaining frogmen recognized their discovery, mission failure and futility of resistance and began to let their weapons sink. They held their arms high in surrender and slowly floated to the surface. Bess surfaced and radioed the Communication Center. Soon, boat lights could be seen approaching from the docks, their floodlights searching the surface.

The security in the boats cautiously loaded the remaining frogmen in the boats one at a time, stripped them of their equipment and tie-wrapped their wrists. Some of the porpoises retrieved the dead frogmen and pushed them up, who were also loaded into the boats Bess circled her arm in the air, squealed instruction and the entire group followed their boats toward the docks. Once the SEALS were secured on the dock, she squealed and said in English, "Thank you. You performed exceptionally well, but there could be a second attack. Please resume your patrols, and please be careful." The porpoises chirped happily and were off again.

Mike had evidently called Camp Gruber for assistance, since a Chinook helicopter landed on the island and a detachment of armed soldiers quickly disembarked and ushered the SEALS away at gunpoint. I was astonished at the efficiency. That engagement could have gone much worse. Actually, the Blue Team had done little in the engagement. Bess and the porpoises had done it all, and they had done a great job of it.

We reentered the Dome, still somewhat stunned by the quickness and decisiveness of the engagement. I was really proud of my water friends and quite confident of their continued ability to defend us. I was also tired and hungry and decided to go see Bob. Damn, he was a good chef. I would have to be careful, since I had already gained a few pounds since arriving on Earth.

Our team went straight to the buffet for food and coffee, then toward a cheering crowd. Mike was waiting and said, "We followed the whole engagement on Bess' scooter camera. Amazing. I called General Kline to come get them, since he represents the government and military leadership. He was only too happy to do so. I guess we will find out more tomorrow at our Conference Room meeting."

Robert said, "I don't think the SEALS will try to attack us that way again. Knowing them, they were probably wired for sound communication and body cameras and the command that sent them saw the quick defeat. They don't have a very good track record with attacks against us. I wish they would just leave us alone."

We continued to chat and settle down, but all that adrenaline still had me hyper. That's when Bess entered the cafeteria, bypassed the food, and came straight toward me. She slipped her arms around me and whispered in my ear, "Are you hyper? I know I am. I'm wound up with adrenaline, and need a release. Maybe we should go up to your apartment and relieve some of this tension."

Peg was still monitoring the satellites, but Meg had heard Bess. I looked at Meg to see her reaction. She smiled and said, "That's a good idea. I have a lot of tension as well. Come on Blane. Let's go with them." Blane smiled, took her hand and followed. Bess took my hand and led me like a puppy, but as we left she took Trix's hand also.

Bess said, "Trix, you better come too. We have a lot of tension." She too followed along.

I had been inside Trix a few time to be milked by her, but that was back when I detested sex and not since I had learned about the pleasure of natural sex. Since my sexual awakening I had fantasied about Trix, but we hadn't yet connected. This attraction was strange indeed, because the majority of our females looked mostly the same, due to our loss of diversity. But, small things, like her abundant orange stripes in her hair made her different and she stood out among our race. I think Bess somehow knew of my fantasy and was making it happen, but not only just for me. Bess obviously liked Trix and wanted her.

Once we entered my apartment Bess, the very assertive girl, grabbed Trix's face between her hands and kissed her hard on the lips. Trix didn't know quite what to do and her arms shot out in surprise but then slowly encircled Bess in an embrace that melted into a mutually passionate kiss. Bess gently pushed her back on the bed and removed her spandex shirt and shorts. Bess admired her body and began to kiss and explore its depths. I simply stared in amazement at how Trix was responding. She was becoming highly aroused, as was I, watching. Bess then spread Trix's thighs. That's when I noticed for the first time that her pubic hair was all orange also. That diversity I found extremely arousing, as did Bess. Bess buried her face in the depths of the smooth silk and aroma of her pussy. Trix began shuddering and screaming out in orgasm, as Bess continued to devour her nectar through multiple additional orgasms. Bess then moved up her body, straddled Trix's face and plunged her dripping pussy down on her mouth and nose. Trix's body stiffened in doubt that lasted only a few seconds before her mouth opened and inhaled Bess' pussy. Trix's inhibitions vanished, and Bess's orgasm started in earnest. After her first orgasm, Bess suddenly reversed her position on Trix's face. Bess continued to rub her flaming pussy over Trix's mouth and tongue, while spreading Trix's orange bush and pussy lips for me. Bess looked at me and grinned. I continued to watch in amazement until my own lust told me to take a hard look at Trix's wide spread thighs and orange covered, quivering pussy. My shorts were off in seconds, and I plunged deep into the quivering warmth. I pounded like a wild man into that pleasure pot, while Trix renewed her suction on Bess. Bess kissed me as I drove into Trix. We all yelled in unison as we orgasmed together.

Bess rolled to her back beside Trix, but I remained still hard and impaled inside Trix. Her legs suddenly wrapped around me, holding me deep inside. I was still gushing and jerking inside her depths, and she made sure I stayed there. Trix eagerly began jerking her hips up against me, forcing me ever deeper inside her. This is when it started. I felt her vagina muscles begin to gently milk my cock, not like the negative sperm milking form previously used. That ancient method was painful. This felt incredibly stimulating. This undulating suction pulled me deep, massaged my manhood and stimulated every inch of my cock. Trix began driving up on me and taking me to new heights of excitement. Her speed increased and pulled harder until we both erupted in loud screams and explosive orgasms.

This time when Trix's legs let me go I fell to the side, completely drained of energy and sperm. I became vaguely aware of cheers and questions among the girls. Bess wanted to know what Trix did to me, so did Meg.

Trix said, "I milked him!"

Peg said, "What? What do you mean you milked him? They hate that."

"You know. I milked him like we used to but much less forceful. I think he liked it."

Blane didn't wait for further explanations. He plunged into Trix to find out for himself.

But I couldn't concentrate. I think I fell asleep.

When I woke the next morning I felt really great. Peg must have evidently finished her shift at the monitor and rejoined us. Meg, Peg and I were tangled together in warmth and affection. I have no idea how long the others continued with their orgy after I fell asleep, but the others were gone, and it was just the three of us. We woke each other and took a shower together. I was beginning to enjoy the shower.

As we were soaping each other I asked, "What happened last night after I went to sleep?"

Meg laughed and said, "A lot. Trix was trying to show us what she did to you. It was exciting to watch, and you evidently liked it a lot. Bess wanted to learn, but we were trained since puberty. It would take Bess quite some time to get proficient. Still, we attacked Blane and practiced on him, but I don't think he minded all that much, that is until we wore him out. Peg even came in in time to help. Poor Blane. He was limping out when we let him go." Meg and Peg both laughed.

We didn't see Blane anywhere when we entered Bob's Cafe. Meg and Peg laughed again at his absence there, and I joined in. He was probably sleeping. Once we finished eating we went up to the Conference Room.

We were apparently late, and the Conference Room was already abuzz with talk. General Kline was there with an older man dressed in some kind of formal attire. He had a strange red cloth tied around his neck. I remember the name, necktie. He looked like a business man from the American movies. General Kline quickly stood and introduced him to me, saying, "Senator Clayton, this is Brin, they don't use last names. Brin is the leader of the Blue Team I was telling you about. You have already met many of the others."

Senator Clayton grabbed my hand and shook it firmly and said, "I am so pleased to meet you and your Blue Team. I've been told that your team is the reason we still have a government and are still alive. Thank you all."

Mike was all smiles, so I assumed this action was to his liking and this man was now considered the government. I said, "I am pleased to meet you, also. Our so called Blue Team is happy to now live among humans. This is now our planet and home too, and we want it to survive. Of course, we want to survive also and will do everything we can to do to live in harmony with humans. Unfortunately, we seem to have gotten ourselves in an internal Earth war. I hope we can end it and live in peace." I didn't know if I was saying the right things to the right people, but it was the truth. Meg, Peg and I took our seats and waited for a reaction.

Senator Clayton smiled. It was not just a smile for show. It was real. He said, "You and your people are extremely welcome here. Apparently, I am the only living representative of our government, so I suppose I am the government as it stands today. I would not be here had it not been for your actions. Without your intervention we would have already lost this war, so you have already earned your place among us, and we owe you and your people much."

I said, "I know little about politics of Earth, but our human friends here." I spread my arms wide to take in the room, "They consider you to be the good guy, so we did also. Besides, you did not try to kill us, like the others. I guess what I'm saying is: Thank you for your welcome."

Mike got the room's attention and said, "General Kline, can you brief us on your activities at Camp Gruber?"

The general stood and said, "Well, our most important occurrence has been finding and bringing in Senator Clayton here for protection. As he has mentioned, he is currently the highest ranking elected official of our government, possibly the only one remaining alive. Once we brought Senator Clayton up to speed, he immediately recorded an address declaring himself temporary president and supporting my claim to be in charge of the military, what's left of it anyway. It has made a difference and many additional military complexes are calling in recognizing this authority. Not the ones we need, however."

"The SEAL team you captured has given us nothing. They remain silent, and we have tried everything to break them. Their Commander is very strong willed, and I'm afraid we may not get any information from them."

Robert interrupted saying, "They are heavily trained to resist interrogation. They will probably die before giving anything up."

I stood for attention and said, "General, can you have someone bring him to me? He evidently can't and won't be forced to share. He must want to be part of us. Maybe I can show him around and persuade him to cooperate and join us."

Startled looks flowed around the table, but the general said, "I can do that, but know he is a dangerous man and extremely lethal."

"I am capable of defending myself, plus Bess will be with me. I'm not worried."

Mike said, "I hope you know what you're doing, but if that's what you want, I will go along with it. I do, however, expect Robert will have security watching … just in case."

I laughed and said, "Well, we need information from him, and we aren't getting any now. We have nothing to lose. Bess and I will wait for him in the cafeteria. Robert, you can join us if you like. Also having been a SEAL might help."

Robert, Bess and I had just got our food and sat down at a table when several army MP security came in leading a shackled and handcuffed man toward us. He was a large man with a solemn and sour face with no real discernible expression. I said,

"Security, please remove those shackles and handcuffs." Their eyes bulged slightly as if to say, really? "I'm sure. Commander, I intend to treat you like one of us. If you want to be treated kindly, you will remain calm and listen to what I have to say. If not, you will be killed outright. We have little time to waste. Now, you make your own decision. First, I suggest you go through the buffet and get something to eat and come back and listen to what I have to say ... or not."

For the first time I noticed surprise in his eyes and possibly curiosity. He stood without his binding, looked around and saw no guards. Resolve, or maybe interest, seemed to settle in his eyes and he walked to the buffet without escort. He returned with his food, sat and began to hardily eat. He said, "OK, you have my interest. Say your piece."

I laughed and said, "It's simple. I need information from you, and they don't seem able to get it from you. As a former Navy SEAL himself, Robert here tells us SEALS are an honorable group, so my assumption is that you are an honorable man, at least I hope so. I also believe you think you are on the right side of our conflict. I hope to show you the error of your way."

"Yes, we are aliens, some of us anyway. We partnered with a human survival team in this complex. We have since partnered with Camp Gruber and have defended them from rogue military forces and gangs. We are now partnered with

Senator Clayton, the only legal government representative, whom your side also tried to kill."

"When we arrived in orbit we used advanced technology to prevent a nuclear holocaust on this planet. In short, we saved the United States and the Earth; but ever since, we have been under attack. There have been nuclear explosion in Washington DC, but not by us. We detest nuclear weapons. The fallout from those weapons would render Earth unlivable, and that would kill us. We are in fact in the process of neutralizing all nuclear weapons. A rogue military coup has taken place in this country, and they used nuclear detonations to eliminate the government. In the process, they have killed millions unnecessarily just to take control after the apocalypse. Those detonations were set off on the ground by teams like yours. We know this because we destroy all missiles launched, many satellite weapons and military planes. We control the air and much of the ground military movements toward us. This is why your team was sent in underwater, but as you now know, we also control the water, at least the water around our community. Bess here led our team that captured you." That got his attention and he stared hard at her. I continued, "She could easily have completely destroyed all of you, and should you try to attack us now, she could still quickly kill you. This is not what we want. We want you to know the truth, because we believe you have been deceived."

"Our advanced technology could have been used to totally destroy our enemy, but we are not here to conquer. We are here to survive. This is a survival community, which I will prove to you if you allow us." I saw doubt flash in his eyes, possibly disbelief and maybe some belief.

The commander said, "What if I don't believe you?"

I said, "Well, if I am wrong about you, then you *are* our enemy. If you don't become part of the solution, then you are part of the problem. You will die, because you cannot be allowed to leave. But, the head of our security, Robert, is an ex-Marine and Navy SEAL. He tells us SEALS are the good guys. I hope so, and I hope you recognize the truth when you hear it or see it."

"Well, commander, that is my speech. Shall we continue our discussion?"

The commander said, "I will continue to listen."

"This is good. We will show you our survival community for what it is and answer your questions" He nodded.

We guided him through the Castle, showing the living quarters and all the facilities, including the communication room. We let him choose the areas he wanted to see. He must have been satisfied that we were not a military organization with war rooms. We showed him the Cave and all the stored food and supplies. We even drove him around the complex of farms, ranches, chicken houses, cattle and dairy operations and storage areas. There was no doubt that this was a survival community.

At one point the commander said, "What if I decide to run while we are out here."

Bess said, "Well, if you got away from us, which you would find difficult, you wouldn't last long. Our satellite is watching, and the laser would find you quick enough." He grinned, which was a sure sign he was becoming comfortable.

Lastly, we took him down to the Dome. The commander's eyes flared open wide at seeing the saucer, then even wider when the pods came to give their welcome to Bess and me. At seeing the porpoises he even backed away, but eventually moved forward to see them more clearly.

The commander asked, "Are these your underwater soldiers in the engagement last night?"

Bess said, "Yes they are our friends and patrol the lake." He just nodded.

I said, "OK commander, it's time for a decision."

The commander was silent, deep in thought. Finally he said, "I believe you. I will trust you and cooperate with you, but me and my men want to become part of your organization."

"Great! Bess, let's call a general meeting."

Most were already there by the time we made it up from the Dome, the general and Senator arriving just behind us. I said, "Our SEAL commander has something to tell us. You have the floor, commander."

The commander said, "First, I want to apologize deeply to all of you. I would have killed you all. Sadly, my team and I have been lied to and duped. Many others as well. I realize that now.

Capt. Holloway, interrupted him during a pause and said, "You are not alone in that, we were lied to and deceived, also. I led a group of pilots, and we were ordered to bomb this complex before we learned the truth."

"Thank you for that. I am a Marine and Navy SEAL. I am Major John Mercer, commanding this SEAL team. Early on my team was brought to NORAD and sequestered before the collapse of civilization. Our command was assigned to General Beasley."

"We were told that America was under attack from aliens, and that you launched nuclear attacks against Washington and some other east coast cities. They said you killed the president and all the government. I believed that and was more than eager to retaliate, and I thought we were doing the right thing and saving Earth. But, after seeing this community and discovering its real purpose, I can't believe those lies. You simply don't have the nuclear technology. From what I have discovered, you are far beyond that level of technology, and it is this group that is trying to save the world. Me and my team want to be part of it."

"Let me know what you need from me, and I will try to help you."

General Kline said, "You have already confirmed that General Beasley is heading up the military coup. We suspected it was him, but we didn't know for sure. Thanks for the confirmation.

We need to know where he is, so we can consider our option for removing him. Where is he commanding from?"

"I was personally given orders by General Beasley in his office at Peterson AFB in Colorado. He could have since moved underground into NORAD, but he seemed concerned about you attacking there. Knowing what I know now, he is probably correct to be paranoid. I think he will remain above ground. Oh, it makes sense now that he wasn't afraid of a nuclear attack, since he was in control of the nuclear arsenal. I should have picked up on that."

I said, "I guess he is not a complete idiot. We could easily take out NORAD with our satellite lasers or other weapons at our disposal, but we would kill a lot of innocent people. Too many are already dying. Still, we must take him out and any others that want to continue the war against us or try to destroy the planet, like he is trying to do. Hopefully, with him gone the coup will dissolve. Those people at NORAD will be needed in the future to rebuild."

Major Mercer said, "I agree with you. General Beasley is obsessed with destroying you at all cost. He must be eliminated. With all your technology, can't you just zap him and teleport him here for execution, or teleport my team there? I would love to take him out."

I laughed out loud and said, "You have watched too many Sci-Fi movies. That technology is not available to us."

Flay jumped to attention, strained tension visible on her face. Total silence filled the room in anticipation, as her unfocused eyes stared at nothing. Flay's face then relaxed, and she smiled. From that look, I knew it would be something good. We waited.

Flay said, "Maybe we do have that kind of technology. I mean, we do use this type of technology for instant communication over vast distances and our time space jumps use this technology. We have just not used the technology for other purposes. We have forgotten how to use it for all its applications. Thank you, Major Mercer for using the word 'Teleport'. That word triggered a sudden epiphany of understanding of instructions my father recently shared with me. I'm not sure even he understood it, but now I do. We can focus this skip technology from our ship to see the target destination, like if we were going to skip, and adjust and reverse the function … thus teleport the selected target back to us."

"Major, if we can allow you to look into the facilities at Peterson AFB, could you direct us toward General Beasley's likely location? Having met with him, you would be able to recognize him when you see him."

A smiling Major Mercer said, "Yes, I can do that, and I would love to assist."

Peg said, "Can we use that technology through obstacles like walls and structures? I remember the rules we follow in skipping. The old ones restricted skipping through asteroid belts."

Flay laughed and said, "I think the old ones misunderstood the instructions and were just being overly cautious. But, I guess we will find out if I'm correct by teleporting this general through walls. If I'm right it will work. If I'm wrong ... poor general. But, do we really care?" Everyone in the room laughed.

We now had a reasonable option for action that wouldn't kill so many. Cheers rang out in the Conference Room.

I said, "Thanks, Flay. How do we go about it?"

"It's simple, now that I understand it. We need to operate it from our ship. I can set it up quickly."

We adjourned to the Dome, with the general, senator and major hugging my back, and many of the department heads followed closely behind them. Once in the Dome, I led them down into the top hatch of Bright One. I turned to watch the wide-eyes as they entered. There was plenty of room in the Control Room, but Flay had me position them all to the rear behind Her. Using her newly discovered knowledge and understanding, Flay began flashing her fingers in an intricate pattern within a blue light. A large holograph image appeared in the air before us, displaying a crosshatch. I had seen this before when Peg and Meg planned the space jumps. Now Flay expanded the zoom area greatly to show most of Colorado. At least I assumed it was Colorado.

Flay said, "Major, I don't know the area. You will have to show me where to zoom in."

The major began pointing to different expanding areas in the display. Soon he was pointing to Peterson AFB, then a building within the display. Finely, the targeting cross-hairs entered an office. Unfortunately, the office was empty. In frustration he ask Flay to pull back the focus until found what he was looking for and pointed to another building. When the view entered the large building many people could be seen seated in an auditorium.

The major said, "There that's the SOB on the stage. Oh, we couldn't have staged this any better. He is addressing his command."

I could see a short, heavy man shaking his fist in the air and screaming at the people in the audience. We did not have any audio, but from his animated movements and wide-open moving jaw, it was quite obvious. I hollered, "If you can, Flay. Get him now! Oh this is perfect."

Flay smiled and flicked her thumb twice through the blue light. Two things happened simultaneously: There was a flash of bright light on the deck behind the holograph, and a bellowing voice said, "I said I want those alien bastards dead, D E A ... uggg"

General Beasley, in person, stood on our deck. Realizing something had changed and looking around, saw blue aliens. He froze in the spelling of "D E A D" with his fist still raised high in the air. It was absolutely classic and extremely comical. The entire Control Room exploded in laughter at the horrified expression that paralyzed the general's face.

I walked forward to let the general get a good look at me, then said, "Hello General Beasley. My name is Brin, and I am one of those alien bastards you want dead. You don't have to spell it for me. I know what that word means and how to spell it. You have been a royal pain in the ass, but your reign is now over. Have you met General Kline and Senator Clayton? They will take you into custody and hold you accountable for your actions. If it was up to me, I would kill you right now." I turned and walked away.

I was replaced immediately by Robert and Major Mercer, who roughly yanked the general's wrists behind his back and handcuffed them together, before pushing him up the ladder. General Beasley said nothing. He had been totally humiliated and broken. He knew it was over for him.

I said, "Flay you did fantastically." All on the deck congratulated Flay, and she beamed with pride, as she should.

Chapter 12
(A Promising Future)

For once things outside the survival complex seemed to be going well. General Kline would dispense justice to the rogue general. I was relatively sure General Kline would use the capture to his advantage in order to try and bring the coup under control. We had done our part, and it was a matter of time before that area of concern would be resolved.

Meg, Peg, Flay and I went back to the cafeteria for more food and coffee. I was really starting to get addicted to coffee, and we had just settled back, enjoying our second cup of coffee when Tina bounced into the chair next to me. She was quickly followed by Flay, and the orange haired Trix. I knew something was up.

Tina acted mysterious and asked, "You want the good news or the bad?"

"Let's start with the bad."

Flay looked downhearted and said, "I have been working with the human doctors, analyzing all the sperm samples from our Apsaras males, and thanks to Dr.. Akiko she sampled all of them. Sadly, our deleted gene pool is producing no live sperm. We will not be able to reproduce any pure Apsaras offspring."

I said, "Well, crap! What is the good news?"

Tina's face broke into a huge grin and blurted out, "The Apsaras females' eggs are fertile. I ran some tests on Meg and Peg, and they are both impregnated, probably many more as well.

Our race has been saved ... partly anyway." When I looked confused she continued, "They are going to have a child. Our race can now continue."

Mike, Nancy and Sue pulled up chairs beside us and started to enjoy their coffee. Tina suddenly burst out, "Mike, you have saved our race. Meg and Peg are impregnated by you."

Mike still didn't grasp the meaning, so Sue said, "Duh. Mike, don't you get it? You impregnated them and they are going to have your babies."

Mike's eyes were wide and said, "How do you know I impregnated them?"

Tina said, "They are impregnated with your DNA. DNA doesn't lie."

I said, "This is fantastic news. We now know our races can crossbreed, at least with your sperm, anyway. This is very good news for our race. Since it worked with Meg and Peg, I'm sure Flay, Tina and Trix are most enthusiastic for you to impregnate them also."

Tina said, "Well Flay is already impregnated by Jeremy, and Trix is impregnated by Robert. But I'm motivated."

Mike's expression of pure shock shown bright; but both Nancy and Sue burst out laughing at his apparent stupid look.

Nancy said, "Brin, we are happy for your people. We are all glad that it is going to work out well for your race. You girls should come over and celebrate with Mike tonight, and Sue, Bess and I can entertain you tonight. Would you like that?" I just grinned ... really big.

I might not be able to impregnate them, but I could certainly keep practicing how to fuck. Happiness flooded me for several reasons. I would be with the Indian girls tonight, and our race would survive. We would have to send a message to the Apsaras Assembly, notifying them of our success.

I had to get my head around becoming a father, even though I was not the contributing DNA donor. I had begun to smile in anticipation, but it broke into a laugh when Nancy and Sue smiled at Mike, and Nancy said, "Bess, Sue and I have been talking, and we have all stopped taking our birth control pills. We want to be impregnated, also. We want to bear your children."

If Mike had a stupid look before, he now had the look of a complete idiot. I started laughing and said, "Mike, do you feel like a race horse being put out for stud?" He just maintained a blank look.

We all knew I couldn't impregnate the Indian sisters, even though they were off birth control, so we decided to go to bed early, while a stunned Mike was being led off by my girls.

It was going to be another fun night.

After a very productive and rewarding day and an enjoyable night, we were all reluctantly up with the alarm and ready. We were eager for today, because we knew General Kline would have a good report, and I was looking forward to it. I was also anxious to finally hear a full report from all the

301

department heads at the morning meeting. The war, which we hoped was now over, had prevented a full briefing, and I was eager to know our survival status.

Bob was in his usual jovial mood, and I noticed him patting the behind of a smiling Kit, our Blue Team chef. Yep, something was going on there, and I was pleased to see them connecting. We got our breakfast and on the way to a table we noticed a smiling Marshal Brady waving us over to join them. General Kline was also there, but he seemed to be somewhere else mentally. His eyes seemed unfocused and he had a huge shit-eating grin on his face. I looked at Marshal Brady as if to say, *"What the hell is up with him?"*

Marshal Brady laughed and quietly said, "I don't know what you and Mike did to those five sisters, but they are wild. Thank you, whatever you did. As soon as I returned to Camp Gruber with them, Kerri and Tammy latched on to General Kline and wouldn't be budged. They let it be known that they intended to live with him. It shocked the hell out of the old man, but as you can see, he must enjoy their attention. He hasn't stopped smiling since."

I said, "What about Tina, Kathy and Sarah?"

Marshal Brady blushed brightly and said, "Well, those three latched on to me. I think I will have to pick only one. They almost killed me last night. I don't know what you did, but they are like nymphs. They can't get enough."

302

Nancy said, "We just showed them the way and what they were missing."

Brady grinned and said, "Well, you sure did a good job."

We finished our breakfast and headed to the Conference Room, which was filling up fast. We had to bring additional chairs in to accommodate everyone. When all were settled, Mike said, "Welcome everyone. It looks like we have a full staff now, and it is time to analyze our status. I think we are all curious about what's happening with General Beasley. Maybe General Kline should go first."

General Kline focused, stood and said, "General Beasley is a broken man and is confessing his crimes. He has no doubt he will be executed. We will, however, give him a formal trial to publicize his crimes, which will be transmitted via the Blue Team's satellite. He is a traitor and is directly responsible for many deaths, unnecessary deaths. He *will* be executed, and Major Mercer has volunteered to shoot him himself. We, Senator Clayton and I, began transmitting a new report detailing our capture of the traitor, General Beasley, and reestablishment of a government at Camp Gruber. Already NORAD and those holdout military facilities have confirmed their support. To be honest, by snatching General Beasley off the stage in front of them, scared the shit out of them. They were afraid they could be next. Any coconspirators are nowhere to be found. At any rate, we are no longer in immediate danger from the military coup, although we should continue to be vigilant. We still have to worry about the gangs, but Senator Clayton has declared them terrorist and ordered the military to shoot them on sight."

"We hope to turn our attention toward survival and possibly eventually reestablishing some civilization. To do that we need and appreciate this community's guidance. You planned well for survival and we hope to survive with you".

I stood and said, "I want to thank all members of this community for making us, the Blue Team as you call us, welcome here. I don't think any of us anticipated having to fight an organized war to save ourselves and the planet. Hopefully, this is behind us now and we look forward to living here and making this our home. Our original purpose in coming here and partnering with you was to ensure our survival as a race. This has been realized in part with the fertilization of some of our females. Our DNA is compatible, as we had hoped. We now know our race will survive. By the very nature of mixing our DNA, we will assimilate and become one with Earth's humans."

"All our Blue Team members have been awakened and have joined with the human departments. My team supervisors report that we have all been assimilated into the various departments and production is high. In some cases we have brought new knowledge and departments into operation, like our underwater fish herding and water grown vegetable production. Blane reports our fish stock and water plants we brought from

Apsaras are thriving in this wonderful lake and many water plants are thriving in Bess' fantastic Greenhouse. Additionally, our proposes have been successful in herding many of the native fish into traps."

"All in all, we are very pleased to be here and are optimistic about our survival"

Robert stood next and said, "I can confirm that all the discussed bridges and some others have been destroyed, and we are monitoring the traffic flow. Taking the bridges out has indeed altered the flow of refugees and had, for the most part, the desired effect. We are continuing to monitor the migration activities and will report any problems. Sadly, the rioting and deaths continue and will for many months. Many have died in the riots, and Dr. Groom predicts many more will die of diseases that will follow. This makes it imperative that we remain isolated and safe, which we will do."

"Trix and her security team are a welcome addition to our security and have reinforced security greatly. They are interfacing well, extremely well actually. Trix and I are mated and are expecting a child." Cheers and applause rang out.

"The only problems we have with the Blue Team are with the canine dogs, but once the dogs get used to their scent, it should work well. We have full camera, infrared and motion sensor coverage of our perimeter and bay, roving canine teams patrolling, various sentry towers, satellite monitoring and security boats at the ready to divert bay-side intrusions. We also have the Blue Team's porpoises patrolling the lake. Our mainline defense remains with the Castle roof-top Rail Gun and EMP Gun and satellite lasers."

"In addition, we added Major Mercer and his SEAL team to our forces. They will be a welcome and formidable addition to our security."

"We haven't had much trouble at our perimeter. We have had confrontations, but most disperse when we show force. Sadly, however, we have killed some roaming bands that tried to gain entrance. We figure that if they cut fences at night to gain access or fire shots at our security team, they are up to no good and are fair game. We act quickly and decisively."

"Almost all members of our community are cross-trained and have been attending Bess' hand-to-hand combat training classes and JJ's firing range. We now have a current defense force and back-up capable of repelling most any attacks, and since we no longer have to worry about nuclear, we are much more confident in our defense. Plus, we have the support of Camp Gruber's attack helicopter force and our own attack saucers to launch against any attacks. In short, we can and are defending ourselves." Cheers

Dr. Groom went next and said, "With the exception of Maj. Mercer and his team, all members of both our teams have been checked out and are disease free and healthy. Maj. Mercer, I'm sure from your military checkups, that you and your team will check out, but I will be wanting all of your team to come by our clinic for blood and fluid

306

samples and dental inspection." At the mention of dental inspection, some in the room chuckled, knowing from personal experience how some of those fluid samples were taken.

When Maj. Mercer heard the chuckles, he opened his eyes wide in curiosity, Dr. Groom smiled and continued, "Don't worry about it, major. It won't be painful. Anyway, as Robert has stated, I am very worried about diseases. That will be the next phase of the collapse. All the decaying bodies and lack of sanitation and clean water, diseases will spread rapidly. It will have to run its course, and there is nothing we can do about it. I estimate 90% of the population will perish. All we can do is isolate ourselves. General Kline, I worry about your operation, and I suggest you do likewise. You can't stop it. Just try to survive so you can be part of the rebuild." The general nodded.

James stood next and said, "Our farming operation is fully staffed and established. All the allocated farming fields are either already supporting crops or prepared to be planted. We have also already expanded our fencing and irrigation systems and cleared other fields. By next summer we will be fully supporting our required food production needs. We have also began to clear and plow fields at Camp Gruber for their food production. The twins' chicken house is already fully providing our egg requirements and in a few months our chicken needs as well. Hog, cattle and sheep production is on schedule. Bess' greenhouse is already providing an abundant supply of vegetables, and it's just starting. We have enough coffee stored to last for years, but Bess is also growing coffee bean plants so we will never run out. Blane's underwater operation can supply far more fish than we can use. Milk harvest from our dairy operation is more than required, and they have begun developing cheese, butter and other dairy products that can be stored. In short, our future supply of food looks fantastic." More applause

Jeremy took the next presentation time. Jeremy stood and said, "All mechanical, electrical, waste handling and water production is going well. Everything is built and operating, and we are mostly on maintenance mode; however, our electricians are modifying the electric grid to power outside our complex. The electrical power generators Brin brought produce many times more power than we use. Soon Camp Gruber, and any others along the grid, will receive power for their complex so they can shut down their generators and save diesel fuel. We are also open to helping out others in need of extra manpower. Just ask." More applause

Mary stood next and said, "You said we are fully staffed, but we have no Chaplin yet. As we all know, our community is not what we would call an overly religious community, but I do get request concerning counseling and spiritual needs. I've also been asked about church services, and it is reasonable to assume many within our group at some point in the future will want to be formally married. I know that the Chaplin scheduled to interview with Nancy didn't show up, and it is probably too late to recruit a Chaplin at this late date; but I wanted the group to know that there still exists a need."

I had no idea what a Chaplin was, but if they felt like they needed one, fine by me. All their previous choices have been great.

General Kline interrupted saying, "I think this is something we may be able to help with. As an emergency disaster group established by FEMA we were required for our staff to have several Chaplains. We can transfer one to your community if you like."

Nancy said, "That's great General Kline. Please, send him or her over to talk with us."

General Kline said, "Yes. We have several. I will send a couple of them to pick from."

Mary continued, "Well, that problem solved. Now as to the Castle, everything else is going great. We still have quite a few unoccupied rooms. I guess this board will eventually answer this questions. Other than these items mentioned, I have no other concerns."

Bob stood next and said, "Our cafeteria is feeding all residents, and most of the food is coming from our own food production. The storerooms are brimming with supplies. I don't think anyone is going without. Still, I have a problem with wasted food. I'm getting pretty vocal about this waste, and I would appreciate all department heads to talk to their people and tell them take all they want but not to pick up food if they can't eat it. The hogs like the extra food, but we need to conserve. I'm at full staff, and we are handling the load quite well. Soon we will expand our menu to include dishes made and provided by the Blue Team cooks. They like our human food, so maybe we will like theirs."

General Kline waited to see if any others stood, and when no one did, he stood and said, "We at Camp Gruber appreciate all you have done to help us. I'm not sure we would have or could survive without your help and assistance. Our survival plans, as designed, were only short term plans. I don't think there were any long term plans considered, but with your help, I believe we too will survive. You can count on our help for anything. James has already began building planting fields, and Jeremy has offered assistance in installing security fencing. We will be sending a security team out to obtain material soon."

With continued silence, Mike stood and said, "These reports all sound fantastic. I believe, baring additional unforeseen circumstances, we will survive. I'm sure we will be forced to deal with many other problems in the future, and we will have to deal with them as they come. We have certainly met all our problem head-on, and we are still here and sound."

"I now declare Phase I of our Apocalypse Project a complete success." Cheers rang out in the conference room. My mind was brimming full of pride, pride in all involved.

Meg and Peg leaned against me and Meg said, "Brin, you made this all happen. It's your plan that you fought so hard to begin, support and defend, and we are very proud of you. Our race will now continue with the birth of our generation's children."

My mind shot forward to a time when our race would have so many children running around the complex, a mixture of Apsaras and human. They would become the beginning of a new race in a new world. I'm sure that would be one or many of the future challenges we would have to face.

The End of Phase I